Rodgers for Constable

They had the votes counted by nine o'clock, and Pat came tearing over to the chicken coop. We could hear him coming from the other side of Barker's; I guess we heard him as he busted out of the schoolhouse and jumped on his horse.

His gun was going off and he was screaming like an Apache when he pulled up in front of us, standing out on the road.

"Hundred and three to twenty-six!" he yelled. "Rodgers for constable. Yeow! Yippee!"

SECOND TIME AROUND was originally published by Random House, Inc., under the title STAR IN THE WEST.

Also by Richard Emery Roberts

THE GILDED ROOSTER

Are there paper-bound books you want but cannot find at your retail stores? You can get any title in print in these famous series, **POCKET BOOKS, CARDINAL EDITIONS, POCKET LIBRARY** and **PERMABOOKS**, by ordering from Mail Service Dept., Pocket Books, Inc., 1 West 39th St., New York 18, N.Y. Enclose retail price plus 5c per book for mailing costs; send check or money order—do not send cash.

FREE CATALOGUE SENT ON REQUEST

(Original title: Star in the West)

Richard E. Roberts

⚓ PERMABOOKS · NEW YORK
Published by Pocket Books, Inc.

Second Time Around

(Original title: *Star in the West*)

Random House edition published September, 1951

PERMABOOK edition published November, 1961
1st printing..September, 1961

This PERMABOOK includes every word contained in the original, higher-priced edition. It is printed from brand-new plates made from completely reset, clear, easy-to-read type.

•

PERMABOOK editions are distributed in the U.S. by Affiliated Publishers, Inc., 630 Fifth Avenue, New York 20, N.Y.

•

PERMABOOK editions are published in the United States by Pocket Books, Inc., and in Canada by Pocket Books of Canada, Ltd.—the world's largest publishers of low-priced adult books.

L

Copyright, 1951, by Richard Emery Roberts. All rights reserved. This PERMABOOK edition is published by arrangement with Random House, Inc.

PRINTED IN THE U.S.A.

For my mother who lived so much of this

chapter 1

You wouldn't think that a crisp, sunshiny day at the beginning of a new year could be the darkest day of your life, but it was, for me.

It was the afternoon of January tenth, 1912. I was standing in the ferry shed at the foot of Cortlandt Street. I wore my brown suit and I had Greg's old walrus-hide bag with a nightgown and clean underwear and some shirtwaists in it, and stockings and another pair of shoes. I was going west —way west to Oklahoma. I'd never been west of Newark, New Jersey, in my life.

Pinned between my corset and my guimpe I had a hundred dollars. I had about twenty dollars in my pocketbook, beside my ticket to Oklahoma City. I had some change, too, left over from paying the hansom-cab driver who brought me across from Brooklyn Bridge where the streetcars stopped under the big, noisy shed.

I was a little empty in the stomach and shaky in the knees, because I kept thinking that when the ferry came in and I got on it, it was going to start me on my way to a wild, strange place called Oklahoma. I didn't know it then, of course, but it was starting me on a far, far way to a lots wilder place—Arizona.

When the ferry docked, I marched on as stiff and straight as I could hold myself, so no one would know how quivery I was.

The ferry smelled of damp wood, cigars and beer and horses. I always liked horses, though I knew nothing about them. Brooklyn, where I grew up and lived, was full of horses. Greg even had a horse and rig before we were married, and we used to go for Sunday spins down the Boulevard in it. He kept it after we were married, too, but when the first baby came—Jerry—his mother sold it. The rig wasn't really his; nothing was really his. Everything was hers—the big brownstone house on Columbia Heights, the store block on Fulton Street that brought in fat rents, the clothes he wore, and, when I married him, the clothes I wore—the baby, almost, too, because she paid the bills.

Greg had one thing. He had his name on the door of the real-estate office that he thought he ran. His name went like this: "William Rodgers & Son." The part from the "&" sign to the end was Greg's name. Everybody but himself knew that he had nothing to say about anything, that his mother ran the place from her second-floor-rear parlor in the house on Columbia Heights. And she didn't like me. Never did. So when Greg died of pneumonia—he was always frail—she told me she would take care of the children, and oversee their education. "I won't turn you out, of course," she said, "but I think I know more about what's good for them than you do."

I had never learned how to do anything that other people would want to pay me money for doing. I could sew good enough to fasten buttons and line the hem of a skirt, but that was about all. Women had begun to work in offices in those days and I thought I might do that, but I found out you had to be able to run a typewriter and take something called dictation by means of shorthand. I wanted to get my children, my and Greg's children, away from that bossy old woman, but I had to be able to feed them and keep them warm. That day I stood on the ferry, Jerry was ten, Cissie was eight, and Tim, with his big, baby eyes, was four. I was thirty.

I was heading west because Greg's best friend, a lawyer named Will Saunders, had stirred me up. "If you can't see any way of getting along here in Brooklyn, Lucretia," he'd said, "why don't you try a new place? Oklahoma City, booming with money and oil, say. Should be something for a woman to do there."

It wasn't a bad idea, I thought. Maybe because as a youngster I'd always dreamed about the West it sounded easier to me than I really knew it would be. Anyhow, I decided I'd try it. I had a small bank account Greg had started for me when we married and in which I'd put my birthday presents and anniversary mementos. I drew all the money out of it.

I drew the strings out of my heart, too.

The kids. I don't know how I did it, but I kept from crying when I talked to them. I said in the days before I left, over and over again: "Now you must all be good and stay here with Grandmother and do what she tells you. Because I'm going away."

It was Cissie who always interrupted me here. Jerry just thought about it, Tim only stared with his great, big eyes, but Cissie asked, "Why, Mom?"

"Because," I'd say, "because I'm going away to find a new place for us to live. It will be different from Brooklyn and it may take me a little while to get settled, so I talked it over with Grandmother and we decided it would be best if you stayed here till I send for you."

After a while they got so it made sense to them, but when I said it again this morning, the morning of the day I was really leaving, Jerry said, "Are you really going to send for us, Mom?"

"Why . . ." I said. "Why . . . Oh, Jerry, yes, of course!"

Cissie's lip started to quiver. Tim was watching her and getting ready to bawl. I swallowed a lump in my throat that was big as a doorknob and managed a watery smile. "Jerry, Cissie, Tim," I said. "You've got to believe me! I'm going to find us a new place to live, and I'm going to get you there. Soon, no longer than I can help. Oh, darlings . . ."

So there I was on the train waiting for it to pull out. I was sure I was doing the right thing for the kids and myself, but I was still so torn between going and staying that I had to hold myself down in the seat so I wouldn't jump up and run off that train. Maybe some women can leave their children—even for so good a reason—and be easy about it. But my heart was aching and pounding, and I would shiver every so often. I tried to make myself think about something else, anything, any trivial thing.

I had an upper berth in the Pullman and I was curious what my seatmate would be like. She got there late, almost as the train was pulling out. She was a few years younger than me, I guessed, and a very pretty girl. She was wearing a wedding ring.

When she got settled, she smiled in a friendly way. I was sitting opposite her, riding backwards. She said, "Wouldn't you rather sit beside me? I'm Mrs. Standish. Jane Standish."

"I'm Mrs. Lucretia Rodgers," I said. "I don't mind it this way."

We got into a conversation then, and I learned she'd been visiting her mother in Boston and was going home to her husband.

"Where do you live?" I asked.

"Oklahoma City," said Mrs. Standish.

"My! That's where I'm going!"

"Isn't that strange!" said Mrs. Standish.

I was so glad I'd met her. I started asking questions twenty to the dozen. She laughed and held up her hand. "No, no," she said. "Oklahoma's not really far west. Oh, no."

I was disappointed and said so. "Oh, no," said Jane Standish, "I know. Why, two years ago my husband had a sort of breakdown—he'd been working too hard—and they sent him out to Arizona. Now, there's the West! It's a wonderful place."

I asked her all about it and kept her talking till the porter lit the lights and outside the sun had long since set over the far edge of the world. When the waiter came through with the first call for dinner, my new friend said, "Oh, let's go have dinner now. I'm hungry and you certainly look as if you need some food."

People were apt to say things like that because I was thin. I'd always been thin, not much figure even after the babies came. But I did have nice brown hair, lots of it, and I wore it piled on top of my head. My eyes were sort of greenish blue, but to offset that I had good teeth and wasn't afraid to smile.

At dinner, I asked Jane—we were first-naming by now—where she stayed in Arizona.

"Oh, a town called Nogales," she said. "It's an interesting city, right on the border. It's got a twin city in Mexico. Hills and mountains all around. About forty miles away is a tiny little place called Canelo. I've got a cousin teaching the one-room school there. Bess Oryx."

"Does she like it?"

"Oh, yes."

Then Jane wanted to know about me, why I was going west, who I knew, all that. She was so friendly, such a nice, genuine person with her big brown eyes shining with kindness that I just started talking and told her everything. I told her how I had loved Greg and how sweet he'd been, how I hadn't wanted to live in his mother's house because I knew she didn't like me, couldn't like any girl her son married because she wanted him for herself forever. I told her how old Mrs. Rodgers had eased a little when Jerry was born, and how she'd let down a little more when Cissie came, and how when Tim was born, with his smile and way of reaching out for you, she got almost human.

Jane asked, "Does she really love them? Do you feel all right about leaving them?"

How could I tell her how I felt and still sound honest? Wouldn't she just say, "Well, then, if you hate to leave them so badly, why don't you stay?" It would take hours to show her how old Mrs. Rodgers and I couldn't live together in the same house, how I had no way of earning a living for my family. Thinking of them, I had to choke down a lump in my throat. Then I said, "Of course I don't feel good about it. But she does love them as much as she can love anything. And I couldn't stay there and let her decide the course of my children's lives. So I'm going west."

"But it seems to me," said Jane gently, "that you *are* letting her decide. . . ."

I shook my head hard. This was one thing I'd thought out, lying awake and staring at the dark ceiling.

I said, "I'll be able to make a place for them. Then I'll take them away from her, maybe after only a year or two.

But if I just live in her house like a poor relation, she'll have all their lives to do the deciding, perhaps make the boys the way Greg was. Oh, he was sweet, and I loved him, but he was so weak and spineless! He couldn't do a thing without her approval. I'll not let her make Jerry and Tim like that."

Jane said, "Well. Yes, I see."

She didn't see at all, though. She had no children of her own, so she couldn't know what it was like to go away and leave them, even though you knew they were safe and comfortable, even though you knew you had to do it. There just wasn't any doubt of that—I just had to do it.

But leaving them was like leaving the biggest part of myself. I felt all hollow and gone inside; I felt lost and hopeless. In my upper berth that night, the train swaying and clanking and banging through the dark night, taking me further and further from them, I did the only thing that could help me. I prayed. I asked the good Lord to take care of them and me, to make it work out all right in the end. "Oh, Lord," I thought, "make it as hard and rough and difficult as it must be, but please, God, let me have my babies back again."

I fell asleep feeling that He would.

In the morning, having breakfast in the diner and looking out at the strange fields and towns that we passed, Jane said, "I've got an idea. Don't you stay in Oklahoma City. You're real pioneer stuff, though you may not think so. You go out to that place where my cousin is. That's the place for you."

I said, "Oh, I couldn't go visit a total stranger!"

Jane smiled. "What was I yesterday afternoon? I'll write Bess. You stay with me till she answers."

I did. I stayed with Jane and her nice husband eleven days till Bess's answer came. She said she'd be very glad to have me visit her and look around, though there wasn't much opportunity in Canelo for a woman who wasn't married or a schoolteacher.

Bess was right about many things, but she sure turned out dead wrong about that!

chapter 2

AFTER I WAVED good-by to kind Jane Standish and her nice husband at the station in Oklahoma City, I was on the train three days. Jane had been a very good friend to me; she was the first Westerner I'd met and she proved to be typical of most all of them. Friendly, helping, easy, kind people who liked others and didn't niggle the way city people did. I'd said to Jane I'd never forget her, and I never did. We wrote to each other twice a year and we've visited many times since.

The third day after I got on the train, late in the afternoon, the conductor came down the aisle and said, "Elgin next, ma'am."

Nobody else got off at Elgin, which was the nearest railroad station to Canelo. The train steamed away down the track and I could have felt lonesome, only I didn't have time. I just stood there, trying to see everything at once. This was very close to Canelo.

My eyes just wouldn't stay on the nearby things, though I did realize that there wasn't any station, just a freight house painted yellow with a platform in front of it, and some sort of building across the tracks.

But I couldn't look at these things, because there were mountains over toward the north. I learned later they weren't really so big, but just then they were the biggest things I could see. Three peaks stuck up. They were round and almost flat on top. They looked like biscuits, like huge, gigantic biscuits. They were even the right color, a nice tan, not too dark, not too light. And some one had put a sprinkling of powdered sugar on them, all white and fluffy on their tops. Then I shivered and I knew it was cold. There

7

was a wind whipping right off those biscuits toward me and in another minute my nose was going to start to run, so I grabbed up my bag and hurried across the tracks toward the building there.

It wasn't even built yet. It was only half finished, but a woman in a gray dress opened the door and said, "Come in out of the cold."

I did. Then I said, "I just want to get warm. I'm going to Canelo."

"B.J. won't come till morning," said the woman.

"Please," I said, "how do I get to Canelo?"

"That's what I'm telling you. B.J. drives the mail and he meets the morning train from Nogales. Gets here around noon. You're not likely to get to Canelo tonight unless someone happens along who's going over that way."

"Oh. Well, then, what do I do?"

"You just got to wait till tomorrow. You can stay here. This is a hotel. I'm Mrs. Young. I run it. Me and my husband."

So I thought, if I couldn't get to Canelo, I couldn't, and I'd have to make the best of it. Mrs. Young put me in a small room at the end of the hall.

After a while, Mr. Young came in, a nice, elderly man with a shy smile, and said he was mighty pleased to meet me, yes, sir, and glad I was staying the night. The sun was down below the horizon and those peaks like biscuits had changed color. They were plum and purple and some tan, now, a beautiful sight with the snow on top turning a little pink.

While Mrs. Young fixed supper, I watched the light change. There was a feel about this place I liked, a feel that, in a way, it was a new place and right for new people to come into. I was even happier about it the next morning. I was excited; I'd slept fine on a good bed, so good I wakened late, and then lay there looking out at the land stretching away from under my window to a gash in the ground that Mr. Young had called an "arroyo." He said when there were rains it ran full of water; the rest of the time it was dry.

There was bright sunshine on everything and the sky was

clear blue. The air just sparkled and snapped so you didn't notice how cold it was at first. Mrs. Young filled me with stewed dried apples, pancakes and syrup and coffee and thick pieces of fat, smoky bacon that tasted awfully good. She apologized for not having eggs; the coyotes had got her hens, she said, and though once in a while a Mexican who lived a few miles away came in with eggs, she hadn't seen him in a week or more.

Then I heard Mr. Young shouting outside and wheels grinding and little hooves pattering. Mrs. Young said, "That's B.J. But you don't have to hurry; the train's not due yet."

I went outside, though. I was too impatient. My suit was warm and I had put on long underwear, but just the same it was cold. B.J. was a nice man with a cultivated voice. He told me Bess was living at the Barkers'. Mrs. Barker was the postmistress for Canelo. We went on talking, and it turned out B.J. was from the east and had moved west with his wife and children for their health and also because, as he said, "I became very tired of city life."

"What city did you live in?" I asked.

"Newark," he said. "Know it?"

I'd seen it once or twice. "I can sympathize with you," I said.

B.J. had a buckboard drawn by a pair of the cutest things I'd ever seen. They were little donkeys, soft, grayish-brown in color, with a pair of long, flappy ears, very pretty, almost sad and at the same time impudent faces, nice dark stripes down their backs with another across their shoulders. "The Mexicans say that's because a burro—donkey to us—carried Jesus into Jerusalem," B.J. told me.

Far down the track there was a hooting. "Train's coming!" I rushed into the hotel and got my bag.

The train came in, all fussy and important, bell ringing, whistle tootling. They unloaded a crate which Mr. Young put in the freight house, and a very skinny mail bag which B.J. put in the buckboard. No one got off, no one got on. The engine puffed and snorted, the train groaned, gathered speed and rattled away up the track.

"Well, get in," said B.J.

He gave me a blanket to put across my lap. I snuggled my hands under it before we had gone very far. That wind was bitter! I was glad I'd worn a heavy veil over my hat, tied tightly under my chin. Even though my eyes were watering at times, I was busy looking at the countryside. It was beautiful, wide open, not a house, not a fence, not a windmill. Just rolling country, stretching away to those mountains behind us. Ahead it swept on and on and seemed to drop away, and then miles away, off to the left, it ran up against a dark, snow-topped wall of mountains, looming there like great big bulls scrunched down and sleeping. Those were real honest-to-God mountains, I thought. They must be; the others had a prettiness about them, but those things over there were rugged and strong.

"How far away are those?" I asked B.J., pointing.

"The Huachucas?" he asked. He said it "Wachugas."

"Why I guess it'd be twenty miles or so. Little more or less."

"They're mountains, aren't they?"

He chuckled. "They're mountains, all right. Wild ones, too. Why there's mountain lion and tigers up from Mexico and *javelinas*—they're wild pigs—and bears and deer of course, maybe even wild sheep, though I've never met anyone who'd seen one of them. And some renegade Mexicans, too, I guess. They're having a revolution down there, you know, and some of the losers slip across the line—shouldn't say slip, they just come across—and hang out there. Bad hombres, too, some of them. All hungry, of course."

"Do they ever come this far?" I asked.

B.J. shrugged. "Might meet one now and then, but there's too many people around here for it to be comfortable for them. That's why I carry this, though."

"This" was a sawed-off shotgun in clips on the dashboard where he could snatch it up quick as a wink. He had a pistol in a holster on his belt, too. "You've got a lot of artillery," I said. I don't like guns; they always make me nervous.

"Oh, the revolver is for the government," B.J. said. "Shotgun's for myself. More chance of hitting with it."

We passed a bunch of cows munching at the grass that came up to their bellies, their rumps to the wind, their tails tucked in tight. One old one raised her head, looked at us, snorted and began to walk away. The others took alarm and started after her. They trotted a ways, then turned and all of them looked at us, heads high, very serious.

The road began to pitch downward again and I could see another road turning off it up ahead. Then I saw the first house, a rambling thing built of rough stone with a shingle roof and a long, narrow porch across the front of it.

"Aggie Gates's," said B.J., pointing with his chin. "Up there, up that road, is the Malloy place."

As we were about to pass the stone house, out of the barn opposite it, right alongside the road, came a woman on a big, high, light-colored horse. He was some sort of gray, but I didn't know enough then to call him a blue roan, which was what he was. I didn't have much time to look at him anyhow, because the woman on him took all my attention.

She was one of the handsomest women I'd ever seen in my life. She had black eyes and black hair, and a white, white skin with real roses in her cheeks. Her hair was piled up under a felt hat like a man's; she had a blue canvas jacket that covered the top of her; she wore a gray skirt and she was riding that big horse sidesaddle.

B.J. tipped his hat. "Good morning, Mrs. Gates," he said.

She just nodded and raised her hand and rode across the road. You could see she had something on her mind, something that didn't allow her to stop and talk, something she was determined to do.

"That's Aggie Gates," B.J. said. "Riding after cattle on the coldest day we've had this winter."

It was cold, all right. But cold as it was, and numb and frozen as I was, I turned my head to look after that woman. Even then, even just that glimpse I had of her, I admired her.

As if he was reading my thoughts, B.J. said, "Aggie Gates is quite a woman. Runs her place herself—well, that is, with Dan helping her. He's her son."

"Why doesn't she let him ride around today, then?" My teeth were chattering so I could hardly speak.

11

"You're real cold," said B.J. "Well, Aggie Gates is a woman who likes to get things done. Remember Ben Franklin, 'If thou wouldst have it done, go!' Aggie always goes."

The road turned sharply and ran up a ridge. There was a big house with a peaked tin roof and a sort of low porch all around what I could see of it. There were outbuildings, too, but I didn't pay much attention to them.

B.J. said, "Here we are. This is Barker's."

A tall man came out and said, "I'm Bess Oryx's beau. I'm John Yoss."

I tried to say, "Pleased to meet you," but my mouth was stiff with cold. I tried to stand up, to get out of the buckboard. My legs were so stiff I could hardly move. John Yoss reached out and picked me up.

"Make a mighty nice armful, don't you, New York lady?" he said.

I thought he was somewhat familiar on first sight, but I knew Westerners were supposed to be friendly and breezy, and I didn't want to act green. But I sort of squirmed around a little so he set me on my feet.

"Here she is, Mrs. Barker," he yelled. "Here's Bess's friend!"

Then he gave a smirk and said in a lower voice, "And maybe a new friend for me, too, huh?"

I didn't have to answer him—and I don't know what I would have said, since it was all so strange—because Mrs. Barker was beckoning from the door. She was a nice-looking, elderly woman with graying hair, as I noticed later. Right then I just wanted to get as close as I could to the big fire blazing away in the huge, rough stone chimneyplace.

Oh, it felt good! I held out my hands and rubbed them. Mrs. Barker brought me a cup of hot, black coffee, so strong it would almost eat holes in the cup. I turned my back to the fire, and sipped at the coffee, and let the heat soak in.

John Yoss began to tell about what a fine cowhand he was. He was a tall, husky man with the most beautiful copper-colored hair, but he had a mean look on his face. His eyes were green but, I thought, too close together. He looked like a man with a chip on his shoulder, but still, I could see that he was the big, bragging kind that some women would take to.

He stood there, talking about himself, throwing me smiles and glances meant to be killing. He was trying just as hard as he knew how to flirt with me. I didn't like it a bit; here he had said first thing that he was Bess's beau, and now he was making a play for me.

Then Mr. Barker came in. He was a thin old man with a face that looked like leather and hands that had fingers like big sausages. He grunted at John Yoss, and looked me up and down with a twinkle in his eye.

"You're Bess Oryx's friend, I guess."

"That's right, Mr. Barker."

"Cold outside," he said, and that was the last word he said till supper time.

A boy's voice yelled, "Ma, when we going to eat?" The door banged open, and in came a light-haired boy about fifteen years old. He grinned at me, and said, "Hello, greenhorn."

"Billy!" said Mrs. Barker. "Be polite."

"Aw, Ma, I was just kidding."

I said, "I don't mind. I am a greenhorn."

Billy grinned harder and rushed out to wash.

John Yoss went back to telling how he was going to build up his own outfit. He worked some on his homestead and some for neighbors, he said.

All of a sudden there was a yell from outside. John Yoss said, "There's Bess!"

What I learned later to call a little old cowpony came tearing up to the porch with a little old girl riding him. She just dropped the reins, jumped off, and came running into the house. She had a sunbonnet tied under her chin and a dark divided skirt with the same sort of denim jumper Mrs. Gates had worn. She ran right over to me.

"Lu!" she yelled.

"Bess!" I shouted.

We patted each other's backs and danced around and cut up generally, just as if we were old friends. Then we had supper and sat around and talked. Mrs. Barker asked me about New York; she'd never seen it, never been east of the Mississippi River, but she wanted to know about it. So I told her the best I could, but how could I describe the Brooklyn Bridge or the Singer Building to a woman who had never seen a suspension bridge or a skyscraper? Billy kept interrupting with all kinds of questions. Pretty soon John Yoss got tired of listening to someone else talk, so he tried to get going again on what a fine fellow he was.

Mr. Barker said, "You go to bed, Billy."

"Aw, Pa . . . ."

"Git along, I say!" Then he cut in on Yoss by standing up and saying, "I'm turning in. We're riding early tomorrow, John."

The way he said it meant, "You better by God haul yourself out of bed come daybreak if you're working for me."

Yoss just scowled and went on talking.

Bess said, "I'm sleepy, too. Good night, John. Come along, Lu."

With the door shut in her room, she said, "I'm getting real tired of that John Yoss. To hear him talk you'd think he was a cattleman with ten thousand head instead of a little old one-man, baling-wire outfit! Why, he's just a homesteader who has to work five months of the year so he can prove up his claim the other seven!"

"That's no way to talk about your beau."

"Did he tell you he was my beau? Well, he does spark some, but he needn't think I'd throw in with him in a one-room 'dobe shack with heifers sticking their heads in at the door." She cocked her head at me and said, "Besides, I thought I caught him kind of making eyes at you a couple of times."

"Well, I guess you did. If you don't mind my saying so —since he is your beau—I didn't like it much."

"Oh, you say what you think!" Bess told me. "John Yoss would like to think he's something special with me, but he's not!"

"Nor with me either," I said, "and he isn't going to be!"

Bess shook her head. "Lu," she said, "the future's a thing

14

no one can predict. But since there's a future coming tomorrow," she went on with a grin, "maybe I better tell you about some of the people here. Mrs. Barker's a real nice woman, though of course as postmistress she's got a big interest in other people's business. But she's goodhearted, and wouldn't really harm anybody. And old man Barker isn't as bad as he looks. And that Billy is a rascal. He used to keep things stirred up at school, too. Now that he's quit, it's a lot easier."

She went on talking about others till she dropped off to sleep. But I couldn't sleep. I was too nervous. This seemed like such a long way from Brooklyn, so different from home. This was a new place, unsettled, open, empty. Oh, it was a far, far place; a far-off, dropping-off-of-the-world country.

Bess woke me up the next morning. "Look, Lu," she said, "it's snowing!"

It was—big flakes whirling down, making the ground white. "Lu," said Bess, "I've got an idea."

No one else in Canelo ever called me Lu. I was Mrs. Rodgers and Rodge, but never Lu to anyone except Bess and later, when he got to know me, Artur Resswell.

"What's your idea?" I asked.

"We're going back to my house. We'll go live there. I like it better, anyhow."

"Why aren't you there now?"

"Oh, Mrs. Barker is a worrier. You know, the revolution made a lot of Mexicans move across the line. Some of them are pretty bad, they say, so they got to worrying about me being alone in my house and just to make them stop talking I came over here."

"Oh," I said. It didn't sound too unworrisome to me. I thought that maybe it wouldn't take much worrying to bring me out of a lonesome house stuck off somewhere all by myself. "Where is your house?" I asked Bess.

"Just a hoot and a holler over the hill. Over longside the schoolhouse. Where it ought to be."

So at breakfast Bess said, "Mrs. Barker, I'm going to move back to my house. I've got someone to stay with me and I'm not afraid."

Billy hooted. "Maybe you're not!" he yelled, "but I'll bet your friend is."

So of course I said, "I'm not, either!"

Billy just grinned, and Mrs. Barker started to make Bess back down. She was wasting her breath, though I hoped she could. But that little old Bess Oryx was from Missouri. She had that mulishness that they grow in Missouri, and she was a pioneer breed of girl from way back. She just ate her oatmeal, drank her coffee and ate her biscuits and fat bacon and syrup—Billy called it lick—and said nothing. But anyone could see from the way she held her head that Mrs. Barker could no more move her than she could have moved the Huachucas.

Mrs. Barker finally sighed and said, "All right. Billy, you hitch up the rig and take Mrs. Rodgers and her things and Bess's over."

So he did.

Bess's house was made of adobe, which are flat, sun-dried bricks. It was plastered inside so the dust wouldn't fall all over everything. It had a peaked corrugated-iron roof. There was a big stone fireplace at the end opposite the door, with a cookstove alongside it. The whole house was only the one room. It had a couple of cots covered with Navajo blankets; skins on the wood floor—coyote, deer, mountain lion. The ceiling was unbleached muslin tacked to wide-spaced beams. I guessed that up above it was just open to the tin roof.

Billy helped me build a fire. He brought in water from the schoolhouse well, and I started dusting the place and cleaning up. It wasn't messy, but Bess hadn't used it for sometime. I worked around settling myself and it till she came in from school in the afternoon.

It got dark, and I got sort of scary. "Shouldn't we put out the lamps, Bess?"

"What for?"

"Well, if any Mexicans or Indians are prowling around..."

Bess laughed. "Look," she said.

Out of the stand at the head of her cot, she took what seemed to me an enormous revolver.

"I'm a pretty good shot," she said. "See that knot in the door, the one to the right of the handle?"

I clapped my hands to my ears, but not in time. It sounded like a cannon going off. It just made me more certain that I hated guns.

"Unsquinch your eyes," said Bess. "I only need one shot."

Sure enough, the knot was gone. There was just a hole in the door. "I'll send one of the boys down tomorrow to nail a piece of tin over it," said Bess.

I slept pretty sound that night, but I woke with an awful start. There was a gun fight going on, right in the room! I pulled the blankets up over my head and hoped Bess would win. I didn't want to be killed by some outlaw.

The shooting stopped, and I peeked out. Bess was lying in bed, reloading her gun, just as calm as if it was Sunday morning in church.

"Did you kill him?" I asked.

"Got two of them," she said.

"How can you be so cool?" I was shaking all over, and I didn't want to look at the bodies, but I asked, "Did they break the door down?"

Bess started to laugh. She rolled around in her bed and laughed. "Oh, Lu," she said weakly, "you'll be the death of me! It's rats or ground squirrels I killed. Look." She pointed up at the muslin ceiling over my bed. It had a sag in it and even I could see something was lying there.

"You mean there's rats up there?"

"Not many," said Bess. "And they'll get out now I got two of them. They just came back since I've been away. Why it's fun to lie here in bed and wait for them to run across! You've got to be mighty quick to hit one."

"Bess Oryx," I said, "I don't care how good a shot you are, if you ever wake me up again like that, I'll—I'll—I don't know what I'll do."

"Next time I'll holler at you first," said Bess. "I'm real sorry, Lu. I forgot your finicky Eastern notions. You better get used to guns. If you stay here you'll see a lot of them, and maybe have something to do with them yourself."

"I'm never going to touch one!" I said, and I meant it.

17

But time proved Bess right and me wrong.

We had our breakfast—coffee and oatmeal. I stood in the door watching the kids come to school. They rode up on horses; some came in buggies or wagons driven by their fathers or a hand. There were about twenty of them, all ages and sizes, and I was sure wishing my Jerry, Cissie and Tim were among them. Bess got herself ready and went over and rang the bell and they all poured inside.

I was working around the house, straightening up and wondering what to do about the dead rats in the ceiling when I heard a rig of some sort outside. Billy Barker yelled, "Mrs. Rodgers, Ma wants you to come over and visit with her."

I thought that was real nice. I got my coat and hat on, and away we went. It wasn't far, really, maybe a mile, and I could have walked it easy. I said so. I said, "When I want to visit her I can just walk over."

"You better not," said Billy. "Some of these here critters can be pretty mean. Old cows get on the prod. Man on foot ain't safe in this country."

Well, every morning Mrs. Barker would send for me, usually Billy, though a couple of times it was John Yoss, and once Pat Malloy. I'd met him at Mrs. Barker's one day.

We were sitting there talking, and I was sewing on some of Bess's stuff that she didn't have time to put in shape, when a horse came up. The man on him crossed the porch, not stamping and jingling the way most of the cowhands did, but sort of bashful and careful. The door opened gently and a red face on a neck like a turkey poked itself in. It had china-blue eyes and it was clean-shaven, but the wrinkles down from the corners of the mouth were dark brown where tobacco juice had trickled.

It said, "Uh-uh . . ."

"Come all the way in, Pat," said Mrs. Barker. "Mrs. Rodgers, this here's Pat Malloy, one of our earliest settlers and the shyest man in seven states and one territory."

"Pleased to meet you," I said.

"Uh—uh—uh . . ."

"Oh, come in, Pat. She don't bite, and you know I don't. I guess there's mail for you, too. Come on in."

He came in. He stood there, twisting his hat in his hands and you could see he was wondering where to spit.

"Why don't you get rid of that cud outside, Pat, and then come back in and have a nice visit with us? Don't get on that mangy old horse of yours and high-tail it, neither. You spit and come right back!"

What he said was a mumble, but it sounded a little like, "Yes, ma'am."

When he was outside, Mrs. Barker said, "He's dying to see you but he's so bashful it hurts. Just don't move sudden or you'll startle him like you would a deer."

He came back in, moving sidewise. He had pale, sandy hair, and his eyelashes and eyebrows were so thin and pale they hardly showed in that scarlet face of his. He was homely as a plucked turkey. I guessed he was about forty years old.

He sat stiff on a chair while Mrs. Barker and I went on about our business. After a while you could feel him let down little by little. He never said a word for an hour or more, then all of a sudden he spoke in a high voice, "Be good grass this spring with all this snow."

Mrs. Barker never turned around. "Sure will," she said.

"Hear Mrs. Rodgers's from New York," he said to her.

"That's right."

"Often wondered how people lived there. I heard they got a railroad running in a hole in the ground. Mighty dangerous, I'd think."

"No worse than a deep mine," said Mrs. Barker.

"Sure, but what's to keep all them high buildings from caving it in? Don't seem safe to me."

"It's safe enough," I said. He gave a little jump.

"Well, I got to go now," he said, standing up. He twisted his hat a couple of times. "Mighty pleased to meet you, ma'am." He didn't look at me. "Anything I can do, you let me know. Mighty glad to do it." He gulped a couple of times, and backed toward the door. "Well," he said, "well . . ."

All of a sudden he was gone. I heard his horse lope away. "More words than I've heard out of Pat in a month," said Mrs. Barker. "He sure liked you real good, Mrs. Rodgers. He could be a good friend, too, in this country."

"Mrs. Barker," I said, "there isn't any work a woman like me could get out here, is there?"

"Why, I don't know. You want to work?"

"I've got to. You're all kind to me and Bess is sure hospitable, but I can't just live here doing nothing."

"You're helping Bess a lot, you know."

"Well, maybe. But I've got to earn some money. I've got to make a place for myself."

Mrs. Barker turned and looked at me. "You know, Mrs. Rodgers, if I was you what I'd do? I'd go down to Nogales next week. You know what's going to happen next week?"

I shook my head no.

"Next week is February fourteenth. And on that day this territory becomes the State of Arizona, the newest, youngest, finest state in the Union! Mrs. Rodgers, there'll be some sights to see that day, and Nogales is a growing city. There ought to be lots of opportunities there for a smart woman like you."

I thought about it a long time. "I guess maybe you're right, Mrs. Barker. But I hate to leave the country for the city. I got a feeling, somehow, that this could be a good place for me. I don't know how, though."

I remembered that handsome woman I'd seen the day B.J. drove me over from Elgin. "How does that Mrs. Gates get along?"

"Aggie's got a ranch. She runs cattle. It's nothing you could do."

I couldn't, of course.

"All right," I said, "I guess I will go to Nogales."

chapter 3

MRS. BARKER had written her sister, the wife of Judge Dunphy, and asked them to take me in. So when the train stopped and I pulled my nose away from the window pane, I found a Mexican boy on the gravel platform who knew where the Judge lived, and took me there—a house halfway up a very steep hill on the west side of town.

Mrs. Dunphy looked so like Mrs. Barker that anyone would know they were sisters. She said, "Well, so here's the New York lady! My, my, I don't believe there's been a lady from New York in this town long as I can remember! Don't give that boy more than a nickel. Come in, come in."

I did, and Mrs. Dunphy said, "Now, Mrs. Rodgers, I'm sorry I don't have a room in my house for you. I figure you want to stay in Nogales a while. But the Joneses next door will be glad to have you. Mrs. Jones said you could stay and take your meals with them and she'd guess three dollars a week would be all right if that suited you."

That sounded reasonable to me, and I said so.

"That's fine, that's fine," said Mrs. Dunphy. "We'll go right over."

When we stepped out the door, the whole town was plain to see. I'd been so busy climbing the hill before that I hadn't turned around and looked.

Nogales was built in a wide canyon. The hills opposite, like the hills on the side where I was, were steep but rounded —no cliffs or anything like that. The bottom of the canyon ran generally north and south. In the very center was the railroad track, the one I'd come in from Elgin on, and also the one that came down from Tucson. The tracks went on south and the canyon sort of broadened out in that direction.

Mrs. Dunphy said, "That's Mexico. That there fence running across the middle of International Street is the border."

The hills on the other side of the line didn't look a bit different to me, and for a minute I was disappointed. Then I thought there wasn't any reason they should be different. The boundary was artificial; the hills were the same earth as on this side.

"Are all Mexicans bad?" I asked Mrs. Dunphy.

She gave me a look. "Never saw one who wasn't lazy as any pig! Can't trust them further than you can see them. They're dirty, too!"

I looked at the hills, the same each side, and I wondered if people weren't maybe the same way—people on the other side pretty much like the ones on this. But I didn't say it to Mrs. Dunphy because I could tell she believed what she said and it wouldn't do any good at all.

Mrs. Jones was a younger woman than me, scrawny as a plucked pullet and so cross-eyed that when she cried the tears must certainly run down her back. She was nice; she fluttered around me and helped me put my things away.

The next day was February fourteenth, nineteen hundred and twelve, and Arizona would officially be a state at twelve noon. Mrs. Jones said she expected there would be considerable excitement, and that she intended to go downtown and see it, just as soon as she got her housework done up. If I cared to wait, she'd be glad to have me go with her. But I wanted to see what the town was like, try to find some prospects of work, look around generally, so I said, "I think I'll go now, Mrs. Jones."

I put on my blue serge suit and my sailor hat and off I went. The sun was shining in the clear, deep blue sky, the hills were brown, but there was a feel of spring in the air. Back home, I thought, it's probably miserable, snowing, raining, wet dirty streets, horses slipping on the car tracks, houses stuffy with used-up air, nothing like this. How Jerry and Cissie and Tim would love this place! What it would do for them! I had to get cracking and find out what there was to find out.

It was exciting to be a stranger in a strange town, even

though it wasn't a very big one. People were hanging flags on the stores; they were talking and laughing. Some of them, men mostly, stared at me. Everybody knew I was a stranger in town. I thought, "Go ahead and look, boys. You're just as funny to me!"

I passed a combination pool hall and saloon. The smell was cool and sour. I remembered beer with Greg on hot summer nights, wine at holiday dinners. Only I couldn't remember Greg so well. While Tim and Cissie and Jerry were so clear and distinct that I could almost feel them— and how I did want to touch them, tousle the boys' hair, pat Cissie's chubby backside!— Greg was getting misty around the edges. I could still see his dear face, but as if there was a foggy glass over it. I couldn't touch him at all; I could remember that he had put his arms around me often, but I couldn't remember how they had felt. I guess it wasn't that I had forgotten Greg—I never could—but I was getting used to the idea of him not being in the world any more.

I passed an ice-cream and candy store, a drug store, a place that sold boots and saddles. Out on the street, a couple of cowmen were making fools of themselves, riding up and down and shooting off their guns. By golly, I said to myself, this sure was the real West.

And I was dead certain sure of it when a burly man stepped out into the middle of the street and just stood there with his hand up. The two cowmen pulled up their horses and looked sheepish. The burly man said something, slow and calm, and they handed over their guns and rode away up the street, even their backs looking ashamed, their hats suddenly floppy, not jaunty.

I couldn't help myself. I walked over to him and said, "That was a brave thing to do."

He took off his hat. He had a slab of a red face with little bright gray eyes half-hidden in it.

He said, "Why, you must be the New York lady. Mrs. Rodgers, ain't it? I'm Tom Patterson, sheriff. Let me know if I can ever do anything for you."

I said I would. He turned away and his coat blew open and the silver star pinned to his shirt flashed in the sunlight. I thought how I'd like to wear a star like that and do brave things. Then I remembered I was a woman and women didn't do things like that. They never wore stars nor carried guns—not that I wanted to carry a gun. If I'd known then that a star like that and a gun were going to get my hands on the kids sooner than anything else could have, I might have saved a lot of worry and work. But of course, I didn't know.

I wandered along the other side of the street and was staring into the jeweler's window, next door to Resswell's Barber Shop, when Mrs. Jones grabbed my arm.

"Oh, Mrs. Rodgers—" all out of breath—"I'm so glad I found you. You've just got to come right down to the courthouse with me. Mayor's going to speak, and Judge Dunphy. Mrs. Dunphy would never forgive me if you weren't there to hear."

I said, "Sure! Sure, I'll go. Let's start."

Mrs. Jones giggled. "Why, you sounded just like a Westerner, then."

I thought that a real pretty compliment, because that was what I wanted to sound like. So we started off up the street, arm in arm.

We hadn't gone far when we stopped. "Look, Mrs. Rodgers, there's a whole crowd of men in front of Resswell's saloon. We'd better go back and 'round by the other street."

She meant to cross the railroad tracks and go along on the other side. I couldn't see the sense of it.

"I don't see why," I said.

"Well, we'd just better. People in this town don't think much of women who hang around saloons."

I'd guessed Mrs. Jones was nice but sort of silly and now I was sure. "We're not going to hang around; we're going right past." I pulled her but she pulled back.

"I don't think . . . Those men . . ."

"Oh, for heaven's sake! I'm not afraid of men! Those men won't bother us!"

Then from way beyond the crowd of men, way up the street near the courthouse, I heard the finest music in the world: a thumping big brass band.

"What's that?" I asked.

"The Army band from the camp. They're going to play at the speaking."

"Well, I'm certainly not going to miss that." I grabbed Mrs. Jones's arm. "Come on, those men are probably watching a pair of fools fight and they'll never notice us."

Mrs. Jones said, "I don't know. . . . More likely, it's free beer. . . ."

"Just put your head back and your nose in the air!"

I dragged her along. I put my nose up as if I was walking down Fifth Avenue on Easter Sunday in a new ostrich-plume hat and boa and a velvet suit.

Mrs. Jones gave a nervous giggle. "You're sure not Western now!" Then she lifted her chin and we sailed on down the board sidewalk.

The men were laughing and talking and now I wasn't so sure we could walk right through them. We'd have to go out in the street, I guessed. But just before I was ready to step off into the dust, there was a commotion inside the crowd.

"Make way, gentlemen. Move to one side please. Ladies want to pass!"

The crowd opened and shoving them around with friendly pats on their shoulders was a big, handsome man with a sweeping mustache the color of old honey. He had very blue eyes and his face was a little red as if his skin was too fair for the Arizona sun. He gave me one of the kindest smiles I'd ever seen.

"Make way for the ladies!" he kept saying and shoving.

"Sure, sure, all right," said the men, moving back. They all had glasses in their hands, and I saw the attraction right away. It was a table draped in red, white and blue with a big galvanized-iron washtub sitting on it, a big cake of ice in the tub and what could only be champagne fizzing and sparkling around the ice.

"Ladies, it is statehood day," the big blond man said. "You should drink a toast to the newest state, to our state, to Arizona!"

A man said, "You ought to be down at the courthouse, too, Art."

The man with the mustache smiled wider than ever. "Not with the politicians, not me," he said. He reached out and the waiter at the table handed him two glasses of champagne.

"Here, ladies," he said, "to the great new young state of Arizona."

I reached right out and took mine. Mrs. Jones didn't want to, but I jabbed her in the ribs with my elbow and hissed, "Be polite."

The man called Art said, "Yes, let us always be polite." He reached back and the waiter looked a little surprised and hurried to fill a glass and hand it to him. He lifted it high. "So!" he said. *"Gesundheit!"*

"By God," said someone, "it's certain sure a day when old Art takes a drink!"

I felt very fine. I loved them all and I loved this place. I wanted to say something, too.

"Arizona," I yelled, "God bless her!"

Somebody shot off a gun, they all hooted and hollered and Art opened the other side of the crowd. We swept through for all the world like the whole darned Floradora Sextette itself.

The band was calling me, but I just had to ask Mrs. Jones, "Who was that? The nice man with the kind smile."

"Arthur Resswell," she said. "My, I hope Mr. Jones doesn't hear of this. Or Mrs. Dunphy. Goodness, we shouldn't have done that."

"Oh, you . . ." I said. But she was right. I mean, we couldn't have done it again. This time was all right; people treated it as a combination joke and dare. I was the lady from New York and so I was expected to be daring and different, and it was my first day in town, and it was the day Arizona became a state and the day they had champagne on the streets.

"Who's Arthur Resswell?" I asked, rushing Mrs. Jones along. I could hear the band getting louder.

"He calls it Artur. Some sort of European. Maybe German, I guess. Owns that saloon and the barber shop and a butcher store. Oh dear, why did we do it!"

I felt awful good, but I almost wanted to shake her. But we reached the crowd at the foot of the courthouse steps and there behind the speakers' platform was the band, all shiny brass. They were just wonderful and they played like angels. I pushed and squirmed and dragged Mrs. Jones along and got right into the front of the crowd, close enough so I could feel that lovely bass drum pounding in my stomach, just shivering right through me. The mayor made a speech, and Judge Dunphy, whom I liked as soon as he came to the front of the platform, spoke on the new State in the grand Union of States.

It was all fun, and the band played between each speech and the flag waved and people cheered and a couple of little boys set off firecrackers under the horse of a drunk cowboy up the street and the horse pitched and the cowboy's friends yelled at him not to pull leather and he swore at them and lost his hat and finally flew over the horse's head into the dust. It was a fine time. I was yelling and hollering with the best of them. I was happy and confident again, glad I was in the West and liking this place better every minute.

Then Mrs. Jones gasped, "Ted's lunch!" She wormed out of the crowd and went running away for all the world like a skinny little pullet after a June bug.

But I stayed to the bitter end when the band came marching down the steps and went banging and slamming and tooting their way back to their camp. It was gorgeous!

Then I went home to Mrs. Jones's and took a nap. The excitement had worn me out. Mrs. Dunphy called over just before I fell asleep and asked me if I'd stop in that evening. She wanted me to meet the Judge.

The Judge was a nice man, a little fat. Behind his glasses he had a pair of tired, kind eyes that you knew had seen too much of the meanness people can do. We sat there chatting and I told the Judge how much I enjoyed his speech. The last light faded out of the sky; it was full dark. The town got a little noisier; more firecrackers and guns went off, and once in a while someone would just open his mouth and whoop.

"They're sure celebrating," said the Judge. "And well they might. Be a long time 'fore another state joins the Union."

"No more land to make one out of."

"Maybe Alaska," said the Judge. "Maybe the Islands. Hear you drank some of Artur Resswell's champagne today."

"Oh, I did! He was nice. What is he?"

"Saloonkeeper, barber, owns a butcher shop," said Mrs. Dunphy.

"I know all that. I mean, where's he from? He has some sort of accent."

"Oh," said the Judge, "he's Austrian. From Vienna, he told me. Came over for the St. Louis Fair, liked it here, moved out west somehow. Barbered and made money, invested it in his saloon, hired his barbers, quit himself, set up his butcher shop. Art's one of our leading citizens, now, and a fine man, too. Doesn't drink or gamble, word's good as his bond, only fault is known as an easy touch on mining claims. Probably owns a share in half the gopher holes in Santa Cruz County."

"Is his wife Austrian, too?" I asked.

Mrs. Dunphy said, "He's got no wife."

"Come on," said the Judge. "Most time for the fireworks. Let's go outside."

After I got into bed that night and said my prayers, I couldn't drop right off to sleep, because I was feeling happy. I felt as if I belonged to this place, being here when it became a state. I was excited and wound up. All of a sudden I realized that Artur was the first man I had looked at as a man in a long time. Greg had been dead nearly a year, and in all that time, naturally, I hadn't thought of those things. And it probably wasn't right to now, only all at once I remembered how his arms would go around me and how he'd kiss me and the good feeling of putting my arms around him, being close and happy, knowing he was a man. I cried; I cried right then and there and was mad at myself for thinking earlier that I couldn't remember Greg. And Artur making me feel that way must mean he was as nice as Greg.

It was no disloyalty to Greg. It was a compliment for both of them.

Next morning, Nogales was a very quiet town. An awful lot of men had wish-I-hadn't-taken-that-last-one expressions on their faces, and when I passed the barber shop there was a crowd of cowmen waiting for rubs and hot towels.

I found the school that morning and talked to the principal, but, of course, that was hopeless, since I hadn't a bit of training.

Back at Mrs. Jones's for lunch, she told me Mrs. Dunphy had something to tell me. I went over there.

Mrs. Dunphy said, "I know you need work, Mrs. Rodgers, so I've been thinking of things you could do. Old Roy Hudgins owns the Hudgins Dairy out there on the Patagonia road 'bout half a mile. He's been looking for a housekeeper would stay with him awhile. Had a bunch of Mexican women, and they'd leave or he couldn't stand them, they was so dirty. I know he'd be pleased to have someone like you keeping house for him."

"That's the last thing I'll try, Mrs. Dunphy," I said. I felt it wouldn't advance me one step toward making a place for my children. I knew I couldn't make a home for Jerry and Cissie and Tim in a man's house. "But you're kind and good to think about me, to bother your head at all, and I thank you."

Mrs. Dunphy said, "Well, Mrs. Rodgers, there aren't likely to be many jobs in this town that you could get."

"I've got to find one, Mrs. Dunphy! And I hope you and the Judge will help me."

"Well," said Mrs. Dunphy, "there's one way you can make your way in this town. The men here want to get married so bad that none of our schoolteachers last more than a year."

"Oh, is that so?" I said.

Mrs. Dunphy drew a deep breath. "Well, Mrs. Rodgers, you could set your cap at someone. Only if you're thinking of Resswell, you'd better change your mind. He doesn't like women. But there's plenty of other well-off men here. That is, if you're able to get married!"

I was sorry afterwards because she meant well in her own cold sort of way. But I lost my temper some.

"Mrs. Dunphy, it's none of your business what I can or can't do! About anything! But I'll tell you right now I had a wonderful husband and he's not been dead very long, and I just can't look at any man!"

I was mad and sad at the same time, and I guess I was mad at myself because I wasn't exactly telling the truth. Last night had showed me that I wasn't. I had no thoughts of any particular man, but I did remember the nice things about a man, the nice things about Greg. It would be kind of good to know again that when a man took my arm to help me into a carriage, he wasn't only doing it out of politeness, but partly because he wanted to touch me and I wanted him to touch me.

Nothing much went on in Nogales between noon and two o'clock. The town almost went to sleep. So I waited till two o'clock, and then straightened myself up and went downtown again.

I saw the proprietor of the Owl Drug Store but he had nothing for me.

When I came out on the sidewalk there was the nice, big, blond man from the crowd at the saloon, smiling at me with his hat in his hand.

"I am Artur Resswell," he said. "And I have learned your name. It is Mrs. Rodgers. You come from New York."

There was something about him that made me feel very American. I wanted to help him because this was a strange land for him. Even though he was a lot bigger than me and even though Judge Dunphy said he was so successful, there was a sort of wide-openness about his blue eyes and a childish sort of honesty in his nice face that made me want to take care of him, to help him. All this made me feel particularly Western, so I said, "You're dern tootin' certain sure right, pard."

"Ha," he said, waving his hat, "already you talk like one of us."

"One of us!" I thought. "That's a laugh!" No one could ever mistake him for a Westerner whenever he opened his

30

mouth. It wasn't only his accent, but the way he put his words together. No American ever talked the way Artur did.

"Well, thank you," I said, and started on.

"But I have something to talk with you," he said. "Please, I hear you are looking for a job and I think I am looking for a lady like you. Maybe you would have a soda with me and I could tell you what I think."

"Why, all right," I said. That was Western, too, wasn't it? Don't have to bother about introductions to go have a soda with a man and talk about a job. Or was it abandoned? Well, not abandoned, but a little too free and easy?

"Then we will step into Pete's here." He waved his hat and kind of shooed me into the Elite Soda Parlor.

There wasn't anybody in it except ourselves. Artur said, "What flavor do you like, Mrs. Rodgers?"

"Chocolate."

"Chocolate for the lady, Pete," he said. "The usual for me."

The usual turned out to be vanilla with chocolate ice cream. I said, "I never heard of a saloonkeeper drinking soda."

Artur smiled. "That glass of wine with you, that is the first I have since New Year's. And then only one, too. I do not drink." He began to eat his soda as if there was nothing else in the world as important.

It almost made me mad for a minute, the way he'd suddenly forgotten me. Then I saw the sense in it. People last a lot longer than sodas, which are only good right when they're made. I'd still be here when both our sodas were gone, so I started contentedly on mine.

Halfway through it, I got the queerest feeling. Sitting here with Artur, eating the first soda we ever ate together, made me think of the day I started west, standing there on the ferry and watching the Singer and the World Buildings get smaller and smaller. Not that this time was sad or hurtful —it was good and it was fun—but it had a sort of separateness about it, a once-only feeling like it had had. I thought, "I guess I'll always remember sitting here in the Elite Soda Parlor with Artur Resswell."

31

And I always have.

I'd no more than spooned up the last bit of chocolate ice cream—I always eat the ice cream last, it's the best part—when Artur said politely, "Please, Mrs. Rodgers, may I smoke a cigar?"

"Oh, yes," I said.

His question took me back to Brooklyn for a moment. Greg always asked if he could smoke when he finished a meal. I don't know why, but something made me wonder what Greg would have thought of Artur. I tried to see Artur through Greg's eyes, but I couldn't manage that. I could only say to myself that I was sure Greg would have liked him just as well as I did. I knew he wouldn't have minded me drinking a soda with him.

Artur carefully put out his match. "You think it is some time you will stay here for?" he asked.

When I straightened that out for myself, I said, "Yes."

"Oh." He cleared his throat. "Please, you do not like it in New York?"

"Brooklyn," I said. "Though it's the same thing. Yes, I liked it there."

Artur gave the tiniest frown. "Then what I heard is perhaps wrong and you are just making a visit here?"

"Oh, no!" I said. "I want to stay here."

"Good," said Artur, "but perhaps you left someone in New York?"

I almost yelled. "I sure did! Three wonderful children!" But that sure wasn't his business, and I saw no reason to tell him. In a minute I was mighty glad I hadn't.

I only said, "My husband died last spring . . ."

"It must be that way, I thought," said Artur. "I am very sorry, Mrs. Rodgers."

I looked at him, and by golly, he meant it! He was genuinely sorry and wasn't just saying it because it was manners to say so.

I said the only thing I could. "Thank you, Mr. Resswell."

"Then you have responsibilities only to yourself, not so?" said Artur.

I nodded. I wondered whether to tell him about the kids

now or not. If I did, he might think that I'd spend too much of my time thinking about them, and not enough on my work, whatever it was to be.

"I am a good reader of character," he said. "Time after time, I say to myself, 'That man is honest; you can grubstake him.' Perhaps three or four out of so many I don't know do not pay me back."

"That's fine," I said.

He nodded wisely. "To myself I said, 'That Mrs. Rodgers, she has to look after only herself or she would not be here.' Now I see I was right. You are a good lady and too good to go away and leave anyone behind who needs you."

"Well . . ." I said. "After all . . ."

I didn't feel too good, all of a sudden. I was just about to tell him how old Mrs. Rodgers was looking after the children a whole lot better than I could at this particular time—better from a food, clothes, and roof-over-the-head standpoint, anyhow. I was just about to tell him that, when he said, "It happened to me."

"Why you poor big old thing!" I thought.

"Yes," he said, "I was only six when my mother left."

If that had happened to him, and happened tragically, as his tone of voice would indicate, I was sure glad he didn't know about me waltzing away from my three!

What difference did it make, though, I thought?

Well, Artur had a niceness about him, a sort of self-respecting likeableness that made you want to have his very best opinion. It did that to me, anyhow. And if his mother had been so bad to him—though there might have been reasons he never knew about—he wasn't likely to want another woman who looked as if she was doing the same thing working for him. At least, I thought he wouldn't. I wanted to hear about that job. Maybe it would be the one that would make it possible for me to bring my children out here.

"It is not good for young children to not have a mother," he said.

I wished he'd stop talking like that. It made me feel as if maybe I hadn't done all I could to stay with the kids.

But I had thought and thought, and tried and tried, and I couldn't. Coming west was doing the best thing I could, I was sure.

So I said, "Yes, I guess so. I have a stepmother."

"That is better than none at all," Artur said.

"Why, yes," I said. "I guess so."

"No," said Artur. "That is not good. . . ." He sat there with a musing look on his face. I wondered what bad times he was remembering, what old hurts and pains. I thought of what Mrs. Dunphy had said about him—how he didn't like women. She might believe that and so might he, but I didn't. I looked at his hands, long-fingered, clean and strong with pale golden hairs all over their backs. I looked at his mouth; it was full-lipped and firm, a good man's mouth. He'd made me remember what a man was like, hadn't he? No, however he might think he felt, he didn't truly hate women. But he was wary of them. The little boy who had been deserted at six wasn't going to take a chance getting hurt again.

Wouldn't he dislike me if he knew about Jerry, Cissie and Tim!

They were none of his business. "You said something about a job?" I asked.

Artur puffed his cigar, took it out of his mouth and looked at the lit end of it in the questioning way men do, as if it could tell them something. Then, he said, "Mrs. Rodgers, maybe I know how you and me can make some money."

"I could sure do with some."

Artur said, "You know that I have a barber shop besides my saloon?"

"Across the street," I said.

He nodded. "Well, for some time I have thought and thought how I could make more money in the barber business and just before you came I have an idea. I will have a manicurist in the shop! This will be novel; many men will come to have their hands held by pretty lady. You will come and work for me. You will be manicurist. Cowmen will ride in from miles around to go to Resswell's barber shop and have their hands held by the lady from New York."

I wasn't so certain of that. "I don't see why," I said.

Artur nodded positively. "You will see. Besides, that is for me to worry. I pay you six dollars a week. That is sure. What manicuring brings in over six dollars we split half and half. Tipping is not a custom here, but if anyone does, you keep it. Now what do you think?"

I hadn't a thing to lose. "It's all right by me."

Artur's nice blue eyes sparkled and he chuckled. "That is fine, fine!" He rubbed his hands together.

"But I don't know a thing about manicuring. How will the customers like that?"

"Nothing, nothing!" said Artur airily waving his hands. "Nothing think of it! Just cut off the big nails and smooth them out a little with file or sandpaper stick and push the skin back around the nails with orange stick. I will have everything prepared and we will start Saturday. That is best day to start because the shop does most business then."

This was the very best thing that had happened since I'd left New York. It began to look to me, that afternoon in the Elite Soda Parlor, that I'd get my children quicker than I thought.

Artur and I shook hands when we parted. I went almost running up the hill to the Judge's house. I had to share my good news with someone.

Mrs. Dunphy didn't think too much of it, though. "Can't say I'd like to be sitting there in a barber shop full of men a-holding hands with some strange man and him breathing whisky and tobacco at me. All them men a-staring and people on the street looking in the windows. No, Mrs. Rodgers," she shook her head, "it's honest work, that I can't deny, but it's not what I'd choose for myself."

"You don't have to, Mrs. Dunphy. You've got a husband to support you."

She gave me a sharp look. "That Arthur Resswell is a handsome man."

I just said, "Yes, I guess he is." I knew what she was driving at, and I certainly wasn't going to give her any chance to think it. It wasn't so, anyhow.

"I've got an idea, Mrs. Rodgers," she said, "that you've led a sheltered kind of life. That's all well and good till you have to take care of yourself like you do now, being a widow. But there's a lot of people around here think Arthur Resswell's such a fine man . . ."

"He is, Mrs. Dunphy, and I don't want to hear any gossip about him. . . ."

"This isn't gossip. This is something I just want you to know if you're going to work for him."

She sucked her lips in and stood there waiting for me to beg her to tell me, but of course, I didn't, and since she wanted to tell me very badly, she couldn't wait.

"I happen to know that Artur Resswell sends money abroad," she said, in a significant voice. "To a family, I happen to know. There are children. . . ."

"Children?" I thought that Artur was exactly the sort of man who would send money to children.

"It's my belief," said Mrs. Dunphy, "that the man's got a family over there in Austria. He might even have a wife!" She looked at me, hard.

Well, of course, he could have, and it wasn't my business or Mrs. Dunphy's if he had. But she had riled me. I asked, "I thought you said he didn't like women?"

That didn't stop her. "Maybe that's why! Ran away from his wife and family . . ."

"Supports them, you said, though, even if he can't stand her."

"Well," she said grudgingly, "yes. But you just watch your step, Mrs. Rodgers, just watch your step."

Artur introduced me to all the barbers after the shop closed Friday night at five. Big black Joe was his head barber, a fine-looking man with a deep, gentle voice that was firm but respectful. You could see he'd tolerate no nonsense. The Mexicans who worked with him respected him, as did the customers. After Artur quit hanging around the shop, Joe watched out for me just as well. When the talk got what he considered rough—and that didn't take long—he'd say in that wonderful voice, "Now, gents, remember we've got a lady in the shop."

The hardest cowboys would lower their voices or stop talking entirely. It wasn't only Joe; it was that they'd really forgotten I was there, and as soon as they remembered it—not just me, but a woman—they remembered their manners.

But that was later.

First came Saturday and nine o'clock, and my first day at my new job. Artur was there. He'd shown me how to lay out my table the evening before.

I was wearing my blue suit and a stiff shirtwaist with a high collar. I had borrowed a little white apron from Mrs. Jones, and when I got to the shop I took off my jacket and put on the apron. I sat behind my table looking cool, I hoped, but my heart was beating fast and I was sure I was shaking and I couldn't understand a thing Artur said.

The table was in the window to the right of the door with plenty of light for working purposes, though Artur had figured it more to be conspicuous for advertising purposes. But he'd been smart enough to rig a thin curtain across the window so it looked private enough for bashful men to not feel shy while their hands were held by a strange woman. I didn't realize how smart Artur had been about all this till the first couple of days went past and I got over my scaredness.

Nothing happened all morning. Men came in and went out with shaves and haircuts, but not a one wanted his nails done, though all three barbers were suggesting manicures and Artur, who stayed right in the shop all day, talked manicure too. I got a little more composed when nothing happened, but Artur looked sort of worried as the time went on. It went very fast for me, even though I did nothing. It always does the first time you do something new, whether it's a job, meeting a new and likable person, making a journey, learning a skill.

Artur sent me home for lunch at twelve o'clock. Mrs. Jones asked how it was going.

"No good," I said, and I was feeling low. "Not a single customer. Oh, I want a cup of coffee!"

I went back to the shop at two o'clock as Artur had told me. At three o'clock I had my first customer. He was a cowboy and he was a little drunk, I think. Anyhow, he took a dare from the friend he'd come in with and came over to the table.

"Would you fix my fingernails, ma'am?" he said very politely.

"I'll be glad to," I said. "Sit right down."

I had to reach over and take his hand. It was practically shaking, which made me feel a lot better. If he was nervous, why should I be? I thought.

He said, "Don't let on I'm snorty, ma'am. My *amigo* bet I wouldn't do this. Ain't going to hurt much, is it?"

"Hurt!" I said. "A big fellow like you."

"I aim to do some dancing at the *baile* tonight," he said, "and I'd sure like to look right purty."

"You will," I said.

He hadn't washed his hands real good in Lord knew when and his fingernails were just black. I forgot what Artur had told me and just took up the clippers and snipped right down to the quick. When I got through, he didn't have a nail to scratch himself with and I figured the dirt would have a chance to wear off. As for doing anything with his cuticle, it was a job for a blacksmith with a hoof rasp. I turned him loose, and he paid Artur, who was handling the cash register, and cracked his friend on the back and yelled, "You're next, *amigo*, you're sure next!"

"What you can do I can do!" said the friend with an expression on his face like he was going to be shot. He plunked himself down across from me.

I caught a sort of queer look from Artur and he seemed to be trying to tell me something, but I had the bit in my teeth as it was, and just rared up and tore away. I hacked his nails, which were as bad as the other's, right down to the quick, said, "There you are," and sat back for the next customer.

It wasn't hard work, I thought, and by that time my first friend was standing outside the door practically yelling like a sideshow barker. "Come get a manycure!" he yelled. "Git your dirty old fingernails chopped off by the lady from New York."

His friend joined him. Artur started over to speak to me,

but they came hustling back in the door with a sheepish-looking cowhand between them, plunked him down in the chair, and each one grabbed a hand and held it out to me.

I whacked his nails off.

Soft job, I thought. I hadn't touched an instrument except my clippers.

Then a fellow finished a haircut and my two friends held him up at the door and pushed him into the chair. I think he would have come anyhow, just wanted a little urging.

Two of them went out on the street and corralled a couple more and before you knew it there was a line of men waiting to have their nails cut, standing outside the window, trying to peer in, and my table was adrift with nail clippings and Artur had gone out the back door of the shop, red in the face, shaking with laughter. I guessed he was tickled to death with the business we were doing.

The rush stopped about five o'clock. I'd done eight dollars and fifty cents worth of manicures.

Saturday the shop stayed open till eight. At six o'clock Artur came back. His eyes were smiling. "Mrs. Rodgers, in celebration you will honor me with dinner at the Border Café, please?"

"That's mighty kind of you, Mr. Resswell," I said. "Thank you, I will."

We'd finished our steaks when Artur told me what he had to tell. "You should not cut all the nails off," he said. "You should trim and shape them. I watched with alarm at first, sure they would complain, but they know nothing, either. Look, Mrs. Rodgers, why did you do it? You forgot what I told you."

I was afraid he was going to fire me. Then I thought he wouldn't have taken me to dinner to fire me. I said, "They were so dirty and hard. It was easier that way."

Artur gave a great laugh. "That is the American way! Easier! But from now on, if you remember to make the man soak his hand in the bowl of water . . ."

"Water!" I said. "My Lord, I forgot about that!"

"So simple," said Artur. "Oh, you are wonderful, dear

Mrs. Rodgers. Please, what do people call you without the Mrs.?"

"Oh, Rodgers, or Rodge. Goodness, I'm sorry, Mr. Resswell."

"Your first name," he said, "please."

"Lucretia. Lu for short."

"Lu," he said, as if he was tasting it and trying to tell whether he'd like it. "Yes, Lu. That is nice. You call me Artur and I will call you Lu."

He did. The only man in all of Arizona who called me Lu.

chapter 4

IT WAS six weeks later to the day that I got off the train in Elgin.

What had happened was this: the manicure business went bad and I quit it after four weeks. Artur had said the novelty of it would make it go, and it did, for a couple of weeks. Then the novelty must have worn off—something he hadn't counted on—and I sat for two weeks with my hands in my lap or reading a book. Finally, I told Artur I wanted to quit.

"But why, Lu? Do you not like it here?"

"Sure I do, but I'm not going to sit here doing nothing and letting you pay me for it."

Artur felt bad about it, and so did I, because I had really made a sincere friend in him. Maybe a little more than a friend—I felt that he thought it was something special. And I must admit I liked having dinner with him at the Border Café on Saturdays, liked him walking me up the hill when the shop closed late, liked talking to him. Artur Resswell was first of all a good man. I mean he was kind and considerate and thoughtful and, I guess, the most honest man I've ever known. He was fun, too; in his mild, sort of held-back way, he could make things seem awful funny. He had me laughing all the time, and that was a good thing for me. It gave me confidence for what I did later, after I'd worked a week for Pete Anagakos as a cashier. He had the same idea as Artur: novelty, pack them in. But he either was smarter—which he really wasn't—or quicker to give up a gamble. He fired me the Saturday that ended that week.

Artur walked me up the hill that night, just the same as the other Saturdays. "Now, Lu, what are you going to do?"

"I've been thinking. I had a pretty good hunch Pete wouldn't keep me on, and I was right. I sat down the other night and I said to myself, 'Lu Rodgers, you've been too impatient, too grabby. You're going at this blind and rushing and bull-headed.'"

"No, no, it is a nice head, a pretty head with its pile of brown hair," said Artur.

I couldn't tell whether he was laughing or didn't understand what bull-headed meant. I said, "Bull-headed is the way you do things, Artur. Like all you Dutchmen, bull-headed."

He chuckled down deep in his throat. "Viennese is not Dutch, Lu," he said. He said that every time I called him a Dutchman, so of course I thought it was a joke to call him one.

"Never mind, Artur," I said. "Let me tell you about this. I've been trying too hard to get set too fast. I'm impatient. I want . . ."

I stopped at that. I was almost going to tell him I wanted my children with me and wanted them as quickly as possible. I don't know exactly what stopped me; I suppose I didn't want to bear the look he'd give me, didn't want him to think about me the way he would when he learned I'd left Jerry and Cissie and Tim back there in Brooklyn. I couldn't make him believe I was going to get them back with me, that I was working to bring them out here.

It was surely a thing he'd be bull-headed about.

I did so wish it hadn't happened to him. Maybe that was why he wasn't married; maybe he couldn't take the responsibility of a family and children. Or maybe Mrs. Dunphy was right.

All of a sudden I found myself asking a terribly impertinent question. "Are you married, Artur?"

He gave me an amazed stare, as he had every right to. But he didn't get mad. He said slowly, "No, Lu, I never was." Then he smiled and cocked his big, handsome head to one side while his eyes got bluer with his smile. "Why should you ask me that?"

"Just curious," I said, "just curious!" I couldn't think of

any other reason to give him. It didn't make much sense for his answer to give me a sort of pleasure, almost a relief, you might say. But it did.

"I think," he said slowly, "people talk." He nodded his head. "People always talk," he said. "I think they tell you I send money home. So I do—I send money home for my sister's children."

"Oh, Artur," I said, "that's just fine!" And I was glad; it was exactly the sort of thing I knew Artur would do. "But I'm sorry for her. . . ."

"Do not be!" he said with the fiercest frown I'd ever seen on that ordinarily good-natured face of his.

"But if she's a widow like me . . ."

"Not a widow!" he said. "Well, you will think I am angry with you. It is not that. It is that I find it hard to remember that she is my sister. . . ."

My hand was on his arm and I could feel how tense he was, so I thought I'd better ask no more about his sister. If he wanted to tell me, he would. If he didn't, asking would only aggravate him. But, Lord, I thought, hasn't there ever been a pleasant woman in his life?

I wanted to ask him that, but I guessed it wouldn't sound very soothing. So I just said, "Well, Artur, let me tell you what I've been thinking of doing."

"Delighted," said Artur politely and warmly, sounding almost like Teddy Roosevelt.

"Well, I want to—make a place for myself in this country and I know how I'm going to. Mrs. Dunphy told me Hudgins, the milkman, was looking for a housekeeper. . . ."

"So . . ." said Artur. "Yes, I have heard, but . . ."

"But that's no way for a woman to make a place for herself," I said. "She never gets level with the man. I mean she's just a hired hand and no more unless she marries him finally. Well, that's nothing I want. . . ."

"No?" asked Artur.

"Nope."

"Never?"

"Oh, I don't know about that. Stop interrupting me, Artur! So housekeeping for a man is no good. But housekeeping for a woman would be different. Good chance there, with the right woman, to become a sort of partner. Work for little, but have an agreement that you share the profits . . ."

"Now, Lu," said Artur, very patiently, "what kind of profits comes out of a house? I mean a housekeeping."

"Oh, nothing to that! Not in town. Don't you understand what I'm saying, Artur? The country—out there in Canelo."

Artur stood still and laughed. I knew he was laughing at me, but he had such a nice laugh and I was sure he liked me and wasn't being mean, so I laughed too.

When he finished, he said, "If you could find a lady out there who wanted a housekeeper or sort of lady hired hand . . ."

"That's it; that's it! Lady hired hand! Woman hired hand!"

"My goodness, Lu," he went on, "you'd have to learn to ride a horse and rope cattle. You can't do that!"

"I can!" I guess I stamped my foot. "I certainly can, Artur Resswell, and I'm going to!"

So here I was in Elgin. I had written Mrs. Barker and asked if there was any woman she knew of who wanted a woman to help her, someone to do housework or anything else. I didn't expect to earn much, either.

Of course, there was really just one woman I had in mind. It was that woman I'd seen the first day I got to Canelo, the woman who went riding after her own cattle on a day cold enough to freeze you stiff, the woman who lived alone: Aggie Gates.

Three days later I heard from Mrs. Barker. Mrs. Gates thought she'd like to try to see how she and me would get along. She'd pay eight dollars a month and found.

A good long time later, Aggie told me what happened. Old man Barker went over to tell Aggie about my letter. He rode up, she said, and hollered and when she came out he yelled, "Aggie, we can't get another man for you, but we sure got you a nice woman!" This was a great joke to him because then Aggie was a widow who had had three husbands.

When Mr. Barker got through slapping his thigh and

bellowing with laughter, Aggie asked who it was. "That woman from New York," said Barker, "the one who stayed with Bess Oryx a while."

Aggie remembered me, though we hadn't exchanged two words.

So Mrs. Barker wrote and I got on the train and when I did, I was thinking, "I'm going home. I'm going to the right place. This is for me!"

Standing there across from the hotel—still not finished—I was thinking this while B.J. loaded up his buckboard with the single mail sack, and then told me to get in, and off we went.

No snow this time. Spring was here and the grass was green and sparkling in the sunshine. The sky was high and clear blue. Over eastward the Huachucas cut off the earth and reached for the sky, tall and dark, running south as far as you could see. The little burros trotted like they knew I was in a hurry and B.J. was talking about what a fine thing it was to be a state.

It was a fine thing, I thought, and a fine thing to start out with the youngest state and start to learn how to live in that state, to learn what you had to do to live the way people lived here.

We came up out of the canyon and a couple of miles more and we would be in Canelo, at the house and homestead of Aggie Gates. I was wearing a blue-straw sailor with a veil and my blue suit and I was sitting there beside B.J. listening to him when a couple of women on horses suddenly came up out of an arroyo. B.J. stopped. "Hello, Clara," he said. "Hello, Minnie! What you doing up here?"

"Looking for a cow. You seen a old brindle longhorn . . . ?"

I wasn't listening because I was looking at them. They rode astride in divided skirts and they both wore sunbonnets. I had a feeling they weren't really looking for a cow and that they hadn't just happened to stop us.

B.J. introduced me then. "Mrs. Dan Langwood," he said, and I knew that was the wife of Aggie Gates's son, "and Mrs. Angus MacBain."

They were polite, but it was like they were choking something down. They said they must go along, and they rode past us and B.J. started his burros. I looked back and they were leaning over, laughing fit to kill. I couldn't see what they were laughing at.

Later they told me they had ridden out on purpose to see the woman who was going to work for Aggie. I guess I looked pretty prim and proper, sitting there stiff in my veil and suit. Because they said to each other, "That old maid! Aggie'll never get along with that old maid!"

I suppose I was prim and strained and straight. Part of learning to get along in the West was to learn not to be.

Then there it was, the low stone house with the long porch around its front and side. There was the barn across the road, and the corral, and the pasture lot. There was the hill across the creek with the cottonwoods waving high and green beside it, the hill behind which Barker's stood. Over beyond the hill, I knew, was the mighty wall of the Huachucas, solid and dark against the sky. But mostly, I was looking at the house I was going to live in.

A rubber-tired buggy stood in front of it with a fat bay horse hitched to it. B.J. said, "That Charles Jackson. He's courting Aggie."

B.J. stopped his team ahead of the buggy and I got out and he handed me my bags and I went up to the house. Two dogs, mostly collie, with a lot of other kinds mixed in, woofed at me but didn't get up. They looked friendly, anyhow.

"Whooie, whooie!" I called, "anybody home here?"

A firm, no-nonsense voice answered, "Come in!"

I did.

My eyes were squinched from the sun outside and I couldn't see very well at first. "In the kitchen!" the voice called impatiently.

I just dropped my bags and ran. I bumped a piece of furniture or two, but by the time I got to the kitchen I was seeing all right.

There she was, there was Aggie Gates, tall and handsome with black hair, red cheeks, and snapping black eyes. She was ironing, and she whirled around, put the iron down on the stove and whirled back.

"Well, Mrs. Rodgers, glad you got here!" She unfastened her apron and whipped it over the back of a chair. "This is Mr. Jackson," she said. "Mr. Charles Jackson."

He was a heavy-set, good-looking man with a handle-bar mustache and brown eyes. He wore a regular dark business suit with a thick gold watch chain across his vest. "Pleased to meet you, Mrs. Rodgers," he said.

"You just put away this ironing, Mrs. Rodgers," said Aggie, "and then you can peel those apples. Put the ironing in the other room on the table, this time. You'll soon learn where it goes, though. All right, Charles, soon as I get my hat we'll go!"

She was out of the room like a flash, graceful and sleek. Mr. Jackson shook his head in admiration. "Sure is a mover, Aggie is," he said. "Don't let her trouble you, that's just the way she is. Mighty fine woman."

Just then I wasn't so sure. When she came flashing back with a big black hat with a red rose on one side, I almost told her I wasn't staying. But I didn't; I guessed I could make a little more of a try at it.

I didn't say a word. She stood there a minute looking at me; then she gave me a smile that was like the sun busting out from behind a cloud, a big smile that wasn't just mouth, but eyes too. She sort of nodded her head.

"I'm going riding, Mrs. Rodgers. You just go ahead with the apples."

All I said was, "All right."

I learned by experience that Aggie always had a job to fit any person who appeared; didn't matter if they were two or ninety, Aggie had a job that needed doing, was suitable to their ability, and that they could start on right off.

I started peeling the apples and putting the peeled ones to soak in a big pan of water. It must have been five minutes later when I realized that here I was standing peeling apples like mad with my hat still on, my bag beside the door, not even a breath taken since I came in.

I said, "Lucretia Rodgers, you're a silly ninny!"

I put down my paring knife, dried my hands on a flour-sack dish towel and looked around the kitchen.

It was even more primitive a room than Bess's place beside the schoolhouse. It was just the rock walls of the house, not covered with anything, just rough as they came from the mason's trowel. There was a great, big, black range that almost took up one side of the room, on the opposite side a sink with a pump and a window over it, alongside it a door that led into a rock-walled storeroom or larder. I opened the door in the wall between the sink and the stove. It was an outside door. A path led away from it past a woodpile and on up a little rise to a small privy that had a couple of scrub oaks growing beside it.

I went into the living room. It had an enormous rough stone fireplace almost taking up one side of it. The other walls had been plastered and painted. There were two windows either side of the front door, a table in the center of the room, and some chairs scattered around. Over in the corner by the kitchen was a cot.

I opened the door at the front end of the room and found what had to be Aggie's bedroom. A three-quarter brass bed and a dresser and a washstand filled most of it. One corner was curtained off for a clothes closet. It wasn't too cheerful, but she had tried; she had ruffled curtains at the windows.

It looked to me as if I'd be sleeping on the cot in the living room. I guessed I could stand it.

I changed out of my suit into a skirt and shirtwaist and found a flour-sacking apron. Then I put the ironing away, finished the apples, tidied up the kitchen and had nothing more to do. I went out and sat on the porch in one of the old kitchen chairs that stood on it. The dogs weren't around.

The porch was just wide old splintery boards about five feet long, laid endwise to the house and propped on logs at the outside. I sat there, sort of dreaming, while the afternoon wore away. Down in the pasture behind the barn were four, five horses. I wondered which one of them I'd be riding; then I got very brave, the way you do in daydreams, and was sure I could ride any of them. It wasn't long till I saw myself just loping along, all up and down the hills, working cattle, yelling, whirling my rope, even carrying a gun and shooting it off in a stampede some wild night with the lightning cracking and the rain a-pouring down and the cattle just running belly to ground. Yes, and shooting the rustlers who had started it all, too! Oh, it was a brave dream!

It was sure interesting, too, because I never heard the horse nor saw it till it stopped dead in front of me. In the saddle was red-faced, china-blue-eyed Pat Malloy, little dribbles of tobacco juice seeping out of the corners of his mouth, his Adam's apple working like a turkey gobbler's.

I was startled enough so that he had time to get out words. "Howdy, Mrs. Rodgers."

"Good afternoon, Mr. Malloy," I said.

His face got even redder. "So you remember me!" he said, like he sure hadn't expected it. I took it that the increased color was due to pleasure as much as embarrassment.

"Of course, I remember you. You're the first real Western cowhand I ever met, Mr. Malloy." Didn't matter whether that was strictly true or not; it ought to make him feel good.

It did. He couldn't get any redder, but his Adam's apple jerked up and down faster. He even stammered a little. "Th-thanks, thanks very much!" he said. "Hear you're going to stay with Aggie."

"I am if she'll have me," I said.

"Oh, she will, all right. She has trouble getting people to stay. Oh, gosh! I mean, sometimes people don't last so long with Aggie. No, no . . ." He was getting more and more confused. "Well, better git along. Ma's waiting for me. Anything I can do, you tell me. Live right over there behind that ridge. Guess you can see our smoke from here."

He tipped his hat, kicked his horse, and started off. He yelled back, "I didn't mean that the way it sounds. I just mean some find her hard to get along with." He must have realized that was just as bad, because he gave a despairing wave and kicked his horse into a run.

In spite of what Pat said I liked this place. It was peaceful and it felt right. The sunshine was so bright, the air so clear. The hills were green. The cottonwoods were feathery with new leaves and their branches stood up tall against the blue sky. I could just see Jerry pounding down the hill from Barker's on his horse, Cissie and Tim on ponies, their faces tan and healthy, their muscles hard, all of them yelling for dinner. Oh, I could practically see them unsaddling their horses in the corral and running across to fling their arms around me! Real, live, hearty, Western kids!

What I did see was a huge black cat coming across the road from the pasture field. He had a bushy-tailed animal in his mouth that must be a squirrel, I knew. He saw me sitting there, because his tail went up the way a cat's tail will when he's pleased and eager, and he moved a little faster, though not much. He was as dignified as a judge and handsomer than most.

"What's your name?" I asked when he crossed the road. His mouth was too full to answer, so he came right up and dropped the squirrel at my shoe. It was stone dead. The big cat said, "Meeyawp!"

I put my hand down and he sniffed it and then rubbed his snoot against it the way a cat does when he's very pleased and friendly. He made me feel more welcome than Aggie had. I scratched him behind the ears and he said, "Meeyawp!" again, but with a different inflection, and jumped up in my lap, turned around once, and settled down, purring.

I stroked his head. "I don't know whether I ought to let you be so lazy," I said. But I let him stay.

He was still there, but very sound asleep, about half an hour later when the buggy rolled up, the dogs running behind it. They came over to inspect me; one of them sniffed at the cat, who opened one eye and lifted a paw in a warning gesture. The other dog found the dead squirrel, snatched it up and went tearing out toward the barn, his friend hard after him.

Mr. Jackson helped Aggie out of the buggy, got back in, and went up the road toward Elgin. Aggie came up to the house.

I wondered if it would have been better if I'd been working when she arrived, but I wasn't going to hop up for her.

She looked at me, saw the cat, smiled very friendlily and said, "So Satan's taken to you. That's fine."

"I like cats."

"Well, now, we'd better get you settled. You'll have to sleep on the cot in there, unless you want to sleep outdoors. You could put it out on the porch if you want to, or round back of the lumber room."

That was a wooden shack built up against the house so it made an ell on the north side. It was used as a storeroom for all kinds of things.

I thought I'd better sleep inside till I got used to the place, I said. But I liked the idea of sleeping out where I could wake up and look at the stars and feel the wind in my face. I guessed I'd do that after awhile, when the nights got warmer.

So I was settled and Aggie couldn't have been nicer. "I'm going to call you Rodge," she said, "and you call me Aggie." She had lots of plans now that I was there. She'd been needing help a long time, she said, and while I couldn't know much about a lot of things, she was sure she could teach me. I guessed I could learn. I meant to make this thing work.

That was my first day in what was to be my home for a long time. There was nothing very special about it, and yet, afterward, looking back, I could see how it was a small pattern of what all the time would be. There was Aggie, first hard and cold and strange, suddenly giving a melting smile, then going away leaving me puzzled, then coming back as friendly as anyone could ask for. And there was the little adventure with Satan the cat, and in the future there'd always be new things like that. And there was my feeling that this was best, what I was doing. It turned out I was right about that.

When I went to bed that night it was pitch dark. I felt a little strange in that strange house, with that strange woman sleeping a few feet away behind the wall.

Pitch dark, and me a little lonesome, a little fearful, not enough to want to quit, but enough so I'd like to have had something familiar and friendly with me. Still, I had almost got to sleep, when I felt a thump on the foot end of the cot. It was a friendly thump; I waited.

Hard little feet walked right up my stomach and Satan smelled my face, then stuck his tongue out and gave me a couple of swipes on the cheek. Then he turned around and curled up beside me, purred awhile, and we both fell asleep.

Well, the days went on and I began to fit in. I learned to do things the way Aggie liked them done, and maybe I taught her a few new ways. I met her son, Dan Langwood, a tall, handsome, almost Indian-looking fellow, who came over with his wife, Clara, pretty as a picture, one of the pair who'd stopped me and B.J. on the way in. The other one, Minnie MacBain, came over at times, too. She was Aggie's sister. She had a couple of children, but since MacBain's mother lived with them, she visited with Aggie pretty often. She was a lot softer than Aggie, easier to get on with, but maybe not as deep a thinker.

In a couple of weeks I began to feel very country and Western. I could see I had a job cut out for me in getting along with Aggie, but I thought that if I worked at it with a will, I'd manage. I was going to make this idea of mine work; I had to make Aggie want me. Maybe I had to make myself want Aggie, too.

There were times I caught myself wishing Artur was around so I could talk it over with him. Before I left Nogales, I had thought that I'd miss him some, but I found I was missing him a good deal more than I'd expected. I'd been depending on him a lot, not for advice or sympathy so much, but for his company, for the way he looked at me. It was a look that told me he admired me and had as much pleasure in my company as I did in his. Once, the evening before I left, I had thought he was going to kiss me, and I hadn't been able to make up my mind whether I wanted him to or not. He didn't, so I didn't have to decide, but once or twice now I wished he had. I thought, too, how nice it would be to put my arm through his, how good a man's solid arm felt.

Artur liked me to take his arm, too. Mrs. Dunphy was

sure wrong about Artur. He didn't hate women. He didn't even dislike them. He was just afraid of them. I had to stop thinking about Artur and how he felt about women, because if I didn't, I'd begin to say to myself, "Hang that mother and sister of his!"

I hadn't done any riding yet. Whenever I mentioned it, Aggie would say, "Oh, sure, we'll fix you up with a horse. Too busy right now . . ."

She had big plans, too. One thing she was going to do was get some chickens so we'd have eggs and meat. "Can't keep chickens when I'm here alone," she told me. "Coyotes steal them soon's my back's turned."

"Coyotes!" I said. "That close to the house?" Because there was a little chicken house sort of tacked to one side of the barn.

"Oh, sure. They just wait around until they see you ride off and then they come down and take a chicken or two. Eat up a whole flock in a couple of weeks."

"Why didn't you tell me this before?" I asked and I was mad, real mad. Last night, for the first time, I'd slept out on the porch. Aggie hadn't said a word about coyotes, about danger; why she'd even helped me move my cot out!

"I think that's real mean, Aggie Gates!" I said. "I might have been bit! They might have eaten me!"

Aggie just laughed at me. "No coyote ever bit anybody!" she said. "And they never come near the house. The dogs keep them away."

"Well . . ." I said. "Well . . ."

I was glad to hear that, because sleeping on the porch was fine. I had lain there last night and Satan came and curled up beside me, and one of the dogs shoved his nose in my face, flopped down under the cot, hit the floor a couple of thumps with his tail, gave a long sigh and went to sleep. I liked it, sleeping out.

After a month, I got braver and moved my cot around back behind the lumber room. It was better here; I couldn't hear Aggie snore. I often wondered how her husbands had stood it, though maybe they snored, too. Here I had the whole world for my private room. There wasn't even the shed of the porch over me; I could like flat on my back and stare up into the black, black sky with the stars blazing away. I could stare up so hard I would almost get dizzy as if I was looking down, not up.

Satan took to sleeping with me every night. He was nice to have because he was warm. The nights could get pretty cold, even though the days were getting warmer. Satan didn't sleep all night, of course; he went off on cat business at irregular times, but he always came back.

During that time I began to find out a little about Aggie, her past, the things that had happened to her to make her the way she was.

We were sitting after dinner one evening. It still wasn't dark enough to light the lamp, but too dark to do anything without a light. Through the kitchen door I could see the remains of the sunset, a dull red glow over the tops of the ridge that rimmed our hollow to the west.

"I wonder what this country was like when the first white men came into it," I said.

Aggie snorted. "You're a great one for wondering," she said. "I guess it was a lot like it is today."

"But there must have been Indians!"

"There were Indians when I came here," said Aggie.

"Here? In this place?"

"No, no," said Aggie. "In the country. I wasn't here when I came into the country. Ma and Pa stopped at Dos Cabezas, a little mining camp. No, if you want to know what it was like right here in the early days, you go ask Pat's mother. Old Grandma Malloy was here when Geronimo was tearing things up. Many a night and some days, too, she and the three boys hid out in the cornfield when they heard Geronimo was loose. He never bothered them, but once he passed down the canyon on Barker's side."

I didn't want to hear about the Malloys, interesting as that might be. I wanted to hear about Aggie. I said, "How old were you when your people brought you here?"

"Me? Why, four, I guess."

"You couldn't remember much, then," I said, taunting her.

"Oh, yes, I can!" Aggie said with a big voice. "Yes, indeed, I can! Let me tell you, I'll never forget that trip...."

"Trip?"

"Yes, trip. We came from Colorado."

"I never knew that."

"No reason why you should. You know it now, though. Pa always was a drifter and a no-good...."

She told me about that trip, then. She went on talking and talking, and it got darker and darker, but I didn't make a move toward the lamp; Aggie seemed to talk better in the dark. Sometimes her voice was sad and sometimes harsh and bitter. Most of the time it was just flat, as if she was telling something she didn't want to think about but had to get out of her.

Her father had married her mother in Alabama, and gone out to Colorado where he had a good log house and a good job running a sawmill. But there were a lot of his relatives down around Wilcox, Arizona; so many that the place was sometimes called the Henry settlement, from the family name, Henry. And Mr. Henry was a drifter, as Aggie said. He decided he wanted to go down into what was newer country than Colorado.

Well, Aggie's mother held him back for awhile, but he was bound and possessed to go to Arizona. So at last Mrs. Henry put in the covered wagon everything she could, a fine old highboy that she'd brought from her home in Alabama with a nick on it where a Union trooper had saber-slashed it in the War, a couple of featherbeds, her sewing machine, and all the food she could get together with what money she could raise. A bucket or two swung under the wagon, and a dog ran in the wagon's shade under the back axle. Aggie's pet cow was hitched behind—even though she was only four she could milk and she had a pet cow.

Aggie's mother cried when they said good-by to their neighbors and that made Aggie cry too, and her sister Lizzie, who was two, began to bawl, and the little young baby, James, probably whimpered but wasn't heard in the general uproar. It was lucky Minnie hadn't been born yet, and consequently couldn't help make a noise. So, crying and sobbing, they left home and started out for Arizona.

It took them three months to get to Dos Cabezas.

One of the horses died after about a month and they hitched Aggie's cow to the wagon, and kept on going. For Aggie's father mightn't have been much, but when he began to move, hell nor high water wouldn't stop him.

They couldn't travel as fast with the cow as with a real team, so the food began to get lower and lower. Mrs. Henry skimped as much as she could, not making much bread—biscuits, that would be. And the cow stopped giving milk, because she was working too hard, so the two girls didn't get very much to eat. Mr. Henry let them ride in the wagon a lot while he walked along beside the team, or ahead, picking the best way to go because in some places there wasn't much road, just a sort of track made by people who had come this way earlier.

One evening they started to camp and a couple of men rode up.

"Stranger," they said to Mr. Henry, "you see that there smoke over there?"

It was a high, thin column of white smoke in the eastern sky, and Aggie said it looked strange and bad even to her.

"Yep," said Mr. Henry.

"Well, stranger," said the men, "that's a bunch of Apaches and you're heading right toward them! You better turn around and come with us. We're riding to get away from them."

"Will you loan me one of your horses?" Mr. Henry asked.

"Can't do that. They ain't broke to harness. You'll have to make out best you can, your own self."

They rode off, Aggie's father calling curses after them.

There wasn't a thing they could do. They might as well camp as try to run. The cow and the horse wouldn't have been able to take them more than a mile or two.

Aggie's mother was tired, tired in her very bones. "If we're going to get killed," she said, "we're going to get killed right here. Because I am not going to move. We'll just stay here and hope that the Lord has intended us to live longer than tomorrow."

Mr. Henry said, "Not much else we can do. But I sure did aim to get to Dos Cabezas."

They thought they stood a good chance of being massacred. Aggie said they made camp and her father loaded up his shotgun and bragged he'd take some of the devils with him, but he was pretty scared. And her mother just built a fire and started cooking supper.

They kept hearing things and they were sure the Apaches were coming closer. After a while, Aggie's mother said supper was ready. She opened the Dutch oven and pulled out a great big batch of biscuits. She had used all of the flour she'd been saving.

"Here," she said, "you children eat as much as you want. You, too," she told her husband. "I'm going to eat all I can and all I want, because I've been hungry for bread for a long time now. The Indians may come, but this night we're all of us going to have all the bread we want."

They stuffed themselves with partly cooked biscuits, and Mr. Henry put out the fire. The Indians never came.

When they reached Dos Cabezas, they had to live under a tarpaulin stretched over a wagon tongue. They lived that way for three years; then Aggie's father went away and never came back.

"He was no good," Aggie said. The kitchen was so dark I couldn't see her face. The fire in the stove was pretty well burnt down, but the coals still gave a glow to the cracks around the ash door.

"He was no good," Aggie said bitterly. "It was the night we were sure he'd deserted us that I thought for the first time what I've thought many a time since. Many a time I've wished the Indians had gotten us, all of us, and killed us and scalped us. I've wished that often and often."

I didn't know what to say. "Well . . ." I said, "Well . . ."

"Rodgers," said Aggie, with an edge in her voice. "I don't know what we're sitting here in the dark for. It's time you got these dishes done and the place straightened up."

She left me there in the dark and went into her own room

and closed the door. I guessed she was mad at me for getting her to talking that way—but it was important to me to know about her past.

Living with a woman who had gone through all that as a four-year-old made me begin to feel very Western, very Western, indeed.

In the mornings, I'd get up first and I have the fire going and breakfast ready. Then I'd straighten up the house and pick over frijoles—take out stones, earth, straw, sticks—put them to soak, do all sorts of odd jobs. And Aggie would be out riding or working with Dan, just slashing around somewhere. I loved to see her on her horse; she rode sidesaddle and she was just handsome—the handsomest thing I ever saw. And of course I'd pester her with, "When am I going to ride? I want to help you with the cattle."

"Too busy now," she'd say impatiently. "Later, later."

So I'd work harder around the house and in the barn, which wasn't as big as the house, built of adobe, and held harness, saddles, grain in sacks, things like that. No animals lived in it.

Then after lunch—Aggie liked her big meal at night, when, as she said, she could enjoy it—I liked to clean myself up. I'd put on something different and comb my hair and figure on doing sewing or some such thing in the afternoon. As the days grew warmer, I got out my white linen dresses.

That considerate and thoughtful Artur had given me ten yards of simply beautiful handkerchief linen, and before I left Nogales I had had it made up into three dresses by a Mexican woman. They were lovely dresses, and now that it was warm enough I was glad to wear them. Of course, I had to be careful with them, not to get them dirty.

Aggie had bought about thirty cows with calves from a place on the other side of the Huachucas. She was locating them by keeping their calves in the pasture and letting the old cows come in from the range to be sucked. An old cow would come in any hour of the day or night, bawling to be sucked. Her calf would be standing there at the gate into the corral from the pasture, blatting every time his mammy bawled. Aggie or Clara or Dan would go down to the corral, close the outside gate behind the old cow, open the one to the pasture and let the calf in. Of course, there'd be a whole crowd of calves wanting in, but somehow they knew the right one. How, I couldn't tell. All calves looked alike to me, just calves, that was all. I'd go along and watch whenever I could, even in the afternoons when I was wearing my white dress and white shoes, and had to be careful where I stepped.

Then, Aggie came down with sciatica. It was a terrible attack and she could scarcely move. Her temper got very short because she couldn't do any riding; she could scarcely even walk around the house. All she could do was sit on the porch and boss.

That kept her pretty busy, though.

The very first afternoon I tried to fix her a specially nice lunch, and she ate it grumbling. I didn't mind; I felt sorry for her. I got her out on the porch and settled in her rocker with a couple of pillows, and did the dishes and straightened the kitchen. Then I changed into my white shoes and dress.

Clara and Dan weren't around and neither was Minnie.

An old cow came bawling down the road and a bunch of the calves trotted up to the corral gate, blatting their fool heads off.

Aggie yelled, "Rodgers, Rodgers!"

I hurried out.

"That old cow's in the corral. You go shut the gate behind her and then let her calf in. He's that one with the funny spot over his eye. That one over there!"

"Well . . ." I said.

"Go on," Aggie snapped. "You've seen it done often enough."

Shutting the gate behind the old cow wasn't hard. But I wasn't feeling happy about going into the corral with her. There was a gate directly into the pasture and I went through that. I figured on opening the gate for the calf from his side.

There were about ten or a dozen calves crowding around the gate and I had to push through them. I got through, though, and they all crowded close up behind me. They were blatting so loud I couldn't have heard a gun go off, and the old cow was bawling for her calf to come suck. Which calf it was, I didn't know. They were all the same to me. They all had funny spots.

I unlatched the gate. It opened into the corral, so the calves all pushed forward, knocked me down; a couple of them trampled on me. They were all in the corral, all trying to suck at the same time, and only one of them the one whose mammy the old cow really was.

I got on my feet right away because more calves were coming up, attracted by the rumpus, and I knew I'd better get that gate shut. I slammed it shut in the face of the first calf and wondered how come I wasn't hurt. I wasn't.

The cow kicked a couple of the bolder calves and was standing there with what I hoped and prayed was her own calf, the right one, guzzling away at her. He was having some trouble—a couple of persistent calves were trying to horn in, and his mammy was moving around nervously.

I was so mad and put out with myself that I forgot to be scared. I drove all the calves into a corner and stood there, trying to figure out how to get them back into the pasture without letting the rest of the brutes in.

Something touched my shoulder, and I jumped.

It was Pat Malloy, very red in the face. He yelled, "Want I should help you, Mrs. Rodgers?"

"You bet!" I yelled back.

He went over and flapped his big old hat in the faces of the calves on the other side of the gate and they moved away. He opened the gate and drove the corral calves out. Then he shut it.

"Thanks," I said, "Oh, thanks."

"Yes'm," he said. "Got to be going. Glad to be of help."

"A cup of coffee?"

"No, no thanks." His face got redder. "I got to go."

He hopped up on his horse and rode away.

I went back to the house. I guessed Aggie must be having a real bad pain because her face was flushed and her eyes had tears in them.

"Good thing Pat came along," I said.

Aggie kind of choked. "Yes," she said. She choked again. "Rodgers, you're kind of mussed."

It had all happened so fast. Now I realized my hair was down. And my white dress felt funny, almost as if it was wet behind. I wasn't hurt, though.

Aggie said, "That stuff won't stain. It'll wash out." She choked again.

"Maybe I'd better change," I said.

Aggie just nodded.

I thought I heard her moan with pain as I went into the house. It couldn't have been a laugh; she felt too bad, and anyway, what was there to laugh at?

I had to change my petticoat, too. I rinsed that out and my dress, and put them both to soak. I was glad I had three dresses, because I had another to put on. I had to wear black shoes, though.

When I went back on the porch, Clara was there. She said, "Hello, Rodge." Then she burst out laughing.

"What's the joke?" I asked.

"Oh, Aggie was telling me something funny. Nothing important."

"That cow's ready to go, Rodgers," Aggie said. "Go let her out, and then turn the calf into the pasture."

I guessed that wouldn't be too hard, so across the road I went. I opened the gate and the cow came out and went away. The calf, his stomach full, was curled up in a corner, drowsing. I kicked him in the rump, not hard, but enough to get him up, and drove him through the pasture gate. No calves were interested in coming in now that the corral was empty of mammy cows.

I wasn't back at the porch before there was a bawling from behind the house and along came a cow, heading for the corral. The cow bawled, the calves began to blat, and Aggie said, "Go let that brindle calf in so he can suck. That's his mammy, crossing the road."

"Well . . ." I said, looking at Clara, hoping that she'd offer to do it.

"Don't be scared of those old cows," said Clara. "Most of them are pretty gentle."

61

I marched across, watching where I stepped, and deciding not to let all the calves in this time. I just went into the corral, closing the gate behind me, and looking that cow firmly in the eye. She looked right back, but she didn't snort, so I went across the corral to the pasture gate.

I didn't see any particular brindle calf in that lot, but there was one a little darker than the rest and blatting maybe harder, so I decided that was it. He wasn't up front, though.

I yelled at him. "Come here!"

All that happened was that the cow bawled harder and another calf shoved in front of the one I thought was right. I wished I had a big hat like Pat, but all I had was a small white handkerchief. I climbed up on the gate and waved it at the calves nearest the opening side. They backed off some, and the ones to the side shoved in. My calf was pretty close.

I opened the gate and tried to hold it just wide enough for one calf. They were too quick for me. Three got through, wiping their noses on my dress as they did. The brindle was one of them.

That wasn't so bad. I was learning.

When I got back to the porch, I guessed Aggie and Clara must have been telling jokes again, because they had that laughing look. "I guess you feel better," I said to Aggie.

"Clara told me the funniest thing," she said. "It took my mind off my back."

I went in to wipe calf slobber off my dress.

Dan showed up a few minutes later and he stuck around and let cows in and out for the rest of the afternoon. Clara and I cooked a good supper and we had a lot of talk after it. Even Aggie seemed to enjoy herself.

I got my dress ironed the next morning, but I mussed two that afternoon, letting calves in and out.

Next day I washed and ironed in the morning, mussed and cussed in the afternoon.

A week later, I gave up changing in the afternoon. After all, it was just a silly New York custom and besides, I was tired of washing my white dresses. A week after that, Aggie got over her sciatica.

"Rodgers," she said one morning, "I'm going to teach you to ride."

"I could hug you, Aggie Gates!" I shouted.

She nodded her head in a satisfied way. "Yes," she said, "you've gotten along so good with those calves, I can see you've got the making of a real cowboy in you."

Her sister Minnie came riding up as we were dragging an old sidesaddle out of the barn. "What you doing?" she said.

"Going to teach Rodgers how to ride."

"Ever ridden?" Minnie asked.

"Oh, no," I said, "but it looks easy enough."

Minnie just smiled.

Aggie showed me how to put a saddle on a horse, and I climbed up and off we started. Aggie had loaned me one of her riding skirts. The sidesaddle felt queer, but not unsafe. With the big horn you looped your leg around, it couldn't feel unsafe.

"Let's go!" Minnie yelled and kicked her horse. I wished I was riding astride like her.

My horse started running and I jounced up and down, up and down. I'd bang against the horn and then bang against the high cantle and sometimes I'd almost miss the saddle altogether. Aggie and Minnie dropped behind and let me lead.

I was pretty sore when we got home, but exhilarated. Riding, even with a sidesaddle, was fun, but I didn't want to ever use that saddle again, and I said so.

Minnie and Aggie laughed hard and long. "We were betting how high you'd go," Minnie told me, "and how hard you'd hit. Aggie won, and that's fair enough because she lost to Clara last week."

"What on?" I asked.

"How long you'd go on wearing those white dresses the calves used for handkerchiefs."

"I thought you had a lot of stick-to-it-ness," said Aggie. "More than you showed."

63

"You mean you thought I was a bigger fool than I am!" I said. "I guess I did look sort of funny."

"Sort of!" yelled Aggie. "That first time— Lord, I had the sciatica so bad and I laughed so hard it almost killed me with pain, but I couldn't stop! You looked so awful funny, Rodgers!"

She started to laugh, and I did, too. I must have looked very funny, and I like a joke too.

"But I do want to learn to ride, Aggie," I said.

Pat Malloy stopped by next morning when I was trying to saddle Aggie's rough old horse with her punk old sidesaddle.

"You going to ride that outfit?" he asked.

"I'm going to learn to ride and ride good!" I told him.

"Then I'm going to help you!" he said, and his face got shiny red and his china-blue eyes popped a little.

He did help, too.

chapter 5

PAT came down the next morning leading a dark bay horse with a black mane and tail. He was saddled with a worn but good saddle.

"Here, Mrs. Rodgers," said Pat, "this is for you. His name is Cowboy."

Aggie and I were standing on the porch. Aggie wiped her hands on her apron and said, "You giving that to Rodgers, Pat?"

Pat turned redder than ever. "No, no," he said. "I'm s-sort of loaning the horse and the saddle. Don't use old Cowboy much nohow. Might as well work a little as eat his fool head off and get fat and sassy."

I said, "Pat Malloy, how will I ever thank you? You're just too good to live." I stepped out and put my hand on Cowboy's nose. He felt friendly. He looked at me with a lot of sense in his eyes. I knew I was going to like him.

"He's a pretty darn good cowhorse even if he is kind of old," Pat said.

"You can't ride astride in a sidesaddle skirt, Rodgers. Where you going to get a divided skirt?"

Trust Aggie to throw cold water on something when she felt like it.

Pat said, "That's something you ladies ought to talk over in private. I'll put Cowboy in the corral, Mrs. Rodgers."

"Now that you've loaned me a horse, don't you want to forget the Mrs., Pat?"

Pat grinned, but he was speechless. He just went off across the road to the corral. Aggie said, "That man's going to get so red and hot with shyness that some day he'll disappear in a flash and a puff of smoke."

I made myself a divided skirt. I took my oldest cloth skirt, a brown mohair, and split it front and back up the middle and double-seamed each split. It wasn't very elegant and it wasn't right but it would do. Still, Aggie was scandalized when I put it on that afternoon. She said, "It looks just like pants, Rodgers. I wouldn't want a man to see you in that."

For a woman who had run through three husbands, Aggie was very conventional.

I said, "Until I can buy the right kind, this'll have to do."

Aggie looked at me. "You're pretty near as determined as me," she said.

I took that for a compliment. "I aim to be," I said.

John Yoss stopped as he was riding past one day. Of course, he had heard how Pat had loaned me Cowboy. Yoss tipped his hat and gave me that lady-killing smile of his. He said, "And how's the New York lady today? Why didn't you tell me you wanted a horse? I'd have given you something better than that old crowbait of Pat's."

"Cowboy's a fine horse," I said as coolly as I could.

Yoss chuckled. "Sure can get a spark out of them pretty blue eyes of yours!"

While I wasn't going to quarrel with anyone, Yoss gave me a feeling I didn't like. There was an awful mean streak in the man, and even when he was laughing and joking, I thought I could feel a sort of coldness behind it although I could believe a different woman mightn't find it that way. I wished he'd go away and let me alone. I didn't believe he was really attracted to me—not with spunky, cute, little old Bess around. It was more that he sensed I was a little—just a little—afraid of him, and he liked to watch me squirm.

He said, "I got time. Come on, I'll saddle up for you and you come for a ride with me."

"No, thanks," I said, "I have housework to do."

"Well, I'll be back to try again, New York lady," Yoss said, riding away with his white teeth grinning over his shoulder.

I couldn't stay off Cowboy once I learned to climb up on him. He was a fine horse, gentle, wise, calm. You couldn't spook him no matter how hard you tried, and people—

cowhands—did. They thought it was fun to scare an Easterner by scaring her horse. At all the dances that summer, when Aggie and I were riding to them, and maybe ten, twelve cowboys with us, they would pretend to throw their ropes for Cowboy's feet—the very most dangerous and terrible thing they could do. They never made Cowboy nervous, though. He'd roll his eyes back toward me as if he was saying, "Look, I know they're damn fools, too. Don't you worry!"

The Sunday after Pat gave me Cowboy, I was riding up the road and here came this buckboard in a cloud of dust—summer was coming and things getting dry—and it stopped and looking at me was a kind face with a blond mustache and a smile that seemed like the gates of heaven. It was Artur Resswell, of course.

"Lu!" he said.

"Artur!"

We both began to laugh. I knew we both felt the same way, that it was sure good to see each other. Of course, I had to sort of hide my feelings by asking, "How'd you get here?"

He had taken the train to Elgin, and hired a team and buckboard there from the Youngs at the hotel.

"I thought it was too long since I had seen you, Lu," he said. "And you have changed. You surely do look Western."

I was proud. I tried to make Cowboy act a little wild, but he was too old and wise. He just stood there.

Artur asked, "Where is your gun?"

"Oh, I wouldn't carry a gun!"

He stopped smiling. "Maybe you should. Maybe it's dangerous here."

"From what, cows?" I said, feeling very brave.

"I am serious," said Artur. "There is more trouble in Mexico."

"Why, Bess Oryx is still living all alone in that little old house of hers over by the school," I said. "And the Barkers aren't a bit worried about her. She's going to leave at the end of summer, you know. Says this country's getting too settled. Going to teach school in Nevada. Westerner! That girl's one if ever I saw one."

I'd have gone right on chattering all day, I guess, if Artur hadn't said, "Still, I am serious."

"Well, I wouldn't think of it! People would say I was a fool! Why, Aggie doesn't wear a gun."

She did carry a rifle on her saddle, though. It wasn't for any real use, she said, she'd just got into the habit of it.

"Come on," I said, "Aggie's home and I'd like you to meet her."

I went ahead and Artur followed in his borrowed buckboard. We'd hardly started when a cloud of dust came tearing down the road behind us, overtook us, passed by with a shout. It was Charles Jackson in his buggy with his fine horse.

And then who did we meet but John Yoss. He stopped his horse in the middle of the road and tipped his hat politely, but his mouth went into a sneer at Artur. I wanted to get rid of him fast, so I said, "Mighty fine day, John." I started to push my horse on past, figuring he'd give room.

"Came over looking for you, New York lady," he said with that mean smile of his. "Figured maybe you'd like to go riding with me being it's Sunday."

"That's very nice of you," I said. "But I expected Mr. Resswell." That, of course, was a white lie. "Let me make you acquainted. Mr. Resswell, Mr. Yoss."

I was proud of Artur. He nodded and smiled from his seat in the buckboard. "How do you do, Mr. Yoss?" he said.

"Heard about you," said John Yoss. "Important, ain't you, down there in Nogales?"

Artur lifted his nice eyebrows, shrugged his shoulders in a way he had, smiled a modest smile.

"So now if you'll excuse us, John," I said.

John Yoss started to cloud up, thought better of it, and decided to act as polished as Artur. "Maybe I'll have better luck next time," he said with a grin that you could see hurt him. "Pleased to meet you, Resswell."

Artur smiled and nodded and we went on. I felt so good

that I couldn't worry, but I did guess Yoss would consider Artur a mild sort of enemy from now on. Not as much as he did Pat because Artur wouldn't be around as much, but still someone else to beat, to crow over.

We had a good time that day. Jackson and Artur hit it off well together, but what was more important, I thought, was that Aggie took to Artur from the start. I wouldn't have said that Artur wasn't being extra special nice—as he could when he wanted to—but the way he did it Aggie liked. With Artur and Jackson both playing up to her, she got very happy and excited. She was a beautiful woman when she felt right; her face came alive and you could see the lovely girl she must have been sort of buried underneath. She reveled in admiration and those two men were outdoing each other in it. Jackson was good-looking, in his heavy way, not fat, but sort of Diamond Jim Brady in the face. He reminded me a good deal of my mother's brother, Uncle Gus, who was a salesman all his life when he wasn't busy drinking himself to death. He had the same sort of charm.

But Artur! Beside Artur, Charles Jackson was only a run-of-the-mill, passable man. Artur had a natural niceness, a considerateness, a good, quiet humor, a kindness Jackson lacked. Artur could joke, but it was never cruel; he could let me poke fun at him and never get the slightest bit irritated.

I guess I was blooming some too. It sure is good for a woman to have a man admire her.

The day was too short, though. Artur began looking at his watch. He had to get back to Elgin, I knew, to get the down train, the one I'd come in on. He said, "I am afraid I should begin to go, Lu. It has been a very nice time. A very fine dinner, Mrs. Gates," he said, "and thank you very much. So pleased to have met you, Mr. Jackson." He turned to me. "Good-by Lu."

I wasn't going to let him go that way. I went down to the corral with him.

He kept his back to me when he said, "You know, Lu, this is the first time I call on a lady and I find it very nice."

I said, "Thank you Artur. I hope you'll come again soon." I wanted to say, "Be darn sure you do come again—and very soon!" but that wouldn't have been ladylike.

"But certainly," he said. "I like very much to see you, Lu."

I guess we both got a little bashful at that, because I let him climb into the buckboard without shaking hands, and wished, when it was disappearing over the rise, that I hadn't. But it was too late then, and anyhow, I told myself, what was Artur Resswell to me but a friend, even though he was such a good, kind, warm sort of one?

A real good thoughtful friend, though. A week later, B.J. brought me a package in the mail. In it was the most beautiful brown-corduroy divided skirt any woman ever wore. It was a perfect fit, too. So perfect that Aggie, with a lot of high and fancy sniffing, went around remarking on it for weeks.

"What I can't understand," she would say—sniff, sniff— "is how that man knew your waistband size so well!"

I suppose it was what you might call a kind of intimate present, but I thought that if Artur wanted to give me presents it was far more sensible to give things like the handkerchief linen and this skirt than chocolates or flowers. What would I do with flowers way off here in Canelo? And I sure needed that skirt.

Well, days before the skirt came, in fact on Monday, the day after the men had visited, Aggie and I got to talking about them. "That Charles Jackson," Aggie said. "He's a charmer all right. Mr. Resswell is nice, for a foreigner, though."

"I thought you liked him pretty well," I said.

Aggie gave me a sharp glance. "I thought maybe he felt sort of special about you, coming out here all this way just to see you, but I didn't know you . . ."

"Oh, I didn't mean it that way. . . ."

"No?" said Aggie. "Well, it doesn't matter. You know, I'm glad you and Resswell were here. Jackson's got about to the point where he's going to start pestering me to marry him and I don't know . . ."

"Wouldn't you like to be married again, Aggie?"

"Three times . . ." said Aggie. "It makes you think, Rodgers . . ."

I was kind of worried. If Aggie married again, what happened to that great idea of mine about a partnership? I wanted to find out.

"Wouldn't it feel good to have a man around the house again?" I asked.

Aggie gave me one of her withering looks. "Rodgers," she said, "don't ever forget there's not a thing a woman can't do as well as a man—except one thing!"

In the days to come, whenever we had to pitch into a particularly hard job, we encouraged ourselves with that idea. We had a sort of warcry: "We don't need a man!"

But Lord, we couldn't have gotten on without a man, many's the time! All that late spring and summer, Dan and Clara were over working with us half the time. There was a lot of riding to do that year, or it seemed so to me because I was just beginning. I got so I could spend a whole day in the saddle, but at first I'd get awful stiff and tired.

Dan had married Clara about two years before I arrived. They made a handsome and happy couple, though Aggie wasn't entirely pleased with them. Her trouble was—and I could see it—that she didn't want Dan married to anyone. She wanted to keep him for herself, though he'd been away from her for years until Doc Gates died. Dan had come home then to help his mother pay off the debts Doc had incurred and keep the ranch going. Then as the ranch got to working, Dan branched off, got married and started his own place. But he still had a big interest in Aggie's and came around and worked a lot. Ran his stuff with hers and all that.

Dan was a grand man. He respected his mother and loved his wife. He didn't swear; he seldom got mad. That dark, almost Indian face of his might tighten up a bit, but he never held it against you. He had one failing, which I soon learned. He loved a joke, as long as it was on the other fellow. On himself, it wasn't very funny.

But he was patient with me. While I learned a lot from Aggie, mostly it was by listening and watching. But Dan

—Pat, too, of course—was always willing and anxious to show you how to do it. And he was generous with praise. He'd slap anybody on the back who tried, whether he succeeded or not. It was the willingness that was important to Dan.

I'd been at Aggie's about a month when the Orwells gave a dance at their house, which was about two miles our side of Elgin. Aggie wanted to go and of course I did, too. Aggie said, "We'll go early because you can't ride good enough yet to go with the wild bunch."

"What wild bunch?"

"Oh, Pat, and Bill Yoel and the Duncan boys and any of those cowhands from south of here. They'd come along about three o'clock and help with our chores and then we'd all ride up together. That's the usual way," said Aggie, "but they ride too hard for you, and since Dan and Clara aren't going, they'll stay here and do the chores for us."

Clara showed me how to roll a white skirt and shirtwaist so they wouldn't wrinkle. There was a way of packing them in a flour sack that held them nicely. You took them to the dance that way and changed there.

Off went Aggie and me right after lunch and we got to Orwells' taking it easy in time for a cup of tea before supper. But first we opened our war bags and shook out our party clothes. I hadn't done mine too well and it was mussed a bit.

"Hang it on the line outside," said Mrs. Orwell. "Sun and air will take those wrinkles out and you won't have to iron it."

She had a clothesline between two posts and I pinned my nice skirt to it. We sat in the kitchen drinking tea and getting acquainted. When we decided it was time to change our clothes, I went out for my skirt.

I only saw half of it.

The other half was inside a cow who was chewing away and trying to get the rest down.

I screeched, I guess, because Aggie came tearing out in her petticoat. "What is it, what is it, Rodgers?"

"My skirt, my skirt!"

I was standing there wringing my hands, but Aggie wasted

no time. She rushed over to the cow, grabbed the skirt with one hand, punched the cow in the nose with the other. "Damn critter!" she yelled, "damn critter!"

She hauled away on the skirt and the cow sort of backed off and the skirt came out. It took a long time; I thought afterwards the tail end of it must have been down in the cow's fourth stomach.

Aggie said, "Why couldn't you do that, Rodgers? You're so damn timid!"

A horse came around the corner of the house with a man on it. It was Mr. Orwell. Aggie let out a screech lots louder than mine and tore for the house, ashamed to be seen by a man in her petticoat. Why, she was silly, it covered her like a skirt!

Mrs. Orwell had an iron on the stove when I came into the kitchen. She sponged cow slobber off the skirt, dampened it and ironed it for me, and it was better than when I'd started out.

So the dance was great fun. They had a fiddler and a couple of Mexicans with guitars and they danced about half and half square and round dances. I didn't know the square dances, but I had to learn and learn fast. There weren't enough women to match the men, so no one was allowed to stand idle.

I danced with men whose names I didn't know—couldn't remember all I was introduced to. I found Pat was a good square-dancer, but wouldn't even try to waltz or do the varsoviana. And John Yoss was there, alone because Bess wouldn't come with him, though she was at the dance.

Yoss asked me for a waltz and of course I had to say yes. I didn't want to dance with him, I wanted to keep as far away from him as possible, but I couldn't insult a neighbor. I could tell he'd been drinking—oh, you never saw liquor indoors at one of those affairs, but the men kept their bottles outside. And when he smiled at me, I could smell it on his breath.

"You're so pretty and popular, New York lady," he said. "It's a mighty hard job getting you to myself."

I was getting kind of tired of being called "New York

lady." I said, "People think I'm getting more Western every day."

Yoss said, "To me you'll always be the greenhorn I lifted down from B.J.'s buckboard that winter day. Just a cute, skinny old greenhorn."

You see, he couldn't be really nice; he had to do his best to rile you.

"Say," he said, "you're a right smart dancer, at that. You know, I got a notion to give up Bess and go to sparking you. What you say?"

He was grinning down at me, and I didn't like the smell of his breath, nor what he said, nor his bragging, smart-aleck manner. I swung hard on a reverse—maybe too hard, because the floor was pretty well waxed. John slipped and fell right down, fortunately letting go of me as he fell. He was up in a minute, and I doubted that anyone saw it happen, but he was furious. Those green eyes of his under his coppery hair were mighty mean.

"You shoved me!" he said.

I was so surprised at this that I had no answer.

"God damn it!" he said. "You shoved me."

"I didn't!" I said.

He reached out his hand for me, but it was pushed aside. All of a sudden there was old Pat. His face was red, but he wasn't stuttering.

"Get outside, John Yoss," he said. He said it hard.

Yoss said, "You meddle with me, Pat, and I'll kill you." He, too, said it hard.

I butted in. "Just a minute, both of you. Mr. Yoss owes me an apology and I'll have it before anything else happens."

We had a crowd by now, but I saw Mr. Orwell and a couple of the older and more sensible men pushing through.

John Yoss looked at the faces around him and knew he was licked. No one could call a woman a liar and get away with it at that time and place. "I guess I was mistook," he mumbled.

"Thank you," I said.

The music was still going and Mr. Orwell urged people to dance. Bess came pushing through the crowd, her eyes just blazing. She stamped her foot and spoke the way she would to a kid in her school. "John Yoss, you get out of here. Go on, get!"

Yoss looked at her a minute, then walked away and went outside. Pat was going after him, but I held his sleeve tight.

"Pat Malloy," I said, "I'm not going to be the cause of any fight!"

Pat's eyes popped and he almost swallowed his chaw of tobacco. He pointed at his mouth and the door.

"Got to spit?"

He nodded.

"I'll go with you."

That fixed him. "Rodge," he said, "there's no use letting that fellow get away with anything. To hear him talk you'd think he was big enough to hunt bears with a switch, but I don't think he's so much."

"I don't believe in people fighting," I said.

I wanted to shake Pat as much as if he'd been my son Jerry grown up and acting foolish.

Just then the waltz stopped and they started a square dance, so I dragged Pat right into a set. Nothing more happened that night, and we rode home peaceably with Pat.

I began to learn more about Aggie's past. It was as if she had started remembering after that first evening when she got so mad and so bitter. And I guess it was good for her to have another woman to talk to. I'm sure she told me things and told them in ways that she never would have told anyone else.

She'd talk at odd times, after breakfast if she felt good, at night, sometimes in the middle of the day when we were riding over to her sister Minnie's for something or other, sometimes when we were working in the fields. That was the year we planted a lot of pumpkins.

Aggie's father had stayed long enough in Dos Cabezas so there was another child—Minnie—before he finally took his foot in his hand and left. Minnie wasn't six months old when Mr. Henry went away.

So Aggie's mother had to make a living. Fortunately they

still had the cow and they sold milk to the Chinese who ran the restaurant. They had to do without, of course, but the money bought flour and frijoles. A couple of times while they were in Dos Cabezas a Chinaman died, and Aggie and Lizzie and James, who could walk pretty good by then, hid out behind the graveyard and watched the funeral. Those Chinese weren't Christians, and they would leave bowls of roast pork and rice, and other good things to eat, on the grave. The children would beat the buzzards and stray dogs to it as soon as the Chinamen's backs were turned and gobble it up. Aggie said they wanted to take some home to their mother but didn't dare.

However, the cowboys liked the kids and they felt sorry for Mrs. Henry. There were lots of cows around without brands and in time they helped her build up a nice little herd. When Aggie was about fourteen, Mrs. Henry moved, lock, stock and barrel to Tucson, where the children could have more schooling.

With them went one of the Henry cousins who had come to live and work with them when their herd of cattle got big enough. His name was Con Amore Henry; he sure must have had a fancy and learned father!

In Tucson they went to school and got on fine for a couple of years. The corral was about a mile from the house, and one day Con, as they called him, was down there for some reason when he had an altercation with a Mexican cowboy, and the Mexican shot and killed him. No one knew what really happened. The trial was held at Tombstone, which was then the county seat. Aggie was one of the main witnesses called by the prosecutor to establish Con Amore's gentle character, though the whole family went to Tombstone for the trial. Aggie was bought a new dress and shoes for the occasion.

In spite of the awful reason she was there, she had a very good time. She must have been an absolute beauty at sixteen, and Tombstone had a lot of cowboys coming in with money to spend. It was a gay town, then; the first play Aggie ever saw was at the Bird Cage, the theater with the row of private boxes with curtains all around the walls. She saw Lotta Crabtree, then famous and popular.

And there was a balcony outside her room on the second floor of the hotel. The cowboys would get under it and sing to her, serenade her, bringing music as was the Mexican custom. She got so much attention, she said, that it really turned her head, and she married one of them.

His name was Langwood, and he was Dan's father.

"Rodgers," said Aggie, "he was the best-looking thing that ever trod this earth. People have said since that we made the handsomest couple ever married in Tucson. But that was all Langwood was—just handsome. I left him when Dan was four. Got a divorce a couple of years later."

chapter 6

I WAS riding pretty good by the beginning of August. Dan would say, "Rodge, you go off over there and get that one in there, that yearling with the brown spot."

Cowboy and I would go around back of the bunch and work in nice and easy, not spooking any of them, and we'd bring him out. Dan would say, "Rodge, you did that as well as if you'd been born to the saddle. Won't be long before you'll do to take along!"

Oh, I'd just swell up at things like that. No king was grander than I was right then. I was always so pleased with myself that I overlooked something which was true and which I knew. Aggie said it one time when I came home whistling and swollen with pride.

"Whatever you do, Rodgers," she'd said, "remember it's your horse does the most of it."

And of course, that was true. When Dan told me to get a certain animal, I just pointed old Cowboy at it and he did the rest. He knew his business and so did Star, one of Dan's gentle horses which I rode part of the time. They knew what they were doing so well they wouldn't let me make mistakes.

But the main thing was I was getting to be more and more of a Westerner. Nice as Dan was, he wouldn't have said "You'll do to take along" if I hadn't shown considerable promise. He was honest, even if he was kind.

I wanted to do all the things they did, and as well or better. That was why there wasn't a job I wouldn't tackle, mean or dirty as it might be.

One job, which was more fun and play than mean, was one I started with Pat. More and more as I saw Pat he made me want to take him in hand. It was almost as if he was one of my boys—Jerry or Tim—only older and maybe needing help even more than they did. Because Mrs. Rodgers was certainly teaching them much the same things I would have—manners, cleanliness, neatness. The other things, the good ones, came natural to them, and I guess they did to Pat, too, though with a rougher surface. Pat was kind and considerate and honest, just as I hoped they'd be when they grew older, just as they had been when I left. So I'd begun to get the habit of saying little things, doing little things, for Pat.

There was going to be a dance the second Saturday in August. I knew Pat was going, and when he rode past Friday afternoon as I was hacking away at some stovewood, I got a sudden idea.

"Hey, Pat!" I hollered.

Pat would always stop, even though he mightn't get out a word for a quarter of an hour. He got down off his horse and came over to the woodpile.

"You going to the dance tomorrow, Pat?"

I knew he wouldn't fail to. It was the send-off party for Bess Oryx. I didn't feel too good about it myself, because I knew I was sure going to miss her, even if we did write each other.

He bugged those china-blue eyes at me. "Why, sure."

"Take your hat off, Pat." I said it just as if he was one of my boys. Pat might be older than me, but I felt far older and wiser than I guessed he did.

"Turn around. Pat, you think any girl's going to dance with you when you've got hair hanging down the back of your neck that way?"

He faced me and gulped. "Nope," he said. "Maybe you're right."

"What you going to do about it?"

"Nothing much I can do." He looked like he was going to cry.

"All right. I'll tell you what we'll do. You see this pile of wood? You cut enough of it to last till tomorrow night—and I'm doing some baking tomorrow—and I'll cut your hair tomorrow—provided, of course, you wash your neck first."

Pat just reached for the ax. "Stand back," he said. "You'll get chips in your eyes."

I went into the house. Aggie gave me a sarcastic smile. "We don't need a man!" she said.

"We did a lot of riding," I reminded her.

"I suppose you told him he was handsome?"

"No. Promised to cut his hair for the dance tomorrow."

"Ever cut a man's hair?"

"Aggie," I said, drawling like a Texan, "I aim to try!"

And so I did.

Pat came over about the middle of the morning. I went out with my scissors and a bowl, and sat him down on the well curb. He was kind of fidgety, even for him. I put the bowl on his head and studied it.

"Now, Rodgers," Pat said in a thin voice, "now, Rodgers, you sure you know how?"

"Oh, sure! Don't give it a thought!"

"Well, now, the reason it got so long is last time Ma cut it she can't see so good no more and she got a chunk off the top of my ear."

"Grew back, I guess. We'll see when we get around there." Same tone I'd begun to use to Jerry before I left—tough, but not really mean.

"Maybe we better not try this." Pat said. "You sound mighty heartless this morning. Aggie been at you?"

"Aggie's fine. Now you just hold still." I had the bowl where I wanted it and I started snipping away, making a line all across the back of his head. When I got it good and deep, I took the bowl off and began to work down toward his neck and ears.

I was about halfway through when John Yoss came up the road from Barker's. "You opened a barber shop, New York lady?"

"No."

"Want to go to the dance with me tonight?"

He didn't get off his horse, which stood there breathing hard and sort of quivering in the legs. Pat said, "What's the matter with that horse of yours, John?"

"Ain't fully broke yet. He was flaunching when I saddled

him, but I took it out of him. Mrs. Rodgers, ma'am . . ." He could sound real polite when it suited him though both you and he knew he didn't mean it. "Mrs. Rodgers, ma'am, I'd certain sure be proud if you'd go with me."

"I've got an escort," I said coolly. I was going with Artur Resswell. "Hey, Yoss, your horse is bleeding at the mouth."

"What's the matter with him?" asked Pat.

"None of your damn business!" said John. "I come here to talk to Mrs. Rodgers, not you, Pat."

He got down off the horse, then, but he didn't drop the reins. "If it's only old Pat, here, New York lady," he said, "I reckon I could argue him into excusing you."

You could see the hackles rise on Pat like a dog scouting a coyote. Right then Aggie came out of the house.

She marched up to us, and said, "John Yoss, I've been looking at that horse of yours. What's the matter with his mouth?"

Aggie could make anybody quail when she put on that stern, no-nonsense manner of hers.

"Oh, nothing. Guess he fought the bit a little. . . ."

"Fought it a mighty lot and got it rammed into his mouth, I'd say! Here, let's see." She took the reins out of John's hands and went up to the horse.

"Aw, now, Aggie," John said, all the bluster out of him. "He's all right. Just you leave him be. He might bite you. . . ."

Aggie snorted. "Bite me! Easy, boy," she said to the horse. She took his nose in one hand and his jaw in the other and opened his mouth. He didn't fight her at all, just stood patiently as if he knew she meant well by him. Aggie had a wonderful way with animals.

The poor thing's mouth was full of blood. "You got a Spanish bit on this brute!" said Aggie. "His tongue's cut most in half! John Yoss, you'll ruin this horse!"

"Well, whose business is it?" he asked, trying to bluff.

"By the brand on him, Barker's!" said Aggie. "And mine! You're not fit to own a dog, John Yoss! I wouldn't trust you with a old shelly, waxy-jawed cow! Now you make a hackamore out of your rope, and take that bit out of this animal's mouth and take him back to Barker's! Get another horse! And get off my place!"

John said, "It ain't none of your business. . . ."

"If I start to make things hot for you around here, how long do you think you'd last?" Aggie asked him fiercely.

John muttered something to himself, gave Pat a mean look, tried to grin at me, and got up on his horse. He started back toward Barker's.

Aggie scowled. "I guess he won't go to wrenching his head around any after that," she said.

"He never took the bit off," I said.

"Didn't expect he would, but I frightened him. Now, you get on with your haircutting." She stamped back to the house.

Pat said, "One of these days I'm going to get real riled with John Yoss. We'll have a sure enough run-in."

"Fighting never proved a thing, Pat. Now sit down."

I got the rest of his hair off neat and short. When I got down to where it hung in a sort of fringe on his neck, I discovered he'd washed up to the ends of his hair, but not underneath. From the looks of that part, it had been dry a long time. "I'm going to get some soap and a rag and warm water, and scrub your neck for you," I said. "You sit there."

Pat did, meek as a lamb, meek as one of my own boys; he just rolled his eyes when I got back with the basin. I scrubbed him hard and washed his ears, and when I got done, I said, "There, Pat, you may not be much to look at, but you're clean!" Then I yelled for Aggie. "Whooie, Aggie, come on out and see the good-looking feller!"

Aggie came out. She stood with her hands on her hips and inspected Pat. "Well, Rodgers!" she said, pursing her lips. "You know, if you'd sort of trimmed the edges down gradual to the bare part, he wouldn't look so much like a wad of cotton on a stick!"

"I see what you mean," I said. "Come on, Pat, sit down."

"I don't want to take up too much of your time," said Pat anxiously. "I guess you got a lot to do."

"Pat," said Aggie, "when a person starts to do something

new they might as well get it right the first time. Now, you sit down there!"

Pat sat, and I went to work again. When I got through, his hair was pretty short, but it wasn't a bad haircut at all. "There, Pat, now all you got to do is tell them who did it!"

"I sure will," he said. "Looks better, huh?"

"You bet," I said. "Now I better go do some prettying. Artur'll be getting here soon."

"He's a fine feller," said Pat.

Oh, Pat was like one of my own kids! Bigger, of course, and not nearly so pretty, and if one of mine had chewed tobacco and let the juice trickle down his chin I would have chopped his head off, but still he made me feel like spanking him and cleaning him up and sort of taking care of him. I think Pat felt almost the same way about me—more maybe as if I was his big sister who had peculiar and sometimes annoying ideas, but whom he loved dearly nevertheless and was going to do all he could for.

It was a good thing for both of us. Pat's shyness wouldn't let him have any womenfolks' company except on that sort of basis, and having Pat around like a faithful, big old dog was very good for me. Besides, I needed someone to keep me from being too lonesome for Jerry and Tim and Cissie, and Pat helped that way.

Oh, the lonesomeness wasn't from being alone, for I was hardly ever that. It was just that I could only think about the kids. I needed someone to talk to about them, and after I thought it over a while, I saw that I was foolish, that Aggie was exactly the person to tell. One night after supper, I said, "Aggie, now I've got something to tell you. Now maybe it'll surprise you, and maybe you'll think less of me for something I've done, or wonder why I didn't tell you sooner."

"Sounds like you've been rustling cattle," said Aggie.

"Well, no. But, Aggie, I want to tell you something I've been keeping from you, but will you swear not to tell another soul? Not Dan nor Clara nor Pat nor any of our neighbors or friends? Will you?"

"Rodge," she said seriously, "you can sure trust me with any secret you want to tell."

"All right, Aggie. I left three children back there in Brooklyn with my husband's mother, and came out here trying to make a place for them."

Calm as calm, Aggie said, "I figured you had kids."

"You did?"

"Well," said Aggie, "kind of the way you handled the cat made me think it. Sure, I won't tell, but what you worried about? It's not a crime to have children, not if you're married, and maybe not even if you're not!"

"Sometimes I feel so bad about it, Aggie."

"Leaving them?"

"Yes. Guilty. Like I had abandoned them."

"I'd bet you had a real good reason."

"I thought I did. Listen . . ." I told her about old Mrs. Rodgers, how I couldn't earn a living, all that.

When I finished she said, "Well, you figure you've done the best for them you could, don't you?"

"I do. But sometimes I get doubts. Oh, Aggie, I want to get them in my arms so bad! I need to look at them and smell them and listen to them yell! It's awful not to touch them."

Aggie gave the tenderest smile I'd ever seen on her face. "Dan was the cutest little shaver running around with his pants hanging down . . ." She didn't finish, just shook her head. She gave a great long sigh. "Yes, Rodgers, I know just how you feel. Or pretty near, anyhow. You figure you're doing right, don't you?"

"As near as I can," I said.

"Well, then . . ." said Aggie.

That was all of it at that time, but somehow I felt better, I felt as if the kids were closer because I'd told about them to one person who lived in this place, so it was a little as if both Aggie and me were making them more here by thinking about them.

John Yoss didn't come to the dance. That was good. I heard afterwards that he rode over to Fort Huachuca and got a skinful, so drunk he couldn't sit in the saddle. He was there till Monday, sleeping it off.

It was good to see Artur. It was the first time since he had surprised me that Sunday I was out riding and met him on the road. Aggie had decided to ride over with the bunch, so Artur was going to drive me over.

I was going like a real lady this time. I'd been twice with the bunch, once to a place even further away than Lucas's where the dance was, and it was kind of wearing. The Duncans and Pat and Yoel and ten or a dozen others would start gathering at our place along about three o'clock. Being on a crossroads, or anyhow near one, made Aggie's a natural gathering place. Maybe two widows had something to do with it, too, because Aggie sure was handsome, and I looked a lot better than when I'd arrived. I'd put on a bit of flesh, and my face had gotten color and smoothed out, and I guess my eyes sparkled a bit, and I took very good care of my hair, which was my best feature.

Well, they'd gather early and help us do our chores, and more and more would ride in, and they'd be rolling cigarettes and squatting on their heels, talking cattle and weather and feed, and a couple or three doing chores and joking, and then all of a sudden . . .

The first time I was standing near the corral jawing with the Duncan boys and planning to go up to the house and primp a little pretty soon. Cowboy was saddled with my war bag tied on. That part was all done; I just wanted to freshen myself. But Aggie came swinging round the corner of the corral and she said, "Rodgers, get up on your horse."

"Oh, my, Aggie! I've got to primp."

"No time for primping. They'll be starting any minute and if you aren't ready you'll lose them."

"Oh, pshaw, Aggie . . ."

"Get up on that horse!"

I didn't want to, but I did. I sat there feeling foolish when all of a sudden someone let out a whoop.

"Yowieeee!"

The Duncan boys came off their heels like they'd been prodded with a hot branding iron; they lit in their saddles quirting and yelling. Old Cowboy caught fire and took off down the road. Here we came, pouring and boiling down the highroad! They were on the road and off it; they were ahead and behind and on either side. They kept hollering and yelling till hell wouldn't have had them! And if you didn't stay with them, or got thrown or lost, it was just too bad. No one took any notice; no one ever knew.

So going ladylike in a buggy with Artur made me feel very citified and aristocratic.

We waited till they went. Artur laughed long and hard at their antics. Then we got in the buggy, and followed the cloud of dust that was getting further and further ahead of us.

Artur said, "You enjoy this, Lu?"

"Those crazy devils?"

"I was thinking perhaps you enjoy riding with me. Unless you have become so Western it is too safe and quiet."

"No," I said, "it's a nice change."

"Good!" said Artur, smiling so hard he might have split his face. He put his cigar back in his mouth, touched up the horse with the whip. I thought of how nice secondhand cigar smoke smelled out here in the wide-open air with the sun setting behind us and the Huachucas, that great, green wall, turning purple and plum and reddish in the failing light.

"Maybe you get enough of this pretty soon?" he asked after a while.

"Oh, no, I like it!" I said.

He looked disappointed. "I hoped you might want to come back to Nogales."

I didn't let him finish. "Artur, maybe it looks like I'm just having fun, or playing at being a cowboy, or something silly like that, but it isn't so. I wish I could tell you what this is for me. . . ."

"Lu, I also wish you could. I would so much like to understand. . . ."

"Listen," I said. "When I was a girl in New York there was always something I wanted to do but I wasn't sure of what it was. Something about traveling, living in a new place, learning how to do things. Since I came to Canelo, I've thought I found it. You don't know what it's like for me, Artur. . . ."

It was so hard to tell because it was all made up of little things—sleeping out behind the house under the sky, cooking frijoles so they tasted good, riding Cowboy so I felt he liked the way I did it, cutting out a heifer, getting an approving nod from Aggie—all the little things that made a big thing: taking up the dare of a completely new life, one that I admired, and licking it.

Artur said, "Yes, yes, there is the sky and the mountains, and people like Aggie and Dan and Pat and your own muscles and brain taking and molding and learning new things. All that, I can see, because all that was mine, too. . . ." He smiled sidewise at me. "It was new country and life for me, too, Lu, do not forget."

I put my hand on his arm, I couldn't help it. "Artur," I said, "then you know I just have got to do this."

He didn't speak right away. He blew out some cigar smoke almost as if he was letting out a long sigh. "Yes," he said finally, "you make me see that, Lu." He gave a great big laugh and waved his whip. "Look out there," he said, "open, empty country. It is for people like us."

"It's full of cows," I said.

Artur laughed again. "Lu, you are too practical sometimes." Then he began to joke and, laughing and joking, we got to the party at Lucas's. It was a fine party; we danced till sunup and Bess was the belle of the ball. Then the wild bunch took off, Bess, looking fresh as a new rose, right in there with them. We followed. I was so tired and kind of sad at Bess's leaving, that I just put my head down on Artur's shoulder and fell asleep.

When we got to Aggie's, she had breakfast ready. It was coffee and biscuits and her special way of cooking beef. She'd take a piece of beef, slice it as thin as she could, and then she had a big old skillet almost red hot with a layer of salt in the bottom of it. She'd throw the lean beef on the salt, and sear it so quick it hardly took a minute. That was tasty eating after all-night dancing and a morning ride. Artur ate enough for two men, patted his stomach, smiled at Aggie, fired up a cigar and climbed into the buggy and went away. "Very many thanks, ladies," he had said. "I hope I may see you soon, Lu."

"You sure can."

Aggie milked the cow—we only had one milker then—and I fed the pigs. Back in the kitchen I was starting on the dishes. Aggie said, "Rodgers, let's have another cup of coffee."

We sat at the table drinking coffee and feeling tired—that good Sunday feeling of just lolling around and letting the time pass. After a while, Aggie said, "You know, Rodgers, it gave me the strangest feeling when John Yoss rode up yesterday and sat there watching you cut Pat's hair. That man's bad. He's a cruel man. I've seen him pack sand in the eyes of his horses because they didn't obey him quick enough to suit him."

"I don't like him."

"I know. Even though he makes out like he'd like to spark you, he doesn't like you. He just wants to think he does. He's the sort of man who always has to beat something and I don't like to think it, but I'm afraid he's picked you to beat."

"Well, he won't, because I'm going to have nothing to do with him, nothing at all."

That was an easy thing to say.

Aggie wasn't paying much attention to me. It was as if she was talking to herself. "When he got off his horse," she said, "I could see Morgan Wiley getting off his over there at Brigham's ranch at Sulphur Springs."

What had happened was this: After Aggie left Langwood when Dan was four, her mother's herd was in pretty bad shape. Run down and neglected. So she left Dan with her mother, and she and Minnie, who was then eighteen and a beautiful blonde, went to see what they could do about building up the herd. They lived in a cave that had a front made of flattened oilcans, and they slept together on a single cot. They rode daybreak to dark, and it took them a year, but they sure got that herd put together.

Of course, they got plenty of help, fine-looking girls that they were. John Brigham, who had a ranch of his own at Sulphur Springs, was one of their best helpers and he got pretty sweet on Aggie. A year later, when Dan was six, she got a final decree of divorce from Langwood and married Brigham. She went to live on his ranch, and Dan went with her.

The three of them had a very happy year. Brigham took to Dan, and Dan to Brigham, and Aggie was happier than she had ever been in her life. She didn't once think of the time she wished the Indians had found and scalped them all. She forgot about her no-good father. She stopped worrying about her sisters and their prospects.

One morning they had finished breakfast and Brigham had gone out back to the specialty shop, the two-holer. Aggie was doing house chores, and Dan was hanging around. They heard a horse come up to the house, and then the voice of Morgan Wiley, a neighbor. "Hey," he yelled. "Hey, Brigham."

Aggie wiped her hands on her apron. She went to the front door. "Morning, Morgan," she said.

"Morning, Mrs. Brigham," He got down off his horse and took a couple of steps toward her, his thumbs hooked in his gun belt. "John around?"

"Well . . ." said Aggie, who always was self-conscious at the queerest times.

"I just wanted to talk something over with him," said Wiley. "If he ain't around I can come another time."

"Oh, he's around," said Aggie. "He's just busy right now. You want to sit and wait?"

"I see he's got some stock in the corral," said Wiley. "I'll mosey over there and look at them."

"Yes," said Aggie. "He brought them in yesterday."

Wiley gave her a look that she didn't understand at the moment. "Well," he said, "tell him I'm over at the corral. No hurry."

He walked over—it was about as far away as the corral at Aggie's place. Aggie told Dan to knock on the door and tell Brigham that Wiley was there. "Just let him know," she said. "Wiley acted a little queer."

Aggie saw Brigham come out, still buckling the belt on his

pants. He went across to the corral and Dan went with him. Aggie turned back to her dishes.

She was just wiping the big china coffeepot that was her prize piece when she heard the shot. She dropped the pot. It shattered into a hundred pieces.

She stood a minute, but there was only one shot.

Then she remembered John Brigham hadn't been wearing his gun. Usually no one at that time went anywhere without his gun, but being called over by a neighbor man and on his own place, he hadn't bothered to come into the house and get it.

She heard Dan yell, a boy's high-pitched, scared voice. "Mama, Mama!"

She started to run.

She ran through the front room and out the front door. There was Morgan Wiley riding up the road away from her. Dan was running across toward her, still yelling, "Mama, Mama!"

She couldn't see John Brigham anywhere.

She just flew across to the corral, and Dan turned and tried to keep up with her.

There was John Brigham lying on the ground, blood all over his chest and more coming. Aggie dropped down beside him and took his head in her lap. His eyes rolled up and he gave a deep, grunting sigh. That was his last breath.

It was a controversy over the ownership of a calf.

John Brigham was the love of Aggie's life. None of the others really mattered.

Dan testified at the trial. He had been swinging on the corral gate listening to the men talk. The lawyer for the defense tried to shake Dan, but he couldn't. That boy of seven or eight drew a map of the corral on a blackboard and he showed where they stood. He and Aggie proved Brigham didn't have a gun. Morgan Wiley was sentenced to twenty years in jail, but those were easy times. He served four.

Aggie said, "That's why I get a bad feeling when a man like Yoss rides up and sits there looking tough. It was a bad thing, Rodge."

"How can one man kill another over a yearling steer?" I asked.

"A yearling steer?" asked Aggie. "Does it have to be anything? How can one man kill another?"

"War . . ." I said.

"War, too. It's still one man killing another, or a man or men killing a lot of other men. I don't believe in killing," said Aggie. "I've seen too much of it. It's too final. It's one mistake you never can make up."

I guess I hadn't thought, till Aggie told me her story and till I saw Pat look at John Yoss, that it was still pretty lawless out here. But I did some thinking about it; it stayed on my mind, and the more I thought, the less I liked it. Only there wasn't much to do about it.

Except, as Aggie said, since Arizona was not only the youngest, but the most forward-looking state in the Union, its constitution provided votes for women, and that was more than the states back east did. So we could vote men into office who were against lawlessness, like that fine Tom Patterson, down in Nogales, the Sheriff of Santa Cruz County.

One thing came out of that Pat-Yoss mix-up and that was I got a regular little trade at haircutting. Pat had spread it around at the dance that Mrs. Rodgers, the lady from New York, had cut his hair, and the next Saturday there were five men wanting their hair cut. I charged them two bits each. That was a dollar and a quarter I earned easy, and in one Saturday afternoon. I asked Aggie if she minded. She said, "Lord, Rodgers, you sure need to make money, the measly wages I'm paying. Anything you can do, you go on and do it and don't bother about me. You finished your chores, didn't you?"

"Sure did."

"Well, then . . ."

So that was a little more money for me and I was happy to get it. I saved up enough after a spell to order a pair of real cowboy boots.

Along in September, we began to bring in the spring calves, brand them, earmark, and alter them. The first time I helped with this was sure interesting and also pleasing to me because they tried to play a joke on me and it didn't work.

We had brought in a bunch of mixed stuff—cows with calves, a few yearlings, odds and ends—the night before. Clara and Dan stayed overnight, sleeping in the lumber room. So we got an early start the next morning. Dan built a small fire in one corner of the corral for the branding and searing irons. The rest of us drove in some calves. We left their mammies outside so they wouldn't get on the prod.

We worked afoot, of course, even Aggie, who was roping. It was nothing like the big roundups they told about where there'd be a couple of fires with watchers from each ranch at them and a cowboy on a horse would rope a calf and drag him up to a fire. A flanker, or two, if it was a big yearling, would throw him down. There'd be a couple of cowboys on horses watching the mammy in case she took a notion to get on the prod and come see what ailed her calf. I sure wanted to see one of those.

But now, here we were working our own little bunch of calves, afoot, at home in the corral, and it was still interesting and very exciting for me. Oh, I got right into the work and loved it.

Clara and I would drive a calf out of the huddle in the corner, Aggie would dab a rope on him, Dan would flank him down, Clara would help hog-tie, and I'd hold the calf's head. First, Dan would pull a little, keen knife out of a sheath on his belt and take off what would have made that calf a bull —if it had been going to be a bull. I noticed Clara was collecting the product in a lard bucket, but so much was going on I didn't remark on this, because the next thing Dan did was cut the earmark. This was a swallowtail in the left and an undercut notch in the right, both of them taking out sizable chunks of ear. And that was where the dogs came in. Before those chunks of ear so much as touched the ground, while they were still in the air, they'd snap them up, go chomp-chomp, and swallow, quicker than it takes to tell.

All this time, I'd been trying to hold the calf's head still, and that first day I had the wind knocked out of me a couple of times by a strong calf before I learned to kneel on their necks and hold them real flat.

Clara would hand Dan a hot searing iron; he'd run it over the cuts to seal and sterilize them, then Clara would hand him a branding iron—a poker with a curved end—and Dan would run a Bar-A all over the side of the calf. That brand grew with the calf, too.

When everything was finished, Dan would pull the pigging string off the calf's feet. He'd get up and blow hard; shake his head, looking a little dazed; then trot over and push in among his pals in the opposite corner of the corral.

It was hard and dirty work, but more interesting than anything I'd done yet, so I was right in there with them. We'd done two batches, when Aggie said, "Clara, why don't you go over to the house and fix us some dinner? I'm plumb starved."

"Can you make out without me?"

"Sure, I'll hand irons."

So Clara went over to the house and after a while we heard her yell. "Whooie, whooie! Come and get it."

"We'll finish this one," said Dan.

"One more would wipe out this bunch," said Aggie.

So we did the other one and then turned them out. You should see those poor little fellers scamper to their mammies, and their mammies nosing around them to see what had made them blat so hard there in the corral! But as Aggie said, "You like beef, don't you?"

So we went over and washed up. I felt kind of tired and I had some new aches, but I was feeling big and proud. Talking big, too.

"Sure held those boogers down, didn't I, Dan?"

"You sure did, Rodge," said Dan with a nice smile.

Clara had cooked what looked to me like a real dinner, not just the usual scratch sort of lunch we were apt to have. There were frijoles, and some stewed corn and potatoes, and a platter of what looked like lovely, brown, round fritters or fishcakes. Only we never had fishcakes so they must have been fritters. I took a couple and cut into one.

It was firm and white. "Scallops!" I yelled. "Where did you get them?"

"Oh, go on, eat, don't bother us!"

Well, of course I did. Scallops they were, all right, only I couldn't figure out how Clara got any. But I was hungry, and everyone else just pitched right in, so I did, too. I was reaching for another scallop—they were the biggest I ever saw—when Dan let out a kind of snort.

He was sitting next to me. His face was red and he was having trouble with his breath. I figured he was choking; had swallowed down his Sunday throat. I pounded him on the back, but he put up a hand.

Clara said, "Let him be. He's just laughing."

"Laughing?"

"Yes. What was it you thought you were eating?"

"Scallops. Only they're not so fishy, but I guess that's from being canned."

Aggie was grinning, too. "Rodge," she snorted, "use your head!"

They made such a thing of it, I got a little annoyed. "Well, what's it all about?"

"Scallops!" Dan whispered weakly. He was still red in the face and holding his sides. "Scallops! Mountain oysters, Rodge!"

"Mountain oysters? Oh, from the calves! I should have remembered what they reminded me of. Lamb's fries." I took another one. "They're right tasty."

You never saw three such disappointed faces in your life. Dan got indignant. "You mean to say you've eaten mountain oysters before?"

"Lamb's fries," I said, chewing busily. "'Bout the same thing, I guess."

"I like that!" Dan pounded the table with his fist. "Here I go to work all morning . . ." He turned to Clara. "It was your idea!" he said. "You thought it would be a good joke."

"Now, Dan," said Aggie, "you had to cut them anyhow. I sure like a good plate of them, and never knew you not to."

Dan thought a minute. He was stubborn, though. "Well, if it's going to be a joke, it ought to be."

"You mean it oughtn't turn around and be one on you?" I asked. I sure felt triumphant that time.

chapter 7

It was along in early November and getting colder when we came in from riding one afternoon, just Aggie and me. Aggie said, "Now, Rodgers, no use unsaddling your horse. You go over to Minnie's, and stay all night, and bring back the team. Then tomorrow, early, we'll go across to the San Rafael, and bring back the load of fodder old Keaton promised me. Don't get it pretty soon, that old rascal'll sell it to someone else! Soon's prices go up he sure will."

"All right," I said, "I'll get the team." I was feeling real good about myself because I was wearing my new boots for the first time and I thought they were mighty good-looking. They were a little tight, but they reached almost to my knee. They were brown with stitching all over them.

"Go along, then," said Aggie, "you can just about make it before full dark." The sun was nearly down but there was time enough yet, I knew that.

Aggie said, "Go right along, and don't hesitate anywhere and don't you take the short-cut over the trail, 'cause I'm certain you'll get lost. You've got about as much sense of direction as a swung chicken!"

That was true enough, only I didn't admit it. Neither my sense of direction nor of distance was much good. Poor, patient Pat would take me up on a high hill and say, "Now, Rodge, you see there. That's due west. From here it's about six miles to Barker's."

Very grandly, I said to Aggie, "Oh, I'll get there!"

"Yes, I 'spose," said Aggie looking sharply at me. "I can almost smell that you're so fond of yourself you're going to try that short-cut. Now, don't you do it! You get turned around once and you'll have to lie out all night."

"That's why I carry matches."

"You and your matches!"

I'd started carrying some matches in my jumper pocket when the weather got cold, and they had all laughed and joked at me, but I just said, "All right, if I ever have to lie out all night I'll be comfortable, anyhow."

So off I went. Cowboy wasn't too tired, but he didn't have bounce like he did in the morning. We went past Barker's and I didn't stop, and past the schoolhouse, which was lonely because the new teacher, who came after Bess Oryx, wasn't a pioneer sort and wouldn't live by herself in the teacher's house. She boarded around, which made a little money for some of the people. But it left the schoolhouse lonesome, with no smoke coming out of the chimney near it, and no one to holler out and wave to.

The road ran right along underneath the Huachucas here, and they rose up dark green and black, almost filling the sky. Across to my left was level country, wide and empty with the sky turning dark over it, only a low, low line of pale green in the west where the sun had gone down.

Cowboy plodded along and I sat up on him proud and happy. I was tickled to death to go bring home a team of horses. All you had to do was lead them; wrap the dally round your saddle horn and they'd come along fine. What I liked was Aggie's trusting me to do it alone—though really it was a pretty simple job.

We came to the short-cut—the trail—and I just said "Shucks!" to myself. I'd kind of lost time by not kicking Cowboy along at a smarter pace. Also it was beginning to get colder and my feet were hurting. The new boots were a little tight; since I'd been wearing them all day, in the saddle most of the time, the blood had run into my feet and swollen them. So I wanted to get to Minnie's as soon as possible.

Out loud, I said, "I've been to Minnie's many a time with Aggie or Pat or Dan or Clara over this trail. Shucks, I can do it easy. I'll take it!"

I turned off the road and went jogging along this narrow trail, just running out into open country. Pretty soon I was lost. I'd gotten off the trail and didn't know where I was, and it was dark enough so I couldn't see any landmarks. The Huachucas were just a great big black mass, no peaks I might have been familiar with standing out, and the sunset afterglow was all gone. I didn't know the stars very well, but I picked what I guess was the Pole Star and started off again in a right-hand slaunchwise direction to the north it marked.

Pretty soon, Cowboy just came to a stop. Then he tried to turn around. I wouldn't let him, though I knew that if I gave him his head he'd take me home all right. But I was not going to do it. If I had to lie out on the bare ground all night, I was not going to let Aggie know I was so green and so silly as to lose my way! I kicked old Cowboy and he moved again.

He stopped pretty soon, though, and that made sense because we'd come to a fence. I knew there had to be a house inside it; in fact, I knew there were a couple of homesteads out here with bachelors trying to prove up on them.

I rode around the fence, and on the third side I came to a gate. It was one of those loose wire gates like a section of fence, and I hadn't yet learned to manage one from a horse, so I had to get down. I opened it, led Cowboy through and closed it again.

I rode quite a way before I came to the little shack some bachelor fellow had built. It was buttoned on the outside, and I knew no one was home because I rode around a couple or three times and hollered. My feet were just killing me. How they could hurt so much I don't know because they seemed no more than stumps between the tight boots and the cold night air.

So I unsaddled Cowboy and turned him loose. I went inside, found a lamp, and lit it. I was plenty cold, tired and miserable. I was so miserable I wasn't even hungry. I tried to make a fire in the stove. There was wood in the woodbox, but I didn't want to use that. I found a pile of chunks outside, brought some in and stuffed the stove, but it would only smolder and not catch. I had no small stuff, and by this time I had lost my nerve and was afraid to go out to hunt some. It was dark as the inside of a cow out there.

There was nothing to do except get into the man's bunk—

a regular bachelor one, built into a corner. I looked at the blankets and they weren't as bad as they might have been. Fair to middling clean, that is. So I tried to get my boots off.

They might as well have grown to me. I left them on and crawled in.

Pretty soon I heard the coyotes. And a coyote may be far, far away, but if you're frightened and not sure of yourself, it sounds terribly near and like a whole mess of them. Of course, they couldn't hurt me, couldn't possibly get in.

I slept off and on. I was cold and I kept hearing noises, and just about the time I'd think the coyotes had finished, a new one or bunch would start up. It was a long, long night.

But morning came.

The way I knew, it got less dark outside the window. Not even gray, just less dark. I got up, lit the lamp, wound up my hair, and hunted carefully to be sure I'd left no hairpins or anything that would let the fellow know a woman—or anyone—had been in his shack this last night.

I said to myself, "Rodgers, you've had an experience. You've laid out all night and that's another bit of seasoning." But then I started shivering, which wasn't so much fun. That was one of the coldest mornings I ever knew.

I went out and called. Old Cowboy came trotting up. He was a good horse; I often wished he was mine and not just a loan from Pat. In fact, I had hinted to Dan and Aggie that I needed a horse of my own. They had plenty; they could give me a good, old, broke horse.

I saddled Cowboy and buttoned the shack on the outside. I climbed up and looked around. The sun wasn't over the rim, yet, but there was full dawn and I could see all right. The Huachucas were behind me and right ahead, no more than half a mile, was Minnie's place.

"Sure fooled myself!" I said. "What a pinhead!"

I headed Cowboy for Minnie's. I wasn't going to tell her I spent the night with my boots on in a smelly bachelor's shack within half a mile of her place. Nor let Aggie know, either. They'd rawhide the daylights out of me. I was pretty mad at myself anyhow. "Experience!" I thought.

Then I thought, "Yes, it was!" And I knew who I was

going to tell about it. I was going to write a nice long letter —not that I didn't always—to Jerry and tell him to read it to Cissie and Tim. The letter would be all about a white woman who lived in Indian country—I'd already turned coyotes into Indians, you see—and how she got lost one night, and lay out in an arroyo with just her saddle blanket under her, and her saddle for a pillow. That would give the kids a real thrill. I wouldn't tell them the woman was me, just someone I knew. That idea cheered me enough so that I rode into Minnie's with a flourish.

Minnie came out. She was then alone most of the time except for her two young daughters, because her husband, who was a carpenter, was off on jobs earning a living, making ready cash for them.

Minnie said, "My God, Rodgers, what was Aggie up to sending you over here on such a cold morning and so early?"

"Well, she wanted the team for today, and she wanted me back anyhow by nine o'clock. So I came early."

"You sure look it!" said Minnie. "You look like you been riding all night."

That was too close to the truth to be comfortable. I said, "Well, I ought to turn around. . . ."

Minnie snorted. She was strong-minded, just like her sister. "The sun's not even up yet," she said. "You had anything to eat?"

"No, I haven't had anything to eat. I wouldn't stop for breakfast."

Minnie thought that was pretty strange. "Aggie sure does make people step," she said.

"She sure does," I agreed.

"Well, come on in. You look most frozen."

Since Minnie had slept warm and was standing there all wrapped up in an old red sweater of Mac's and even then looked chilly, I guessed I must look frozen, all right.

I had a good hot breakfast. Minnie got the team up, and off I started with their harness on their backs a-jingling and a-jangling, their big old feet going clomp-clomp on the short-cut trail. I wasn't afraid of it, now that I could see.

The sun came up and warmed our backs, and Cowboy

stepped a little faster because he was going home, and the dally—the lead rope—tightened over my thigh for a moment till the team picked up their feet. I was proud as a peacock again, and twice as happy, so happy I began to sing.

"You bet," I sang, "I'll lick this place. This West was meant for me. I'm as happy as a sailor lad when he puts out to sea!" Silly, of course, but fun. And then I sang, "Down went McGinty to the bottom of the sea," a song my father used to sing, one that Jerry always asked for before going to bed. Pretty funny lullaby, but it suited him.

He was the kind who would take to this country, I thought. I wasn't so sure of Tim, even as a baby—which he was practically still—there was something delicate and refined about him. But it would be good for him. And Cissie—there was a girl! I could see her topping a little pony with her yellow hair flying in the breeze, just pouring leather into her mount, yelling and screaming with joy. Oh, I sure had to keep working on Aggie and get to be her partner, bring my kids out here!

We were almost to the road, when we came to the place where the trail dipped into a draw. It turned sharp here, and went up the opposite bank at an angle. Cowboy, same as most cow ponies, liked to go up a steep place in a sort of jumping lope. He tried it, but the team hung back and slowed him down. So we were just about walking when we came out on top.

There was a man standing there. Standing, I said; he was afoot. I remembered Pat: "Men afoot are dangerous. There's something wrong with a man doesn't have a horse. Likely he's a Mex renegade or a outlaw."

This man was Mexican. He had on a straw hat, a dirty blue jumper, and khaki-colored pants. He had those sandals they wear—huaraches, they're called—on his feet.

I saw this in less than a second. I don't think he had seen me before I came out of the draw, because he was only half turned from a small fire he'd been squatting at. There was the carcass of a new-born calf the other side of the fire, cut into.

He turned fully around. I kicked Cowboy hard. The darned

team took this minute to hold back again. The rope snapped taut and almost cut my leg in half, but it gave such a jerk that Cowboy spun a little, and the team began to move.

What really moved them, though, was the Mexican. He jumped at them. Coming from the side that way, he just naturally spooked them. He did what Cowboy and I couldn't. We were off toward the road in a cloud of dust.

He took a couple of jumps after us, but gave up almost at once.

I didn't call a halt, though. Further I could get from him quicker, better I'd be pleased. So I ran the team all the way to the schoolhouse, which was three, four miles.

It was mighty good to come over the ridge and see the house across the canyon with smoke coming out of the chimney. I jingled up the road and put the team in the corral. I unsaddled Cowboy and turned him into the pasture. He had earned that.

Pat's dun horse was standing by the gate. I went busting into the house. Pat was having a cup of coffee with Aggie. Aggie said, "Well, you got here at last."

I looked at the alarm clock on the shelf over the stove. It was only half-past eight. "It's early," I said, "and I most didn't get here at all."

"Lost your way in broad daylight?" asked Aggie with a lot of sarcasm. I saw it wasn't one of her good mornings.

"Nope," I said, trying to sound calm and all-in-the-day's-work. "A renegade tried to steal the team."

"I'll bet Minnie chased him off!" said Aggie.

"Wasn't at Minnie's. Was when we came out of that little draw just before the trail turns into the road."

"I told you not to take the trail!" said Aggie.

"What was he like?" Pat asked. He didn't sound excited, just curious.

"Oh, regular Mexican. Big straw hat, dirty clothes. Afoot, too, I guess. Didn't see any sign of a horse."

"Well," said Pat, "if he was way over there afoot he ain't likely to come bothering over here. Just as well you didn't stop for him, though."

"Yes," said Aggie. "I'd sure hate to lose that team."

"Well, sure," said Pat. "I better be going, now. You people are busy."

He moseyed out, and Aggie said, "Now we'll go hitch up and get moving right away. It's a long haul across the Canelos."

We got the team hitched to the wagon. We got into our coats—surplus army overcoats, good and warm and big. We started down the road toward the Canelo hills and the San Rafael. When we passed the corner where the road turned toward Barker's and the school, I looked back at our house. Here came Pat, not fifty yards behind us. I waved and he waved back.

I said to Aggie, "Pat's catching up with us. You suppose he wants something?"

"Darned old fool," said Aggie.

Pat didn't overtake us. He turned at the corner and headed toward Barker's. He was balancing something on the saddle in front of him which looked like a shovel to me.

"Now, what would Pat be doing with a shovel?" I asked Aggie.

"Prospecting, most likely," said Aggie without interest. She slapped the lines on the team's backs. "He was carrying on about doing some this morning."

When we came across the pass on the hills, the wagon lurching and creaking on the rough, rocky road, I caught my breath. I still wasn't used to space and bigness, sweeps of sky and ground, and far distant ranges of mountains, blue like sleeping bulls on the horizon.

We got home with the load of fodder about sundown, and we did the chores, and got up to the house. I'd been walking some, which started my circulation. The fire was warm. With Aggie's help I got my new boots off. She was a little suspicious, and I knew that some day the story of my lying out all night would have to come out. She and Minnie would compare notes. But I thought I'd wait awhile.

A couple of days later we rode over to Minnie's for something. We turned off on the short-cut trail, of course, and when we came to the draw, there were the ashes of the Mexican's fire and the remains of the calf. Not much, because buzzards and coyotes had been at it, but enough to make Aggie curious.

"I wonder whose 'twas," she said. She rode over to look.

"It was a mighty young calf," I said, "maybe not branded."

She just snorted. "You wouldn't know a calf from a yearling!"

I was going to make a quick retort when I saw something. "What's that?"

"What?"

"Sticking up out of the ground there."

Aggie took a good look. "It might be a root," she said. "Only there ain't no tree around. It might be a shoe."

That was what it was. The toe of a shoe—not a shoe, a huarache—sticking up out of the ground. About half of it, back to the instep, and there was a foot in it. Remains of a foot, that was. Foot was fastened to leg, too, you could see where the coyotes had scraped away at it.

Aggie said, "Guess that's your Mexican, Rodgers. Looks like he tried to stop someone else."

It made me sick at my stomach. "Let's go, Aggie."

We'd ridden almost to my bachelor's shack, before she said, "Don't take on so, Rodge. This is a new country. It's bound to be a little rough."

"Lawless!" I said. "Just plain lawless!"

"Oh, come. He probably tried to stop some tough hombre like John Yoss or Pete Stolley, here—" she pointed at the shack. "They wouldn't have much patience."

I was upset. "They could have buried him decent and deeper!" I said.

"No tools, or no time."

"If it was Stolley, he could have rid back for a shovel."

"Probably did—if it was Stolley, which I'm not saying. But you'd need a pick, too, and Stolley's just a homesteader. Probably not a pick on his place."

"It makes me sick! Who knows if the man was a criminal? It sounds like a thing John Yoss would do. I'd sure like to catch the fellow who did it!"

"Rodgers," said Aggie, "you ought to be a peace officer."

Pat stopped by that evening and we told him about it.

Dan and Clara were at Aggie's too, for dinner. They were all laughing and joking at me. "Rodge, you ought to run for sheriff!" said Dan. "One word from you and they'd behave, all right!"

I was over my mad by then, so I joked right along. "I'd clean out all the Indians, if I was," I said.

"Indians?" asked Pat, looking startled.

"Oh, Geronimo's dead a long time, Pat," I said. "But I'd like to know who killed that Mex. Doesn't matter, though. Nothing I can do about it. But Indians, yes." And then I told them the story I had written Jerry, about the white woman in Indian territory who had to lie out all night. Before I was half finished they were laughing fit to kill, because they knew who I meant.

"Rodge, you're getting to be more and more of a Westerner all the time," said Clara.

Pat was solemn, though. "Darn good thing that spig didn't see you riding past that night. Darn good thing he didn't see you light up in Stolley's cabin."

"Ah, shucks!" I said. "Pat, you're an old woman!"

"Just as well dead, that fellow," said Pat, shaking his head stubbornly. "I sure think so; just as well dead."

Clara finished it. "Pete Stolley's not that tough. I'll bet it was John Yoss. The story will come out some day."

"I don't want to hear it," I said.

"Not likely you will," said Pat.

As we got into the winter, the nights grew colder, though the days were glorious—sunny, clear, crisp, with the bluest blue skies I'd ever seen. Aggie and I were getting to know each other better, and I felt that a friendship was growing that was outside and beyond the business of working for her, or becoming a partner. I was right about that, and it was a friendship that endured through many long, long years, though there were times that I doubted that we were truly friends. Aggie could be the ugliest person in the world if she didn't feel right. There was the drive she and I made to Hereford later that fall.

Aggie had swapped some she-stuff for a Jersey bull along

in the spring. She figured crossing him with her bald-faced cows to get some nice milking heifers. He was small, but mean as all Jerseys are. I wouldn't go into the pasture on foot and I didn't like to take a horse, either, for like as not he'd go for that.

Aggie bred him to six or seven cows. She wasn't as cautious with him as she should be, I thought. One morning she went down to see about a calf she was weaning with a blab board—a thin board fastened to the nose that won't let it suck—and she didn't come back. So I went down looking for her, and found her walking up the lane, mad as a wet hen—and she was wet. Her back half, as exact a half as if it had been measured, was just mud and water. That Jersey had butted her into the creek. She said he had sneaked up behind her and when she turned he was so close he couldn't hook her, just butt. He butted her right through the fence and into the creek flat on her back. Didn't hurt her, either.

"He goes to Hereford next week along with the rest!" was all she'd say.

She was taking a mixed bunch of stuff to a man over in Hereford who had a buyer further on. And I went along to help her.

Clara was there that morning, and Aggie was so worried and upset she was mean as twenty devils. Clara whispered, "My, I'm glad, Rodge, I'm not in your boots!"

Pat helped us get them up over the hill past Barker's to the main road to Fort Huachuca. There were about twenty-five cattle with the Jersey among them—heifers, cows, calves, a few steers that weren't much account. Pat left us there and Dan had told us how to cut a corner before the Fort that would save us time and miles.

You've got to drive cattle slow, and we didn't make much time, so as we stopped and ate our scanty lunch—jerky and biscuits—Aggie was remembering Dan's directions. But she didn't seem to be sure of them, and she asked me what I thought they were. Well, I still had very little sense of direction, and what I told her was so far wrong in miles that it was pitiful. But somehow she took my idea of our route, though she should have known better. And as we went on and on she got madder and madder. The afternoon wore away and the cattle were hot and tired and one little old calf that wasn't big enough really for such a trip and shouldn't have gone only his mammy did so he had to, too, lagged and lagged at the rear, his tongue hanging out.

Pretty soon Aggie yelled, "Get down off your horse! That poor little thing, we're going to kill it before we get there!"

So we'd stop for a while and let them breathe. Then we'd start again and after a while that poor little booger would be stumbling again. Aggie'd yell, "Get down off that horse, we ain't a-going to drive these cattle any further. We'll kill that little fellow, that poor little thing with his tongue hanging out. We're going to kill it before we get there. It's all your fault, Rodgers, every bit of it."

"Darn you, anyhow! You're the old country woman. Why didn't you listen to what Dan said instead of depending on me?"

Darkness fell long before we were near our destination and Aggie got uglier and uglier. I thought, "Clara sure knew what she was talking about this morning, all right."

And one time when Aggie finished swearing, I said, "This is the last time I ever drive cattle with you, Aggie Gates, the very last time!" But of course it wasn't; I drove them often again.

Somehow we got there. The man had heard us coming and had a lantern hung out in the corral to guide us, and he helped us get those poor tired cattle in, too tired to give any trouble.

We were sure glad to get out of the saddle, and when we went into the house, the man's wife had a good hot supper waiting. Aggie perked up and was just as sweet as if she were a girl of sixteen who'd been brought up in a convent all her life. Butter wouldn't melt in her mouth. You'd never suspect that she'd spent the day belaboring me.

It was the same the next day. We rode back over that trail that had been so long and cold and worrisome and Aggie was just as if we'd never done it. As if it had been a dream. She laughed and joked and made plans for the future. Of course, she had the money from the cattle in her pocket; that might have made her feel different. And no trail seems as long coming back as it does going.

There was a dance at the schoolhouse at the end of that week. Artur came out from Nogales to take me to it. Charles Jackson came to take Aggie, too, and the four of us started out at the same time for the short drive to the schoolhouse. In that sort of sporting way of his, Jackson shouted, "Bet you five I beat you to the schoolhouse."

Artur just shook his head.

"Come on, be a sport!" Jackson yelled.

Artur said calmly, "You have the best horse, I know."

That was fine. I didn't want a race. I felt so pleased at being near Artur, riding beside him, that I didn't want it to go too fast, no faster than it had to, in fact. It had been a month or more since he'd been to Canelo. He looked just as nice as ever, maybe a little more handsome, or maybe that was because I'd only been seeing men like old Pat and the other neighbors.

I told him it was good to see him.

"Well, Lu," he said, slow and deliberate as always, "I still have my wish that you were living in Nogales."

I shook my head.

"Oh, yes, I still wish it. But I know you cannot until you have satisfied yourself here. You are a very determined lady, Lu."

"You make me sound awful."

"I think you have a pretty good idea of what you are like." Artur smiled at me.

I wondered for a minute if I did; I had the idea of what I was, but how could I tell if it was the right one? I asked Artur that.

He considered my question for a while. "I don't know," he said finally. "But I think you know; maybe, better I say you feel it. That is it, I think, you feel it."

"I always know what to do, if that's what you mean," I said.

Artur nodded his blond head. "That is it, Lu."

I was sorry that we came to the schoolhouse, then. I liked

to talk to Artur that way. It was a fine feeling to sit close beside him, the lap robe over both of us because it was chilly, almost the beginning of December. But naturally we had to go right inside, once we reached the schoolhouse, because no lady could sit outside at a dance with a man.

Dancing with Artur was next best and in some ways better than sitting beside him. He was a wonderful waltzer and a vigorous square dancer. He could keep at it just as hard and just as long as any of the cowboys, and he didn't wear spurs to catch your dress. The boys kept their spurs on purposely so they'd jangle when they got to stomping in a Mexican *baile*.

They kept their spurs on for that, but they didn't wear their guns. Many of them didn't come with a gun—after all, Arizona was a state and getting pretty tame—and the ones that did took them off and hung them in the storeroom.

The kids were bedded down there, because schoolhouse dances were much more family affairs than the ones held at people's houses or the dance hall. Families came in farm wagons, the whole caboodle of them, and the kids were sent to sleep on the desks shoved back against one wall to make room for the dancers, or in the storeroom. When you wanted to go home, you had to hunt around among the kids for your coat, because they'd use the coats for covers. That was one reason I never felt bad that my old army overcoat was the only one I had; nothing could happen to it. Anyhow, I liked the idea of bringing your kids to a party; I intended to do it when I could. First, I thought, get your kids out here.

The men might go out and pass a bottle or two at this kind of dance, but one of the big features was the wonderful cakes those women would make and bring. They'd brew coffee on the stove in great, big roundup pots, and that was fine refreshment.

We were all hopping around merrily when Yoss and the Duncan boys arrived. John Yoss unbuckled his belt. He had a gun on it, which he hung up high on the wall of the storeroom. It was the only one there; no other man had worn a gun.

Yoss was drunk, all right; he thought he owned the place the way he stood with his thumbs hooked in his trouserband, his coat thrown open, staring around with those green eyes of his. Green eyes and copper hair, that was John Yoss.

He saw me. The music had stopped, and I was standing with Jackson and Pat. Artur had danced this one with Aggie. Yoss yelled, "Hello, Rodgers!" and started over.

Pat bristled right away. It certainly wasn't polite, no matter how well he knew me, to yell my name right across a dance floor, and with no handle, either. Yoss had never called me Rodgers before, but always, "Mrs. Rodgers," when it wasn't "New York lady."

"He's got a snootful," I said. "Don't get edgy, Pat."

"I got a mind to beat him to a frazzle," said Pat.

"Now, you behave," I told Pat. I was glad Yoss had hung up his gun; I remembered the huarache sticking out of the dirt.

Yoss arrived. "I'd sure admire to have this dance, New York lady!" he shouted.

"It's promised." I was just as cold as I could be.

The music began. Yoss grabbed my arm and swung me around. I didn't want to make a scene. "Just keep quiet, Pat," I said. This dance was with Artur, anyhow. It was up to him to come around and claim it. I wasn't mad at him, even if that might sound so, but he should have been johnny-on-the-spot when the music started, not talking with Aggie and Clara.

His face made me laugh when we danced past. I wasn't enjoying John Yoss's dancing; it was crude, to say the least, and this was a waltz, of which he had little idea. But Artur's mouth was practically hanging open. We had moved halfway down the floor before he shut it.

He'd thought everything out in that time in his slow and deliberate way, but once he had decided what to do, he moved fast. We hadn't reached the end of the floor when he was tapping Yoss's shoulder.

"What you want?"

"Mrs. Rodgers promised me this dance."

"Well, she's dancing with me."

That was the last thing John Yoss said for some time. Artur took him by the back of the neck and the seat of the pants and spun him around. I spun, too, but Yoss let go of me then, wanting to writhe around and grab Artur.

Only he couldn't. He was big, but Artur was bigger—and stronger. Artur pushed Yoss ahead of him toward the door.

There was a barrel of water outside the door, kept there in case of fire. A few of us watched Artur lift Yoss in the air, hold him over his head a minute, then reverse him, and plunge him head first into the barrel. It all happened so fast the music never stopped and most people didn't see it.

Artur turned and grinned at me. "Now, Mrs. Rodgers," he said very politely, "the favor of this dance . . ."

What else could I do? I went into his arms and we began to waltz beautifully. I could hear Artur's heart pumping a little hard, but steady and firm. I was worried, though.

Pat came sidling up alongside us with Mrs. Eckleberry from the Grant for his partner. "The Duncans are taking him home," he whispered hoarsely at us. "I got his gun."

So that was all right and we could go on and have a good time. Because when Yoss cooled off, since hardly anyone had seen it and the ones that did wouldn't throw it to his face, he'd probably think a whole lot before he tried to make trouble with Artur, who was so well-known and respectable, and always hobnobbing with the mayor and the sheriff in Nogales.

Still, it made me more firmly convinced than ever that John Yoss had killed that Mexican. I don't know why, but it did.

Pat danced with me later, and I said that to him. He just wagged his head in a way he had, looking like a mournful old turkey with his red face and pursy mouth. "Maybe," he said, "maybe so."

chapter 8

JOHN Yoss had kept bothering me. He'd come and try to get me to go riding with him, he'd act like he was going to visit at the house every time he passed by—and maybe he would have if Aggie hadn't begun to wear a special face for him. He turned up half the places I went, and he and Pat bristled like strange dogs when they met each other.

Aggie said one day, "Rodge, that man's sure got himself believing he's in love with you."

"Oh now, Aggie!"

She nodded her head in her positive way. "He has. I don't mean he is, truly, because I doubt John Yoss could love anything but himself, but he's made himself believe it."

"I don't like him," I said.

"Then you better let him know it."

"Well, I can't do that . . ."

I didn't want to be bad friends with anyone, even though I didn't like him. I thought that Yoss would get tired of his game if I just gave him enough time, and then he'd quit by himself and there'd be no trouble. I was pretty sure it was more teasing than anything, and, maybe since Bess had gone, an attempt to get himself a steady girl. Not that Bess had been, but he'd been able to say so.

Maybe he said that about me, I didn't know. I didn't want him to, because I didn't want Artur to get to thinking I was a flirt or, like some widows, interested in just catching another man. Still, there wasn't much I could do about that.

I went across to Barker's for the mail one day and John came by on his horse just as I was leaving. I was sure he was going to stop at Barker's the way he was heading, but he said he was going my way, so I had to ride along with him. He started boasting about his spread, how he was soon going to build it up as big as anyone's. He said he was a young and ambitious man who was going to get ahead.

"That's fine, John," I said. "Everyone should want to make something of themselves."

"Yes, sir," he said, wagging his head, his cold green eyes watching me like snakes, "yes, sir, and I figure I've got a mighty good reason for wanting to get ahead. Nothing like a woman to bring out the best in a man, nothing like it."

"But Bess is gone," I said. "Oh—maybe she's coming back?"

He scowled at that, his good temper gone quick as sunshine when a thundercloud swells over the horizon. Then I could see him just pull his face back into a smile. "Nope," he said, " 'tisn't that."

This was my turn to keep still.

After a while he got impatient, specially since we were almost at Aggie's. "Wouldn't you like to know who?" he asked.

"Oh, I'm not curious."

John Yoss trying to wheedle was almost funny, only it wasn't safe to laugh. "Come on, guess," he said.

"Oh, I'm a bum guesser."

Aggie came riding around the corral on old Blue right then and John muttered something under his breath. It sounded like, "Damn!"

"What'd you say, John?" I asked as innocently as I could manage.

"Nothing. Well, see you again." He whirled his horse and went back toward Barker's.

Aggie said, "Well, well, company!"

I said, "I'd rather ride alone."

"Most anyone would," Aggie said.

But I couldn't put Yoss off forever. It was some time after Thanksgiving when he came by one day and caught me in the corral shelling corn for our turkeys. Aggie wasn't in the house, either, but off riding somewhere. John got down from his horse and said, "Looking mighty pretty today, New York lady."

"No different from always," I said.

"Well, maybe it's because you always look so pretty to me."

I turned my back and went on shelling corn.

"Sure hate to see you cutting your hands up with that old corn," said Yoss. "Wouldn't let a woman of mine do it."

"But then I'm my own," I said.

"Been wanting to hear that," Yoss said. "Was kind of worried—not about old Pat so much as that Nogales fellow."

I was mad. I said, "I don't care to discuss my business with you, John Yoss."

He just walked around where he could look at my face. He smiled and said, "Now don't go getting mad at me, my pretty Rodgers. I guess you know how I feel about you."

Quick as I could, I said, "I don't know nor want to know anything."

"That ain't friendly." Yoss's green eyes got steadier and brighter. "Look here. I'm as good as anyone else. I'm a strong young fellow with a good future. I can do anything anybody else can and do it better, by God. You got no call to laugh and fleer at me. By God, I don't like it!"

He was almost yelling when he finished; that temper of his had gotten the better of him.

"What do I care what you like? I just want . . ."

"You don't know what you want," Yoss said. "I'll tell you what you want. You want a man and a place to raise some kids. You want a place to live and call your own, not working for some sour old widow woman like Aggie Gates. Well, by God, I'm offering it to you! Hook up with me, and you and me can make a place for ourselves!"

I never had many proposals, but that was the queerest one I ever did have, shouted at me in a mad voice by a man with a mean face and eyes that would bore holes in rawhide.

I said, "I've got just what I want, John Yoss."

He gulped down his temper. "Aw, now, Rodgers, don't go getting on the prod. I talk kind of fast sometimes, I guess, but I don't mean nothing. Why, I've got the biggest

113

heart in the country. What I'm trying to say is I figure it's about time I had a woman in that place of mine to keep it up for me and kind of make it feel like home. You're the woman I want in it."

I shook my head. I wasn't upset or angry any more, just sorry. There was truth in what he was saying. He was so filled with himself he could never ask nicely like any ordinary man. But he was telling the truth about how he felt. I didn't think it was me he wanted—no particular person, just a woman, though probably he'd feel prouder to rope and tie the stranger from New York than a home-grown heifer.

"Look, John," I said, "don't get mad. I lost my husband not so long ago. He meant a lot to me. I'm not ready to think about another man yet—maybe never."

Yoss couldn't believe you, couldn't allow that what you said was simple and straight instead of complicated and crooked. I suppose it was because he was crooked himself.

"It's Pat!" he said.

I almost laughed in his face, because if a man was going to feel outdone with any woman by another man, Pat was the last and least competitor he should pick for his own pride, if for no other reason, such as that Pat couldn't possibly fall in love or look at any woman.

"It's no one," I said.

"Then what's the matter with me?" That was the nearest I ever heard John Yoss come to pleading.

"No, John. I said no one."

Yoss wouldn't give up. His eyes got stormy and I could almost see his coppery hair bristle. "What about that fellow from Nogales? By God, it's him!"

"It's no one," I said without a shake or quaver.

"Rodgers," Yoss said, and his voice was cold and hard, "I don't like being turned down. I guess you and me won't be such good friends no more."

"I'm sorry about that, John. Why don't we just forget what we've been saying and go on like good neighbors?"

"To hell with you!" he shouted, stamped out of the corral,

climbed up on his horse and spurred and quirted it down the road.

When Aggie got home, I told her John Yoss had proposed to me. "Guess you had good enough sense to tell him 'no'," she said.

"You bet I did. But he hates me for it."

"Probably do something that'll make him hate you more before you're finished," she said. Neither of us knew how true that would be.

Well, it was getting on toward Christmas, and long before this I had begun to worry about presents for the kids. I'd talked it over with Aggie months ago, and she'd said, "Long as you're out West here, why don't you give them things from here?"

So I had started collecting Christmas presents for them long before summer was even over. I hadn't bought but one or two things, the rest I'd swapped for or just found. Everything was Western. For Cissie I had a beautiful soft serape, one of the things I'd had to buy, and a hummingbird's nest, a lovely, tiny ball of fluff, with two dinky little eggs still in it, all on a twig that Pat had cut off one of the cottonwoods by the creek. That was for Cissie, too. Also for her there was the only other thing I'd bought, a genuine hand-made piece of Navajo jewelry, a silver and turquoise necklace. It was light and delicate and the colors would be just right with Cissie's honey-blond hair.

Tim was harder to pick for. That wild young devil of a Billy Barker had shot an owl, and I talked him out of one of the legs he had nailed to a storehouse door to dry. The big outstretched talons and the soft floating feathers that came right down to the knuckle would be interesting for a boy, I hoped. Pat gave me a nice cured rattlesnake skin with the buttons threaded to the tail, and that went to Tim. In return for doing some sewing for Clara, I had gotten a woven horsehair hatband with a silver concha.

Jerry, I guess, came off better than Tim. His prize item was a piece of Indian pottery I had dug up myself. The Sowerses were sinking a well and they told me if I'd help—this half joking—I could have whatever I found. Their place was on the site of an old Indian village and even the adobes in their house were full of knuckle bones and teeth—human, of course, since the adobe had been dug in the old burying ground these Indians had used maybe a couple of hundred years ago. So I went over one day and I had luck. I turned up a brown clay dish, shaped like a round-ended canoe. It was just old brown clay without decoration and it had a nick where my spade had struck it, but it was an interesting thing to speculate over. The three Sowers boys said it was the best thing that had been found on their place. I was sure Jerry, who had imagination, would spend hours wondering what sort of food it had held, who used it, who made it, how long ago, all that. And for him I had a length of horsehair rope, begged from Aggie. Also for Jerry, I swapped an apple pie to the Barkers for an Indian club or ceremonial stick or whatever it was. It was a stick with a cow's tail sewn around it so the long tuft of hair hung off one end.

Getting things to give the kids was fine, but when I thought about them opening the packages without me, I felt different. I wanted to be there so bad; I wanted to see their faces when they looked at all this strange stuff. One day I said to Aggie, "Having children is all very well, but you leave an awful big chunk of yourself with each one."

Aggie just gave me one of those long glances of hers. Finally she said, "That's what mothers are supposed to do."

"It hurts, though."

"Little hurting is good for the soul." She got her broody look on.

Because of that I spoke quickly. "I only wish I could be with them. Be the first Christmas I've missed . . ."

"Probably not the last," said Aggie. Then, because she really was kind, she said, "But maybe next year you'll be with them."

I was too low at that moment. I shook my head. "Sometimes, Aggie, I feel like I'd left them forever."

"Rodgers, you just stiffen that wad of jelly you call a spine and face up to things!" Aggie yelled. "What's the matter with you, can't you take a little trouble?"

I didn't look at her as I said, "Oh, Aggie, it's just you

ought to have your children with you over this holiday . . ."

Then I went on about my chores and we said no more that day, but there was a great big aching spot in my heart for Jerry and Cissie and Tim—and Aggie knew it. She was specially nice from then till Christmas.

Well, the kids were easy to give presents to, but Aggie, Dan and Clara meant I'd have to spend some money. And then there was Artur. I wanted to have a gift for him. Only I didn't have much extra money.

I'd earned some money hair-cutting and still could earn a little more. I had my eight dollars a month from Aggie. But I had needed clothes for myself, and I'd bought a warm dress and a couple of blue-denim jumpers and a heavy sweater. That took a good deal of money, and then I'd had to have long woolen underwear. It was all that kept a body from freezing in the winter, Aggie said, and she was right. I wore it to bed, even.

I was still sleeping outdoors, behind the lumber room. I had a tarp over my bed and many a morning I'd wake to find a couple of inches of snow on it. Satan slept with me every night. I don't know why he didn't suffocate, but he'd get into bed with me and crawl right down under the covers to the bottom where he'd sleep all night. Cat business could wait till spring, he made plain; winter nights were for staying in where it was comfortable. He kept my feet cozy and warm; his soft fur was grand to wiggle my toes in.

"Sleeping with a cat!" Aggie would sniff.

Clara would grin. "Yes, just a cat!"

Then Aggie would snort and turn on her. "You're like all young married women. Nothing else on your mind."

"Satan suits me!" I'd say as airily as a duchess.

"You're sure old-maidish for a widow," said Clara.

That would always get Aggie. I think Clara did it on purpose; there wasn't much love lost between the two of them at that time. Aggie hadn't forgiven Clara yet for taking Dan away from her. So she'd say, "You've got a fine opinion of widows, Clara. Wait'll you have a baby or two."

"Yes," I'd say, "just wait."

"Oh, pooh! You don't know nothing about babies. How

many did you ever have?" And Clara would snap her sparkling blue eyes at me.

I never answered that. I could trust Aggie, but no one else. I didn't want it to get to Artur.

Well, I still had Artur's present to decide on. Aggie and I had agreed we'd give each other sensible presents, and we did. I'd decided to give Dan and Clara a clock—I found it in one of the mail-order catalogs, a Seth Thomas mantel clock in a square mahogany case with a handsome brass face with black figures. They didn't have a mantel in the one-room shack they were living in, but that was all right. They could put it on the bureau.

I had pored through both the catalogs. We had Sneers Rawbuck and Monkey Ward—we called them that for fun—and not only one copy of each, but three.

Those catalogs had made good evening reading all through the fall. We'd come in tired as dogs from riding all day and have our dinner, sometimes just Aggie and me, sometimes Dan and Clara, too, and we'd grab up a catalog and sit there by the blazing fire in the big rock fireplace and see what we could get for the other fellow's Christmas. Though, as I said, I couldn't seem to find a thing for Artur.

The trouble was he didn't need anything. After a while, Aggie knew I had everything else settled and she guessed, or knew darn well, what I was trying to find. So one evening, she said, "Rodgers, you're going to wear those wish books plumb out! There's no use worrying your head about something for that man. Just don't give him anything."

"I'm almost certain he's going to give me a present, and a good one, too."

"Yes," said Aggie, "he is. And I know what it is." She raised her hand. "Nope, no use badgering me, I wouldn't tell you if you got down on your knees. But it doesn't signify that you've got to give him one."

"But I want to give him something, Aggie. I feel that I want to make him a gift. But I just know he's got everything a man could need or want."

"That so?" asked Aggie. "I'd guess he could stand a little of you. . . ."

"Oh, Aggie!" I said. "You make me sick!"

"Don't act so maidenly. You've been married. Oh, all right. Stop blushing. Get half a dozen handkerchiefs and work his initial on the corners. That's a personal touch."

"Handkerchiefs! They're so—so ordinary."

"Never saw a man who had enough yet," said Aggie. "Always snuffling and sniveling. You want Artur to go around like Pat, wiping his nose on the back of his hand?"

"Of course not! He doesn't."

"Then give him handkerchiefs."

"He's got handkerchiefs. He doesn't wipe his nose on his hand!"

"Well, then, he hasn't got enough. You want him going around like old Barker, pulling what looks like a rag he's cleaned out the hen house with out of his pocket?"

"Good Lord, Aggie, Artur doesn't do that either."

"Well, he might." She wagged her head. Right now she was looking like a witch, a haggard, handsome old witch. Aggie was always that way, beautiful when she felt right or some man was around to challenge her; nice when she just felt good; awful, like now, when she was feeling low about something.

But of course I didn't ask what bothered her. I just said, "Maybe you're right. And the initial would be a personal touch. Only I can't embroider."

"I can," said Aggie. "I'll do them for you, Rodge."

Goodness, I thought, I still don't know her. Those hands that could hold a high-headed horse like Blue, dig worms out of an infected animal, cut up a steer, rope a calf, milk, wring a chicken's neck, hold a dying man's head—those hands could embroider, too! I felt ashamed of myself; I should at least have learned that back in Brooklyn.

But all I said was, "Oh, that's too much bother for you."

"No, it ain't," said Aggie, positively. "I like Artur and I like you, Rodgers. Also I think you and him would make a good pair. Being married isn't a bad thing. I ought to know."

"You should," I said. "But I'm not thinking about it."

I wasn't, either. But Aggie said, "You'd better, then. It's a cold world for a woman alone."

"We don't need a man!" I yelled, a little embarrassed.

Aggie smiled. "Lots of the time that's so. But they can sure smooth the path for you if you handle them right and have luck. They sure can! And Resswell looks at you like a boy looks at a pie."

So we sent off the order to Sears or Montgomery Ward, I don't remember which. And when the handkerchiefs came, Aggie worked away at them and did the six in three evenings. As beautiful an AR as you could ask to see. "Don't ever let on you didn't do it, Rodge," she said. "I mean that!"

"But if he asks me?"

"Just pass it off. Make nothing of it."

There was something I had made a lot of, though. And that was what I wanted for Christmas. "Now, boys," I said every time I had a chance—this to Clara or Aggie or Dan—"Now boys, the thing I want is a horse of my own."

"You got a horse, Rodgers," Dan said, teasing. "You've got two, Cowboy and Star."

"I don't own them," I said. "That's what I want, a horse I can own."

"I suppose you'd like him branded with your brand," said Clara. "The upright R, let's say."

"He doesn't have to be branded," I said. "Just really mine."

And that was the thing I wanted most of all, because in spite of my boots and divided skirt, and the pair of spurs Pat had given me, and the quirt Dan had donated, I thought I couldn't feel like a real, honest-to-God Westerner unless I owned my own horse.

So I talked about it all the time, and Dan would nod wisely, and Clara would smile, and Aggie would just go about her business, silent or talkative, but none of them ever paying any real attention to my longing for a horse of my own.

Aggie, Clara and I worked hard all the day before Christmas, getting ready, because we were going to have a big party. Artur was coming, of course, and Jackson. Pat and his mother would be there. Minnie and her daughters. Those were the ones we knew about; there'd be sure to be lots of others. So we stuffed the last two turkeys out of the six Aggie and I had managed to raise, and we fixed pie and cake and all the stuff you have to have for Christmas.

The weather had turned warm as it often seemed to about that time of winter. Clara and Dan stayed over, sleeping in the lumber room. I slept out back as usual. We all went to bed, but got up one by one to sneak into the living room and fill the other fellows' stockings, being good enough not to look to see what was put in ours. Aggie did that first, then I did, then it was Clara and Dan's turn. And Dan was the last, and I could hear him through that flimsy old lumber room wall when he got back into bed. He'd whisper, then Clara and he would laugh hard as they could, then whisper again and laugh some more.

"Some kind of joke," I thought, "and it's sure to be on me. Well, I can take it; I'm a good sport."

Christmas morning Dan had his old battered alarm clock set early so he could wake up and yell "Merry Christmas" before anyone else. And he did; he yelled a yell that Pat Malloy must have heard, that must have wakened old Mrs. Malloy, who was half deaf.

I woke up and lay there thinking how nice it would be to have Tim and Cissie crawl into bed with me instead of just old Satan, but Satan was good, too, though not the same, and I reached down and gave him a pat to make up for thinking small of him. But still and all, it would have been a mighty fine thing to see Jerry's face when he unpacked his presents, and listen to Tim squeal with surprise, and have Cissie give me a great, big, smacking, wet kiss because she was happy.

So I was the last one into the house, and I guess that was the way they wanted it, because Dan had started yelling, "Hey, Rodge! Hey, Rodge!"

And Clara chimed in with, "You better hurry, Rodgers, better hurry!"

I hurried, then. Because I was sure it was a horse. I'd wanted one so bad and I'd let them know it. Dan got up early, I figured, to get him out of the corral or barn or wherever he had him hid, and tie him to the fence. I surely didn't expect to find a horse in my stocking. I wasn't that big a fool.

But when I got inside, there the three of them were, in the living room, in front of the big old fireplace where we had pinned our stockings. There were the stockings hanging full of lumps and bulges, and there were parcels like the clock I'd gotten for Dan and Clara that wouldn't go in a stocking. But on one corner of the fireplace, this is what I found:

A heap of horse manure with a fine, oh, a fine, rope whirled around it, and a sign, "Santa Claus brought Rodgers' horse, but he got away."

They busted out laughing their fool heads off. I couldn't look up for a minute. It was too sharp a joke; their rawhide was too stiff. It made me feel all bowed up. But I got a grip on myself, managed a watery smile, and said, "Well, folks, this is sure going to be a lesson to me, as the man said when they started to hang him. After this, I'll get up earlier."

But they tormented me all day about it. They told it to every visitor who came, and each time all the rest listened and laughed. It was a funny, funny joke for them, and each time they all laughed and made fun of me. I took it, though. I wasn't going to spoil Christmas. But I couldn't hide it too well from Pat, when he came over, and Dan told him.

It was about the tenth time Dan had told it, but he was still busting himself with laughter. Artur hadn't come yet, and I was plumb tired of the joke, and feeling real sorry for myself, and I guess it showed. Pat looked at Dan like he was crazy.

Pat got very red in the face but he spoke straight and he didn't stammer. "You did get a horse for Christmas, Rodgers. Cowboy's yours, he's yours I tell you, and I'll give you a bill of sale just as fast as I can get pen and paper! You got a horse for Christmas, Rodgers; now you stop worrying. You did get a horse for Christmas!"

"Oh, Pat . . ." was all I could say.

His face was so red! "I mean it!" He gulped and tobacco juice ran down his chin. "I ain't a-going to have nobody spoil your Christmas. By God and by giddlin's, Cowboy's your horse, Rodgers!"

Of course, the rope was Dan's real present, and it was a good one, not just the rope itself, but what it meant. It was as if Dan said, "I know you'll make a cowboy, Rodgers, so here's your rope." And Aggie had given me more long underwear, and Clara gave me two fine shirtwaists she made herself. Clara was good with her needle.

Then Artur and Jackson arrived in a cloud of dust, each with his own buggy, and Jackson brought some bottles—which had to be drunk out in the open. Aggie wouldn't allow liquor in her house, though she'd drink it.

Artur had a big, round box for me. He held it out with his nice smile before we ever went into the house. Pat was uncorking one of Jackson's bottles, and Dan and Clara and Minnie were all standing around. "Open it up, Lu," said Artur. "Open it."

There was no mistaking what sort of a box it was, of course. It was a hat box, but inside it was a magnificent fawn-colored Stetson twenty—a twenty-dollar Stetson!

"Oh, Artur . . ." was all I could say. I thought of my piddling little handkerchiefs, then I looked at Artur and I could see in his clear blue eyes that whatever I gave him would be as good as diamonds to him. Right then and there, I had a pretty good hunch that Artur Resswell loved me.

But if he did, I didn't know what to do about it. I just didn't know. Greg, I'd never forget Greg—it wouldn't be possible—but it seemed so long since I'd had his arms around me. Then there were Jerry and Cissie and Tim. How would Artur feel if he knew about them? I could feel my face getting hot. I hoped he wouldn't notice I was blushing, wouldn't ask why. I couldn't tell him I felt guilty, somehow, dishonest. Toward him, of course, I wasn't being fair and open and good, the way he was, but I couldn't. I didn't dare. I wished I knew what to do about him.

Artur said, "I hope it fits you properly."

Clara said, "If it doesn't I'll be glad to have it, fit or no fit!"

"That's a lot of hat," said Minnie. "You sure you can stand up under it, Rodgers?"

"Oh, Artur," I said again. "You're so nice. So thoughtful!

How did you know I wanted this more than anything in the world?"

I saw Pat looking at me, and I said, smiling, "Except my own horse, of course." I just couldn't hurt Pat, even for Artur. Besides, I knew whatever I said wouldn't bother Artur. Pat's eyes showed too much; I felt again how alike he and Jerry were. Oh, one was a boy, of course, and the other a man, but I wanted to take care of them both. I wanted to protect Pat just as much as I did Jerry. I wasn't going to have either of them hurt.

"And I've got my own horse, now," I said. "Pat gave me Cowboy this morning. Didn't you, Pat?"

"The one Santa Claus brought got away!" Dan yelled. "So Pat gave her old Cowboy!"

Pat was turning red again. "Sure did!" said Pat. "Don't mind, do you, Resswell?"

Oh, Lord, I didn't want that. No necessity to go putting Resswell's brand on me in public that way, and anyway, how was Pat to know how I felt about Artur? I didn't—much—myself.

But Artur rose right to it. "Why, it's not for me to say, Pat. What Mrs. Rodgers does concerns her. Of course, I'd be upset if anyone did something she didn't like. I have great respect and admiration for Mrs. Rodgers."

"That's fine," said Pat. "Yes, sir, them's my sentiments, too. Any friend of Rodgers is a friend of mine and vicey versey." He nodded, real hard, spat, and went back to working on the bottle.

"Please, Lu, try the hat on," said Artur.

"Oh, of course . . ."

It was a perfect fit. I don't know how Artur did it—figured what size I'd take—because I had a lot of hair, a regular haystack of brown hair, and I wore it a good deal like a haystack, piled up on top of my head. The hat was just right, though.

"It's so . . ." I wanted to say "expensive," then I realized that to Artur this wasn't as expensive as his handkerchiefs had been to me. So I said, "So pretty."

Pat had the cork out of the bottle now, and he took a swig.

"Here, Art," he said, holding it toward him. Artur started to shake his head, then put out his hand and took it.

"Yes," he said. "Just one, for Christmas." He took a very small swig.

I reached for it. "Me, too," I said, "for Christmas."

"Leave some for the rest of us," said Minnie.

Pat stood there looking at me. "Nice hat. Mighty nice hat. But, by God, Rodgers, you can't wear it standing up tall like that!"

"How do you mean?"

"All sugar-loaf shape! No dents! Look, you can do like the old fellers in Texas, hit it a crack on your knee and that's it. Or you can put a gully running down the front, slaunchwise from the peak, like up North. Or three dents to the peak, that's good Arizona. Or—you going to have to use a chin strap, 'twon't jam down on all that hair, so then you can do it Mexican."

"How's that?"

"Push the top down and then hump it up around inside. Flat, like."

"No, I want it Arizona style."

"Here, give me," said Dan.

I handed it to him. His fingers moulded it just as if it was putty. I liked the way he fixed it. "That's fine!" I said.

Then I took Artur inside and gave him his handkerchiefs, and I had been right; he was just as pleased as if they were the world's finest cigars or a diamond ring or whatever the most expensive thing a body could find in the wish book was.

"You got to use them, Artur," I said.

He folded one and put it in his breast pocket, four corners sticking out. It looked nice.

I left Artur then, with the rest of the company, and went back into the kitchen to help Aggie. We were getting near dinner time when there was a lot of yelling and shouting outside and we went to look.

There was Uncle Tom, all spruced up, come down from the mountains on his mule with a jug of whisky tied to his saddle horn. He had been sampling it, too, the way he was weaving and bobbing in the saddle. He started cracking jokes with everybody.

"Light and rest your saddle, Uncle Tom!" Aggie shouted.

"Stay for dinner," Clara said.

"Sure will!" said Uncle Tom. He slipped down off the mule and started passing his jug around. Then he saw me.

"Mrs. Rodgers, ma'am," he said, polite as could be, "here's a Christmas gift for you." With that he reached into a flour sack on his saddle and pulled out the God-awfullest, scrawniest, little old puny black kitten you ever saw in all the world.

"My Lord, Uncle Tom!" I said, "he's certain sure going to die!"

He shook his head till his beard wagged. "Runt of the litter," he said. "All for you. Joke, huh?"

I took the kitten into the kitchen and gave him a saucer of milk. I fixed a flour sack behind the stove where it was warm and he just curled up there. I doubted he would live, but if he did, I wondered what Satan would think of him. The kitten was blacker than Satan was; every least last hair of his was black, and Satan had a few whites on his chest.

We served up dinner. We carved the turkey in the kitchen and set platters on the long table Dan had rigged from planks in the living room. There were thirteen of us to dinner and we sure ate hearty. Every so often Uncle Tom slid off his chair and slipped outside and took a pull at his jug. By the time we finished with the pies, he was feeling no pain. He began to joke about how he'd given Rodgers a Christmas present but hadn't gotten one in return. Even if his was a scrawny little kitten, he said, he ought to get a present, shouldn't he?

"Sure," I said. "What would you like?"

That tickled him, because he had something in mind, I could tell, and I supposed it was another joke of some kind. I liked jokes, even if they were on me, and didn't mind helping. The horse, though, that had hurt even though it certainly wasn't meant to.

"Well," said Uncle Tom, "I've heard, Rodgers, that you've gotten kind of a reputation for cutting hair. I'm wondering if you could trim my beard."

"I sure can, Uncle Tom. I sure can! Just wait till I get my tools."

I got my comb and scissors. I took Uncle Tom outside and sat him down on the well curb where I cut all the cowboys' hair. Most of the men came out to watch, but the womenfolks stayed inside to do the dishes.

So I winked at Artur and Pat and Dan. I said, "Better take another pull on that jug of yours, Uncle Tom. This might hurt."

He laughed at that, but he took another pull.

And he was just drunk enough to not realize what I was doing. No mirror, of course, to look in.

I trimmed his beard to a point, nicely, the way he kept it. But I made the point come way over to his right side, way, way over off the corner of his chin, about where he carried his jug on his saddle.

"There," I said. "How's that?"

"Good," he said, wagging his gray head. "Real good. Thank you kindly, ma'am."

The men were all laughing, but Uncle Tom didn't realize what I'd done. Later he rode off, pleased as Punch with himself, and spent the night at Barker's, but they didn't tell him, either. It was some time before his beard grew right again.

I felt sort of mean, but he had been careless with that poor little kitten and I figured a joke on someone else beside me would be a change, anyhow.

When Artur left, I walked down to the corral with him while he got his horse and hitched it to his buggy. It was his horse and buggy, now; he stabled it at Elgin and rode out by train.

I stood there, watching him hitch up. I thought of what a good day it had been, how kind everyone was, how they loved one another as people specially should at Christmas. The sun was down and the stars were coming out. Aggie had lit the lamps in the house and the Duncan boys had come up with their banjos. People in the house were singing with them. I wished so bad the kids were here, and all at once I felt I was doing them a sort of wrong in denying I was their mother.

"Artur," I said.

He turned to me with a smile. "Yes, Lu?"

I thought I'd tell him and just see what happened. Then I remembered the feel of his arm that night in Nogales when he said, "I find it hard to remember that she is my sister. . . ."

"Artur," I said, and I stepped close to him and touched his hand, "Artur, I know it's a queer place and time, but somehow it's important to me. What did your sister do to you?"

"I will tell you," he said, very precise, but not asking me why I asked, not questioning. That was a wonderful thing about Artur; he could tell when you needed something and the fact that you needed it was enough for him. He didn't have to ask why, and chew it up and hash around until you were sorry you had asked. He knew a sincere need when he saw it, and he gave to it.

Now he said, "My sister did the same thing that my mother did. My mother ran away from my sister and me when I was six."

"Your father . . ." I interrupted.

"Him, too," Artur agreed, "but that is another thing. It is the children I think of, Lu. A woman should not desert her children for any reason!"

"No reason at all, Artur?" I asked faintly. "Not even if she's sure it's good for them?"

"No!" he said. His voice was very fierce. "And then my sister—she does the same thing. She runs away and leaves three little children. Gives them up for a man!" He waved his hands scornfully.

"Maybe she loved him."

"Ach!" he cried. "The children!"

"But didn't your mother or your sister ever try to explain?"

"Words! Words! What do they mean? We show our love, our responsibility with the things we do, not with words. Words are cheap, easy! It is how we behave that proves what we are. Not what we say!"

I'd never heard him speak so positively. This was a thing he must have thought over and over. I felt so sorry for him. I could almost see him as a little tow-headed youngster, not able to figure out why his mother had left him. And even if he knew the reason, I could see now it wasn't going to make any difference to him.

"But every woman is not like your mother or sister," I said very carefully.

He shook his big head and smiled at me. "You, Lu, are not like my mother or my sister."

But he would think so, I knew. And I knew how it would hurt if he despised me.

He was looking down at me, expecting an answer. I raised my face. I said, "I hope not, Artur."

I meant that from the bottom of my heart. But I was really sure I wasn't.

"It was a very good Christmas for me, Lu," said Artur. "The best I can remember."

"I'm glad," I said.

Then because I wanted him to take away more than my poor little Christmas present, I put my arms around his neck and kissed him. His mustache tickled my nose; it felt good. All of a sudden, I got into a sort of panic, pulled away from him, and ran for the house like a silly young girl. But I turned at the door and waved.

Artur waved back. His buggy whirled off down the road, and I went into the house.

chapter 9

WE GOT through the winter. Spring came at last, and I was very glad to see it. My, that was a cold winter! Some mornings I'd think I never would get warm again.

We always did the chores before we had breakfast, and we didn't wait for the sun to come up. The ridge to the east blocked the early sun, and as Aggie said, "Wait for that sun to get over those ridges and the day'll be half gone!"

I'd get the fire started and a pot of mush on the stove. Then I'd go out to the corral where Aggie was milking. I'd take the sack of pumpkins I'd broken up the evening before and go down to the pigpen in the pasture. It was about a quarter of a mile, and though I had stout shoes and gloves, my hands and feet would be so numb by the time I got there that I didn't know I had any.

Aggie had a lot of spells of gloom those months. She'd get sullen and smoldering. She did a lot of riding and I thought it was to get off by herself as much as anything. Jackson was bothering her; she didn't know whether or not she wanted to get married again. "Be the fourth time," she'd say. "Never seemed lucky with it."

Then she told me about Doc Gates, her third husband. They called him Doc because he was a veterinarian. That was how Aggie came to know him—she had some real sick horses one time and Doc fixed them for her.

"He was a big, fine-looking man," she said. Her tone was very bitter, and I wondered why. "Big and fine-looking, and a great talker. Very jolly. I thought it would be good for me to have someone like that in the house—laughing and joking and carrying on. It was fun, too, for a while."

She went into a broody silence, her black brows pulled together in a heavy frown. Finally, she heaved a long sigh and said, without looking at me, "He was killed by a runaway team in his buckboard. Plunged into a deep arroyo and busted his neck. There've been times, there were times, when I've wished it had happened sooner."

"Why, Aggie!"

"Don't 'why, Aggie' me! You never knew Doc Gates. Well, anyhow, you see what I mean about luck."

"That's nonsense! People make their own luck."

Aggie would give me a look. "Maybe it's the same thing. Maybe I make it the way I want it." She'd fall silent and her eyes would turn inward and I could see she was thinking back to that time when the Indians nearly got them when she was just a little girl. And wishing they had!

"Maybe you make it the way you want it, too, Rodgers. Maybe you and Resswell—he could be good luck for you, you know."

I'd shrug my shoulders.

"You think he wouldn't stand for those kids of yours? Maybe so. Lots of men wouldn't take to another man's children."

"Oh, no," I said, "he'd like them."

"You seem pretty sure of that."

"I am. Anybody'd like Jerry and Cissie and Tim. It's their mother Artur wouldn't like."

Aggie gave a sharp laugh. "He likes you right now! He just sits and moons at you!"

"Now he does," I said. "He wouldn't then."

"Rodgers," said Aggie, puckering up her mouth as if she'd bit into something real tart, "Rodgers, you're hinting and skirting around some sort of mystery, and you've been here long enough to know how I feel about that."

I sure did. If Aggie really got interested in something you had no rest till she'd wormed it out of you. That had bothered me at first, just as a lot of her other traits had bothered me. It really didn't, any more. I felt different about Aggie. I felt that she was my friend and I was hers. No matter how we might quarrel, we had a regard for each other—love in the Christian and friendship sense—that couldn't be broken by anything either of us did to the other.

So I told her about Artur and his mother and sister. When I had finished, she said, "Rodge, you got a real mean one there."

"You can see, can't you," I asked her, "that I can't just tell him about the kids because he'll never believe I left them for their own sakes, because there was no way I could have them with me. He won't believe I'm working here so I can get them back to me some day."

"Would you want them on this place, Rodge?" Aggie asked.

I looked at her for a while. I was still a hired hand, I thought, but I was getting closer all the time. I understood Aggie pretty well, but not all the way through.

I said, "How can I tell? It's not possible to even get them out here, yet. Railroad fare . . ."

"Won't always be so hard-scrabble," said Aggie. "One of these days your ship'll come in."

Just hearing about another person's troubles usually cheered her up, the way this had. So I was partly reinforcing that, and only partly being truly gloomy, when I said, "Yes, loaded with sugar—but with a leak so bad it's all melted and turned to syrup and running out!"

"Oh, come now, Rodgers, it won't be that way at all. It'll be full of gold and silk and plum pudding. My goodness, who'd think I could say such foolish things at my age!"

"Oh, well," I said.

I did get into a mood of feeling dismal—worrying about Artur and the kids and what Aggie meant by asking if I wanted them here on the ranch—so I was glad when Pat proposed a prospecting trip.

It would be just him and me, he said. We'd take a wagon with a chuck chest full of flour, bacon, beans and coffee. We'd go west, clear across Santa Cruz County, into the Baboquivari Mountains where Pat knew some likely spots to pan for gold. Go for ten days or so, and we'd lead our horses behind the wagon so we could camp and then strike out into places you wouldn't be able to go in a wagon.

Before we were through, though, I learned there weren't many places Pat couldn't go in a wagon.

Well, of course, I was wild to go. One of the biggest things I wanted to do was prospect. "Oh, we're not likely to find nothing," said Pat. "Maybe pick up a nugget or two, maybe find a pocket of nuggets. But we got to go soon while there's water in the washes or we won't have any to pan with."

Aggie said, "Sure, you go ahead. I'd go if I didn't mind sleeping out at night. Probably get lumbago again if I did."

I was pretty independent but I had enough Eastern ways left in my thinking to consider what ten days alone in the mountains could do to a woman's reputation.

"Oh, pshaw!" said Aggie. "You could go to Timbuctoo with Pat and he'd be too shy to look you full in the face!"

It was Dan who objected. Dan was almost ten years younger than me, but he treated me as if I was his kid sister most of the time. He was very good to me and thoughtful. He said, "No, no, Rodgers, you shouldn't do it."

"Why?"

"Well, what do you think people . . . ?"

Aggie said, "Dan Langwood, everybody that knows Pat knows the last woman he got within arm's length of was his mother when he was five years old. The ones that don't know that don't know him. As for Rodgers, everybody knows she's a prissy old maid at heart even if she does have a handle to her name. There's not the least harm in it, and a lot of fun."

Dan was stubborn, too. "No," he said again.

So I said, "All right."

But I could be stubborn and I wanted to go. Aggie and I cooked up a fine story for Dan about a trip to Tucson. Aggie was as bare-faced a liar as ever lived when she wanted to be, though she maintained she never told an untruth in her life. Pat and I packed the chuck wagon, and one fine morning off we went.

We headed across the Canelo hills and into the San Rafael valley, then along a good road which Pat said ran nearly due west and would take us into Harshaw, a mining town.

We went through Harshaw late in the afternoon, turned off on a road past a lot of mines. This road petered out to no more than a broad trail after a while. We came to a little canyon off the one our trail was following and turned into it. Pat said there was water at the head. We made camp in a good, clear spot, and Pat took a bucket and went up for water while I made a fire. We were in the Patagonia Mountains, he said, and would get out of them the next morning. We'd come over twenty miles.

Next morning the trail disappeared. Pat just went straight ahead. We jolted over hills and under trees and followed a cowpath or two. Once Pat had to put his rope on the wagon tongue and help the team with his horse, though it was a good team. I held the lines and we went up this rocky place, nearly as steep as a flight of stairs. That was the top. We started going down. I could see out ahead for miles and miles—just rolling country, with way off on the horizon mountains sticking up. It was beautiful, beautiful!

Two days later we were right in the heart of the Baboquivaris. We had come most of the way on old trails, avoiding roads as if they were poison. We slept under the sky in our blankets and it was magnificent. Pat was a good companion; when he said something it made sense; when he had nothing to say he kept still. I guess I chattered enough for both of us.

And I kept thinking how wonderful it would be to have Jerry and Tim along on a trip like this. Jerry specially, because he was getting to the age where any boy longs for the outdoors—to be roughing it. He would have been just bug-eyed all the time. Particularly when the whole purpose of the trip was finding gold.

Well, we found a likely camping place in the Baboquivaris with plenty of water. It was a good, steep-sided canyon with a real creek flowing through it over great ledges of blue stone that looked like it had been smoothed and molded by a gigantic thumb while it was soft. There were rock doves up in the cliffs; mornings they called back and forth with that lovely, liquid coo which seems to come from deep in their chests.

"Now," said Pat, "there's some dry washes up toward the head of this canyon I always meant to look into."

We puttered around for a couple of days and found a stray nugget or two, small ones about the size of a dwarf pea. Pat was happy, but I wasn't. I wanted to make a strike. I saw that just prospecting was enough for Pat, but I wasn't so interested in that. I wanted to find some gold, and I said so.

"That ain't the way you do it, Rodgers," said Pat. "Why, there's men have been moseying around these hills for years and years and never found more than a pinhead. It ain't the finding . . ."

"Not for you. But I could sure use some."

Pat shook his head. "Take it easy. There's something about looking too hard that brings bad luck."

"Nonsense!" I said.

"All right," said Pat. "But it's better to be just looking at the hills and the sky—because then you see things like that."

He pointed, and all at once, up on the hillside something long and grayish-tan moved, and our horses, standing further down the wash in the shade, snorted and flung up their heads.

It was a mountain lion, and a big one. He went up the hill like oil, just pouring around the rocks and scrub oak. In two seconds he had disappeared over the top.

I was shaking. "Gosh, Pat, he might have got one of us!"

"Nope," said Pat. "Lions never attack a man. Coward, or maybe smart, they are. They go after calves and colts and that's about all. Now, as I was saying, you're just standing loose and easy and chewing tobacco, and you spit, like this, and then . . ."

His blob of tobacco juice had started a miniature sand slide in the wash bank. Where it had trickled away, the sand was sort of dark and discolored. Pat squatted down. "Give me that pan," he said.

I handed him the iron pan and he scraped this discolored sand into it. We went back down to the creek in the canyon, where he took some water in the pan and began to whirl it around. He kept this up, a little sand and water slopping over the edge at each twist, till he had a streak of black sand strung along the corner where the rim of the pan turned up off the bottom. Along the edge of the black sand was a fine, fine yellow line, thin as if you'd drawn it with a pencil.

"Color," said Pat.

"Gold!" I yelled.

"Well, yes," Pat gave me a wide, snaggle-toothed grin. "But a mighty small jag of it."

"Let's go back and dig out some more."

"Sure, but it's just a pocket, and not much of a one at that."

He was right, of course, but we never got to prove it, because we had only washed a couple of shovelfuls when it came on to rain. A regular gully washer, too, and it soaked us to the skin. Got so wet even I was ready to go back to camp, though I was bewailing the loss of our mine.

"Washed all away!" I hollered. "Every darn bit of it washed away."

"Don't let it bother you," said Pat. "Wasn't enough there to matter one little bit. But I'll tell you this. Where you find dust, there must be somewhere it came from. Further up . . ."

"Let's go back!"

Pat said, "Even my saddle's wet. I'll go back tomorrow."

That made sense, of course, and anyhow the day was almost gone.

Next morning, my corset was still wet. Oh, we rode in corsets in those days, Aggie and I, and even women as young as Clara. Old-fashioned bone corsets, they were, with lacings up the back, hooks like they used to put on shoes, so you could tie yourself in nice and tight. Mine was still wet, and I couldn't get along without it—at least, I thought so—even though I weighed only one hundred and twenty pounds and stood five feet nine in my stocking feet. Aggie and I were the same height and weight and could wear the same clothes.

So I got all my clothes on, and went and stood over the cooking fire, holding that corset over it so it would dry. I guess I thought I'd fall apart if I rode without it. And I stood there turning it this way and that, and it wouldn't dry. So I got tired, and old Pat, squatting there on the other side of the fire, waiting to cook some bacon and flapjacks, but not able to do it yet because my corset might drip in the pan—old Pat, squatting and trying not to see what I was doing, made me mad. So all of a sudden, I said, "Here, Pat, you take a chance at this! I can't get dressed till this gets dry."

I leaned over as if I was going to hand the corset to him.

Pat would rather have held a pair of mad rattlesnakes than any woman's corset. He gave a sort of strangled cry, jumped up and ran down to the creek.

I said, "Oh, shucks!" and threw the darn thing into the wagon, and started cooking breakfast. Pat came back looking very sheepish. We sat and ate silently. It was a good, friendly silence, though, the sort in which one fellow admits he's been joked, and the other says he won't do it again—for a while, anyhow.

Since the corset was still wet, and I wanted to find my gold mine, I pinned it to the side of the wagon and decided I'd just hold myself together with my own muscles.

Maybe it was being all loose and relaxed without that tight lacing, or maybe it was the rain the day before, but we found our pocket. Pat always said I found it, but I think he took me where I couldn't help but stumble over it.

Anyhow, we panned out some nuggets and some dust. One of the nuggets was large as a lima bean. I was so excited I couldn't speak for a while, and long after Pat said we'd gotten it all, I kept digging and panning to no avail.

In camp that night, we looked at the gold. "Think it's worth five thousand dollars, Pat?"

He gave me a pitying look. "Couple of hundred, maybe."

That was disappointing. "You sure?"

"Certain sure. No use being foolish 'bout these things."

"Nope," I said, "I guess not."

I sat there staring into the fire, thinking how ten or twenty pockets like that and I could get the kids out here. I might have been talking out loud. Pat said, "That was more luck than anything. Men have gone ten years without that good a strike."

"I suppose . . ."

"Don't get to thinking you could do it again."

And he was right. We didn't even find dust the next day. But that night, Pat had his big idea. We were sitting there by the fire, full of beans and bacon, with now and then one of the horses stamping off among the trees where Pat had strung up a rope corral. Overhead, the stars were out, big and bright, nearly hanging on the canyon rim; back in the hills a coyote howled, lost and lonely.

I said, "It's sure beautiful . . ."

Pat said, "I been thinking something, Rodgers. You a Republican or a Democrat?"

"Golly, Pat, I don't know. Never thought about it."

"Well, you've got to be one or the other."

"I don't see why."

"Can't vote next fall without you're something."

"Shoot, I'll decide when the time comes."

"Way I figure," said Pat, "is that you're a Republican. And I'll tell you why." He spat a long sizzle of tobacco juice into the fire. "You're a Republican 'cause John Yoss is a Democrat."

"You're going to run for office?" I asked Pat.

"Not me!" said Pat. "But you are."

"Mayor of Canelo, I suppose?"

Pat shook his head. "Constable. There ain't no mayor, as you well know. Constable. That's what John Yoss is going to run for next fall. He's got a pretty good chance, too, but you and I can beat him."

"How could I be a constable?"

"By getting elected. Now, look here, Rodge, everybody knows you and likes you. People'll vote for you if you give them a chance. First thing, we won't tell a soul, yet. You've got to learn to shoot. You can throw a rope now, though it's got the wobbliest loop I ever did see, and you're a good rider for a woman, particularly one that ain't grown up with horses. But you got to learn to handle a gun, both afoot and in the saddle. And I'm going to teach you."

"This is all silly," I said. "And you know I'm scared of guns, Pat."

"You'll get over that. By God, Rodgers, this is a good idea, and I've got a better one! Tom Patterson's sheriff of this county. He's a Republican, and I swung a lot of votes for him out around Canelo. I'm going to get him to make you a deputy, come September or so. That'll swing the whole damn election! We'll make John Yoss look like hell in a dry year with the folks moved out!"

"I can't . . ."

"Now, Rodgers, you can so! You like a joke as good as anybody. This here'll be the biggest damn joke ever played in the whole damn state of Arizona; it'll be plumb famous in no time!"

"You haven't done it yet."

"We'll start right now. Look a-here. . . ." He unlimbered his big old .45 Colt and started to take it apart.

"I'm going to turn in, Pat. I'm tired, and I'm not sure whether this has been my lucky day or not. Found some gold, but found a sort of no-account proposition, too."

"Aw, Rodgers," he said, and his old, red face was just like a boy's when you take his baseball away. "Aw, Rodgers, we could lick that John Yoss like one, two, three!"

"I'm turning in."

I did, but I woke early in the morning. I lay looking up at the sky, my Arizona sky, still gray, the sun somewhere miles away to the east, not yet over the horizon. But up there in the rock walls the doves were stirring and waking, talking sleepy-like to each other, a kind of question in their voices, asking, "You still there? Where are you?" A little wind drew down the canyon; it brought a whiff of good honest horse smell to me. A wisp of ashes and burnt-wood smell from the fire came with it, though it looked as if it was out. I heard a new gurgle in the creek I hadn't noticed before. I felt the ground under my sleeping bag, good ground, good Arizona ground.

After sleeping on it, Pat's idea seemed better than it had last night, and that's the test of a good idea.

"Pat," I said, "I'll do it!"

"Rodgers," he said, "that's sure fine!"

I thought that John Yoss would really hate me now—and with reason.

We tried one more day of prospecting with no luck. We decided to go home. We'd stop in Nogales and sell our gold. Pat made me promise I'd buy a gun and some shells with part of what I got. Since a gun was part of being a peace officer, I was willing, though I didn't like the idea. Pat said we would talk to Tom Patterson while we were in town. I wanted to talk to Artur.

We broke camp early, and the team, which had been resting, pulled us up out of the canyon in jig time. Out on top, we could see the sunrise, the eastern sky turning pink with the distant mountains just a black, irregular screen for all the great light pouring over their tops. Pat was mighty tickled; he sat there chewing and spitting and clucking at the team. He found a road after an hour or so and stayed on it. It took us into Nogales in time for a late dinner at the Border Café. Mrs. Jones put me up, and Pat decided to sleep in the wagon at the livery stable. We went down to Resswell's Saloon where Pat routed out Artur for me, and left the gold in his safe.

Artur and I went back to the lobby of the Montezuma Hotel, but Pat stayed at the saloon for a couple of snorts. Artur was more glad to see me than surprised. He said, "Lu, you are a remarkable lady. Prospecting with Pat, roping cows, even flying would not surprise me."

"Suppose I got to be a peace officer, would that surprise you?"

"No," he said. "Nothing will. Not ever. And I think for you to be a peace officer is a very good idea. But you must be careful not to get into trouble."

"Oh, I won't," I said. So then I told him all about it. I finished by saying, "Pat thinks of it as a joke on John Yoss. Well, it will be, but to me it's not just a joke."

"What do you mean?" Artur asked.

"The more I think of it, the more I know it will be the biggest thing I can do in this country. Ever since Aggie and I found that dead Mexican, I've wanted to do something about lawlessness."

"That is what I mean by trouble," said Artur. "To serve in a sort of honorary way, that is one thing. But to crusade, to fling yourself into it heart and soul, that is another. I am worried about you, Lu."

"You wouldn't mind, would you?"

"Of course not! It would be a great responsibility, though. Perhaps too great a load."

"No," I said, "women can carry loads." I looked straight at him. "Women can be responsible, too. You'll see."

"Oh," said Artur, "it is just that I will be a little fearful and worried over you if you do it."

"Well, it's a long time off, and I may not get elected."

"But I think Pat is right, you can win an election. And now, Tom Patterson will make you a deputy. I wonder, might you not be the first in the United States?"

"Golly, I don't know! Wouldn't that be something!"

I thought of how proud Jerry would be if his mother was the first woman deputy sheriff in the United States. But the chances were, I was sure, that some of the old-time mining-camp or cow-town girls had been deputies. Maybe if I could win the election, though, I could be the first elected woman peace officer. There was a better chance of that, for only a few states had female suffrage.

"Well," said Artur, "there is one good thing about this. Whatever happens, you will wear a gun."

"Oh, Artur!" I said. "You are sweet! I can take care of myself all right, honest I can."

He smiled. "It appears so. Now, can we go and close the Border Café with a cup of coffee?"

"Of course we can."

Pat and I sold the gold at the assay office the next morning. We got two hundred and twenty-two dollars and sixty-nine cents for it, which we divided evenly except for the odd penny, which Pat insisted I take.

"Because you done something to bring us luck," he mumbled, turning red and going wall-eyed with embarrassment. He meant to joke, I knew, about the corset pinned to the wagon and me feeling free and easy, like he said people should when they were looking for gold.

Then we went to Rodriguez's hardware store and bought me a gun. A Colt double-action .38. Pat said a .45 Peacemaker was too heavy for me, and that if I ever had to use it, a .38, at the close range I'd probably be at, would be just as effective. "The main thing, Rodge," he said, "isn't to be able to hit a target, but to have a gun. On a man it would be dangerous, but with a woman, just having a gun lets her run a bluff that not many men would call. Man would feel foolish to get into a gun fight with a woman."

Then I banked the rest of my money. It felt good; it was a long step toward getting the children out. My bank account, which had been living scrawny on a poor diet of two- and four-bits with an occasional dollar, got fat all of a sudden.

We found Sheriff Patterson in his office under the courthouse where the jail cells were. Pat introduced me and told him we wanted to talk private, so the Sheriff closed the door and reared back in his swivel chair with his thumbs stuck in his suspenders. He gave me a wink from his steely gray eye, and said to Pat, "Don't tell me you're planning to get married."

Pat turned scarlet, his Adam's apple bobbed up and down like a hen picking up corn, and he began to stammer. "Ain't s-s-s-s-so!" he got out at last.

The Sheriff and I laughed a little. Finally he said, "Well, I didn't think you did, Pat. But what can I do for you?"

Pat couldn't talk very well, yet, so I said, "Did you ever think it might add distinction to your office, Sheriff Patterson, if you had a female deputy sheriff? Arizona is the youngest state in the Union, but it is an enlightened and forward-looking state, fitted to become a leader among its sister states. Its constitution granted women the right, the duty to vote, and yet, when has a woman held elective office in this state?"

The Sheriff gave me a long, calculating glance. "Mrs. Rodgers, you sound like quite a politician. But the office of deputy sheriff isn't elective. It's appointive. I make the appointment."

Pat had hold of himself, now. "That's right, Tom. You sure do. But Constable of Canelo Township is elective."

"I don't see the connection," said Patterson.

"Just that there's a fine chance the Democrats will grab that office off again next fall."

"Who's running?"

"Sheriff," I said, "you're trying to pull the wool over our eyes, aren't you? You know darn well that John Yoss is going to run on the Democratic ticket because old man Barker don't want the job any longer."

The Sheriff gave me a tight grin. "All right, I'll call. Everybody put their cards on the table."

"It's this way," said Pat. Then he told him how he figured to beat John Yoss with me. "She needs the start being a deputy sheriff would give her, Tom. You can see that. It's a new idea even for what Mrs. Rodgers calls this forward-looking state to have a woman for a peace officer. But if you give the people the lead, they'll throw in with us. They'll come a-running."

Sheriff Patterson sat there with his thumbs hooked in his galluses, thinking.

"You'll be running next year yourself," said Pat softly. "A good strong Republican ticket in the township wouldn't hurt a little bit."

Patterson said, "I don't know if I want this job any longer. I guess I do, though. Well, that's nothing to you. Yes, Pat, by God, I'll appoint Mrs. Rodgers deputy when you say it's time. But for God's sake, teach her to shoot! I don't want to make a joke out of the sheriff's office!"

Pat gave him a whack on the shoulder. "That's what I expected from you, Tom. I'll make a sharpshooting gal out of old Rodgers or bust her trying! Put it there!"

We shook hands all around and left.

Outside, Pat said, "See, I told you so!"

I stopped at Judge Dunphy's office to say hello.

"Mrs. Rodgers," the Judge said, "you're a far cry from the nervous, thin, worried woman who came out here. You stay here long enough and the country will make a pretty fair Westerner of you."

I wanted to tell him I'd soon be more of a Westerner than he'd ever dreamed, but Pat and the Sheriff and I had agreed the whole scheme was a dead secret—except for Artur, who had promised to never say a word.

I had dinner with Artur that night, a regular Border Café dinner of steaks, fried potatoes and canned corn. There was apple pie and coffee for dessert; their Chinese cook made surprisingly good apple pie. You might say that wasn't a very interesting sort of a dinner, but it somehow seemed very special to me. It was nice to be in a different place from Aggie's, or out there in the country, and while I loved every bit of that, this made me realize I needed more folks around sometimes, too. And the thought of that lovely gold turned into figures in my bankbook made me feel that I was getting somewhere. Artur's nice face across from me, the way he looked at me, even the tone of his voice, made me light and gay and happy. I felt so good I wanted to laugh at something, so I told him how I'd been Canelo's crazy woman last summer, and I didn't worry if I'd told him about it before.

It was along toward the end of the summer, and Aggie was going down the pasture for something. She said, "Get Dinkum, Rodgers, and come along with me." Dinkum was Dan's old burro. He was awful old, over thirty, but he could still trot and carry a light weight like me.

The pasture was just full of sunflowers, and I kept picking them and sticking them all over Dinkum and myself, everywhere, in my sun-bonnet, in the sleeves and neck of my dress, around the saddle, in the bridle, all over, till Dinkum and me looked like a haystack of sunflowers. Even Aggie, who was feeling kind of sour, had to laugh at us. When we finished what we had gone to do and got out to the gate, I said, "Aggie, I'm going to ride over to Barker's and visit with Mrs. Barker."

Well, I had nearly reached the turn-off where the road ran to Barker's and on to Locheil and Fort Huachuca when a couple of Negro cavalrymen came up behind me on those fast-trotting government horses of theirs, and they yelled, "How do we get to Locheil, lady?"

I squinched down to one side in the saddle, and made a horrible face and crossed my eyes. They rode up, one on each side of me, saying, "How do we go to Locheil, lady? How do we go to Locheil?"

I sang at them. The sunflowers and the sun, and neat little old Dinkum and the big, blue sky had kind of made me boil over, bubble up, so I sang at them. "You da—amn fools, you go up tha—at hill!"

They kind of shied at that and one looked at the other. They put spurs to their horses, and they went up the hill at a high lope. I rode into Barker's laughing fit to kill, and told old man Barker and Mrs. Barker what had happened.

About four weeks later, the daughter of a man named Batchelder got married and they had a big dance and party in their two-story barn, a thing unheard of in that country before. They had music from the Fort and a lot of the officers came. Old man Barker had made a trip to the Fort a couple of weeks earlier, and one of the officers he knew, a captain, had asked him if there was a crazy woman in his part of the country. Old man Barker had said, "Oh, sure, there is."

So the captain was at the dance. And Aggie and I were there, of course, and I was feeling very good because I had a new black dress from Sears. Rawhide with a red rose on the shoulder, and I was wearing the first rouge I'd ever owned.

Old man Barker came up with this very handsome captain. Barker said, "Here's our crazy woman, Captain. This is our loony with the sunflowers."

Old man Barker stood there and laughed and laughed.

I was flustered for a minute; then the captain said, "But you look very charming, not crazy."

"The power of the moon is on the wane," I said. "And in my right mind I wear roses."

So he asked me to dance, and I did. But that was one of the country's biggest jokes for a long time, Rodgers getting caught in one of her crazy stunts.

Artur and I laughed over that for a while. "Lu," he said, "you like a joke on yourself as well as anyone else."

"Maybe better," I said. "I figure I can find them as funny as the other fellow does, and lots of people can't do that."

Artur nodded. "Pat was in the saloon when I left. He gave me a message for you. You are to return to Canelo by train. He has still much of that money left and it is burning in his pocket."

"Oh, Artur," I asked, "can't you stop him?"

"Don't worry about him, Lu." Artur gave me a nice smile. "I will see that no harm comes to him and not too much of that money is spent."

"Thanks, Artur."

"It is not for you to thank me. Whatever I do for you, I do because I want to."

"I guess that's true for everybody," I said.

"Oh, maybe," said Artur. "But I mean this in a different way. I want to do things for you." He stopped and looked across the table at me. I could almost read his thoughts on his face. They went something like wondering if he should tell me that he had a very special feeling about me, maybe even whether he should say he loved me.

I didn't know what I'd say to that, and I really didn't feel ready to consider the question. I guess some of this may have showed in my face, because his changed.

"You do enjoy things like this with me, don't you, Lu? Even though it is not very grand?"

"Oh, yes, Artur. I'm always happy when you come out to the country, and I like eating at the Border Café with you."

"That is good," he said solemnly, "because I want to go on seeing you and doing these things with you, even if they are a little foolish."

"I don't see anything foolish about it!" I told him, indignantly.

He gave one of his nice laughs. Shaking his head, he said, "Lu, you are priceless."

"Oh, sure," I said. I thought I knew what he meant, but I didn't intend to give him a chance to say it. He would accuse me of changing my mind since first I didn't want him to say how he felt about me, and then I got annoyed when he ran down the things we did together. Men always love to accuse women of inconsistency.

"Not many women would leave a great city and come out to this rough place. Not many women would try to make it their home. That is what you are doing, aren't you?"

When I nodded my head, he said, "See, you are priceless, then."

"A good thing there's only one of my kind, you mean."

"I mean I know I am a lucky man to know you, since you are so rare."

That was nice, but how rare or priceless would I be if he knew I'd left not only that big city, but three children in it? A small part of me wanted to tell him just to get it over with, just to be finished with worrying. But the rest of me wouldn't find the way he'd act afterwards fun enough to be worth it.

What was I going to do?

Why or how, I don't know, but into my head came the simplest solution, the one way to fix everything.

Bring the kids down!

With them here with me, Artur couldn't fail to understand that I loved and wanted them, and hadn't really run away from them. And Jerry, Cissie and Tim were such fine children he'd be sure to love them!

Oh, the kids with me would fix everything!

It was easier said than done, of course, but at last I knew how to handle Artur.

I just felt so fine I wanted to jump up and down.

"You know," he said reflectively, "I have thought that a good ladies' clothing store would succeed here in Nogales. Why don't you come back to Nogales and open one, Lu? I'll put . . ."

I stopped him. "Where I'm going to make a place for myself, Artur, is right out there in Canelo. I think in another year or so, I can persuade Aggie that I'd make a better partner than a hired hand. We're good enough friends to go partners right now, even if we do rile each other at

147

times. But I'm hoping if I give her enough time and enough hints, she'll see it herself."

Artur shook his head. "Sometimes you are so impractical. What would it advantage Mrs. Gates to make you her partner? What could you bring to it?"

"Oh, it'd be better than just me working there." I didn't have an answer to that question yet, which was the main reason why I hadn't spoken to Aggie about the whole business. But I would get an answer. I had to. It would be a big step toward getting the kids here.

"Also," said Artur, "have you thought of what will happen if Mrs. Gates marries Mr. Jackson? I am sure he wants to marry her."

"I'd thought of that, too, but I hadn't wanted to. "Artur," I said, "it isn't humanly possible to plan every step of your way. And anyhow, what are you trying to do, discourage me about the whole idea?"

I must have sounded mad, because Artur gave me a pleading little smile. "Only to encourage you to move into Nogales where I can see you more often and learn more about you."

Because he'd brought up so many difficulties and such strong ones, he'd made me worry, and because of that, I said shortly, "You wouldn't much like what you learned. Now it's time I went up to Jones's."

"Can I walk up the hill with you?"

I was sorry I had been snappy, so I said, "Oh, I would like that, Artur."

Walking up the hill to Mrs. Jones's reminded me of all the times we'd done it in the spring. It was nicer than ever to feel Artur's solid arm under my hand. It didn't matter what you said, I thought, a man is a pretty satisfactory kind of thing to have around. The right kind of man, that was—Artur's kind. I guessed if he thought I was pretty rare, you'd have to say that his kind was certain sure scarce!

I gave his arm a little shake. "It's a good old world!" I said.

Artur chuckled deep in his chest. He really was a smart man; he didn't say a word. We just walked on in silence till we stopped outside Mrs. Jones's.

"I will come to help you on the train in the morning," said Artur. "I wish you could come to Nogales more often. I'd like it very much."

I didn't know who was around to hear, so I put my mouth up close to his ear to whisper, "Being deputy sheriff might mean I'll have to come to town more often." I did whisper that, but Artur smelled so good I took a real deep sniff and it startled him so that he jerked away.

Then he chuckled. "You're a strange and wonderful woman, Lu," he said. The way he said it made me shiver, though it was a warm evening.

But I politely said, "Thanks for a very nice time, Artur. Good night."

When I got home next day at noon, coming down from Elgin with B.J. and his burro team, Aggie and Dan and Clara were all there, and coming in with B.J. like that, as I'd have had to if I had been to Tucson, confirmed Aggie's story, so whatever Dan might have suspected about Pat's expedition was wiped out, especially since Pat didn't get home till three days later.

But Aggie went into a perfect frenzy when I arrived. She began giving all hands jobs and chores. She snapped at Dan and almost took Clara's head off. They hurried up and did a couple of the things she told them to, and then went down to the corral, got on their horses and rode away.

As they were sneaking off, Clara whispered to me, "I'd sure not like to be in your shoes this afternoon, Rodge. The old woman is sure on a tear!"

"Well," said Aggie, as she watched them ride down the road at a good pace, "sure took them long enough to get a hint!"

She gave me the nicest smile. "I had to get rid of them before you could tell me what you did, didn't I? Now, you sit right down and tell me everything."

She was just as glad and excited as I was about finding the gold. "You're real lucky, Rodgers," she kept saying. "Real lucky."

But when it came to my brown-paper parcel, she wouldn't be satisfied till I opened it. Even the little present I had

149

brought her from Nogales, a pair of black silk stockings, very exciting and seductive, didn't sidetrack her. I had to open that bundle.

"Can't I have any privacy?" I asked.

Aggie shook her head. "Not while you live with me."

When she saw the gun and holster and shells, she firmed up her mouth. "You know how I feel about guns, Rodgers," she said. "I don't like the idea of you carrying one. Now, why should you carry a gun?"

"Oh, you'll see, you'll see," I said airily. But I couldn't win. She had the story out of me the next morning. You couldn't keep anything from Aggie any time she wanted to get it out of you, not unless you hit her with an ax and moved into the next county. Then, most likely, she'd rise up and follow you.

So about eleven o'clock the next morning, worn down and a little mad, but liking the old devil all the same, I swore her to secrecy and told her Pat's scheme.

She was all for it.

"I won't breathe it to a soul!" she promised. "It's the very best idea anyone ever thought up! I wouldn't have given Pat Malloy credit for such a top-notch scheme! Why, Rodgers, you've got to win. It isn't just getting to be deputy, after all, that's a matter of one man's opinion you'll do, it's to get the crowd to say a woman'll do to ride the river with. It's time and past that women got the consideration they're entitled to. By giddelty-golly, we're going to bust this part of the country wide open on this one! Rodgers for constable! Let's see the man who can look me in the eye and say, 'no'."

I doubted there were many who could.

chapter 10

WITH SUMMER coming there was lots of work to do. Clara and Dan and I spent weeks riding every day. Sometimes Aggie would ride with us, sometimes not. I know all three of us loved her dearly, but it was a relief when she stayed home. Because you never could ride to suit her. Either you went too slow or too fast; if Dan wanted to go one direction, Aggie wanted to go another. Clara would sometimes say under her breath, "Hope the old devil doesn't go, hope the old devil doesn't go."

But crotchety as she might feel, Aggie did not give away my and Pat's secret. She helped cover up for me. Dan and Clara would often stay overnight, almost always when we were going to ride next day, and they'd get inquisitive when I'd straddle old Cowboy or Star, who was practically my horse anyhow, and ride off over the rise.

"Oh," Aggie would say, "I sent her up to borrow a fine needle from Grandma Malloy." Just as if Grandma Malloy —poor cross-eyed old soul—could use a fine needle, let alone owning one. Tears in Pat's clothes were mended with safety pins if they got mended at all.

Or Aggie'd say, "I want Rodgers out of the house. Tired of her underfoot day and night!" That sounded very plausible to them. Or she'd give one of a dozen or two other reasons; Aggie had no trouble thinking up lies when she needed them, only she called them excuses.

I kept my .38 at Pat's. He taught me how to handle it, how to draw it from the holster slung on my right hip, bring it up, snap the trigger when it was in line with what I was trying to hit. He taught me the other way, too, bringing it higher than the target and then lowering it to plumb center. This was slower but more accurate. We practiced a couple of times a week; but it was along in June before Pat let me fire a single shot from it. By that time my wrist was strong and limber. At first it had ached like a tooth after an hour of draw, swing, snap.

Grandma Malloy would sit on the doorstep of their house and watch us. She took snuff; she'd sit there with her lip bulging out with the stuff and look at me out of her bright blue, crossed eyes—you could never be sure she was really looking at you or where or what, but you'd think it was you. She'd sit there and watch, and sniff now and then, because she didn't approve of all this nonsense.

"Never meddled with no revolvers," she'd say. "Handled a shotgun—that's the proper shooting iron for a woman. But mostly it's best not to bother with none. Why, many's the time when the boys and me spent the night hiding out, down there in the old cornfield. We'd heard Geronimo was out, and Mr. Malloy would be away on business, and them boys just little shavers. Best thing was to hide out, not try to chuck no bluff with them Apaches."

"This ain't got a thing to do with Apaches, Ma," Pat would say.

"I know, I know. She's just making a fool of you, Pat Malloy. She'll put her strings on you one of these fine days, and then you'll see!"

Poor Pat would fire up redder than the sunset and whisper to me, "Don't you pay no attention to Ma, Rodgers, she just likes to rawhide people."

I thought Grandma Malloy wandered a little in her mind, though, of course, I didn't care what she said. But I had a hard time keeping my face straight when she said, "Mrs. Rodgers, trouble with you is you're fidgety. What you need is a baby buggy, and it full!"

Me, the mother of three!

In June I graduated to shooting tomato cans perched on fence posts. I got so I didn't squinch my eyes up tight when my gun went off; I got so I could knock a can off a post from twenty paces, about once out of five times. I thought that was pretty bad, and so did Pat.

"You're just not a natural marksman, Rodge," he said. "But you'll do, all the same. It's time we went down to Nogales and got Tom Patterson to swear you in like he said he would."

"When do you want to go? I got to tell Aggie." I knew she was all for it and it would be all right with her, but that was the polite thing to do, ask for time off.

"I want to go down day or so before the Fourth," said Pat. "We'll break the news at the picnic."

Canelo was having a Fourth of July picnic down at the swimming hole below Aggie's pasture. The water came out of the ground in a great big pool, deep enough to swim a horse in, and that was the start of the creek that ran away north to Elgin. There would be fifty or sixty people there, eating cake and home-made ice cream fooling around and singing and swimming, maybe, though that would be kids mostly, wearing cut-down overalls for bathing suits.

"That's a fine idea," I said.

"Not only that you're a deputy," said Pat, "but that you're going to stand for election for constable."

"You think that's not too soon?"

Pat shook his head very decidedly. "Give them plenty of time to think about it. Plenty of time for smart fellows to think up good jokes on John Yoss fighting with a woman for the job of constable. 'Must need it mighty bad' and that sort of thing."

So we went down to Nogales by train, and Tom Patterson swore me in. Artur and Pat watched. The Sheriff was so sincere and solemn that it became a ceremony with a lot of dignity.

Patterson smiled at me after I took my hand off the Bible. "It's a pleasure to do this, Mrs. Rodgers," he said, "and that I mean. I'm confident I can depend on you, and that you will discharge the duties of your office with efficiency and honor. And now I wish I had a better badge than this hunk of tin to pin on you."

"You have," said Artur. He handed the Sheriff a tissue-wrapped little box. Patterson opened it. It was a silver star with a little ball on each point. Across the middle it read,

"L. Rodgers." Starting on the lower left-hand point, as you faced it, and reading around, a word to each point, it read, "Deputy Sheriff Santa Cruz County." Straddling the notch at the bottom was "Ariz."

I was terribly, terribly proud, and so touched by Artur's thoughtfulness that I was afraid I was going to cry. But I didn't have time, for the Sheriff said, "Handsomest badge I ever did see." He very politely pinned it to the lapel of the old blue suit I was wearing.

He put his hands on my shoulders and said, "I swore in plenty of deputies, but never one which was a lady, so I never had this chance before, and by God I'm going to take it!"

And with that he kissed me smack on the mouth. "I'm not marrying the law," I said, "only defending it."

So we all laughed, and Artur said this was a very happy occasion and he'd be proud to set them up for all hands, and Sheriff Patterson guessed he could close his office for a short time. We all went down to Resswell's Saloon, but outside the doors Artur stopped and looked at me. I looked back at him.

Pat said, "Oh, hell!"

The Sheriff said, "Plumb forgot it was a lady deputy!"

I said, "Go on in, boys. Don't mind me. Pat, hoist one for me."

Because, of course, I couldn't go into a saloon. No lady could in those days.

Artur touched my arm, and said, "Just a minute, Lu. Come on, gents." He took Pat and the Sheriff in and came out almost at once. "You and I will go down to Pete's and have a soda," he said.

Pat and I got back to Canelo the next day, and the day after was the Fourth. People had gathered down at the swimming place by eleven o'clock. Artur and Sheriff Patterson had come out together, and the Sheriff was down there greeting everybody, a bow for the ladies, a good handshake for the men. Some of the men had bottles and they'd go behind the wagons they'd brought their families in and have a drink. The Sheriff had to have one, too.

Artur stayed at the house with me, till Pat came up to say the women had the tables all set and everybody was thinking about eating. He said, "John Yoss is there, too. He's got some snakebite remedy inside him and thinks he's the belle of the ball. Going around campaigning already! We'll make a sorry sight of him."

"Don't you start any trouble, Pat."

He put on his hurt and innocent look, bugging his china-blue eyes till you thought they'd pop. "Who, me?" he asked. "I never start nothing. It's that old John Yoss."

"Just the same, I'm asking Artur to ride herd on you, Pat. And I'm mighty glad the Sheriff's here. Can't nothing much happen with him around."

"I don't guess nothing will," said Pat. "But John Yoss looks sort of snorty to me. You're sure a sight, Rodge!"

I was wearing my good divided dark-brown corduroy skirt and my cowboy boots and a white shirtwaist. I had tied a red bandanna around my neck though folks—cowhands either—seldom wore them. I had the Stetson Artur had given me on my head, my silver badge all shiny pinned over my heart, and my .38 in its holster swung on my hip. It wasn't loaded, though Pat had put shells in the cartridge loops on the belt.

"Come on, Art," said Pat. "Rodge, you follow us down. Just mosey on in and start saying 'hello' to everybody."

Pat had timed things very well. People were seated at the long tables made of boards they'd brought in their wagons, and they were just about to start saying, "Thank you for the beef, neighbor," or "Please pass the pickles." Sheriff Patterson was standing up at the head of one of the tables and when he saw me, he threw his hat in the air and yelled, "Yeeow!" He kept his dignity doing it, too.

Everybody turned around. "Gosh, Pa, look at Mrs. Rodgers!" one of the Sowers boys yelled.

"What's that star on your shirt?" Uncle Tom hollered.

"Folks," the Sheriff shouted, "Allow me to introduce my new deputy, Mrs. Lu Rodgers!"

With that, Pat threw his hat in the air and howled like a wolf. He had posted Billy Barker to set off about a bushel

155

of firecrackers, and the calves which had been watching through the pasture fence with the curiosity calves have high-tailed it for safer parts. People were yelling and clapping. Some of the men with sense hurried over to their teams just in time to prevent a stampede. It was real noisy around there for a few minutes, noisier than that spot of land probably ever was or will be again.

They quieted down after a while, and began to eat. About halfway through, when people were having seconds and thinking about the cake and ice cream, John Yoss stood up at the center of one of the tables. "Friends," he said, "I got to hand it to Sheriff Patterson for his forward-looking ways. Appointing a woman to be deputy is right in line with the thinking of this forward-looking state of ours which gave females suffrage and the right to vote from the beginning . . ."

Someone asked, "What's the difference, John?"

Yoss waved him away. "Yes, sir," he went on, "and with all politeness to Mr. George Barker, who has been our constable well and truly, I'm sure you folks will be glad to know that whatever shortcomings a woman deputy may have, next fall me, John Yoss, will be constable and able to keep the law and order in full force in the township of Canelo."

"Don't you expect no opposition, John?" Dan Langwood asked.

Yoss threw back his copper-thatched head and laughed. "Why, Dan, I'm a Democrat. You know how the people of Canelo think about Republicans."

"They like me all right, I guess," said Sheriff Patterson, "and I'm a Republican."

"Sure, we like you fine, Sheriff, but we ain't going to vote for you," said Yoss. "Not even if you have made Rodgers a deputy."

The way he said my name, I didn't like it, though everyone called me by it without the Mrs. But not John Yoss.

I said, "There's a handle to that, John Yoss."

He stared at me and sneered. "Well, now . . ." he started.

Aggie had a voice that scratched like barbed wire when

she wanted it to. "I don't vote for a man who is disrespectful of ladies!" she said.

The women began murmuring and digging their husbands in the ribs with their elbows.

Yoss was fairly quick at times. "Why, of course I respect the wimmin folks!" he said. "I just got talking fast. I'm right sorry, Mrs. Rodgers."

Pat stood up, red as a beet. He stammered a little. "Learn to s-s-say that ri-ri-right handy, John Yoss." He grabbed the edge of the table with his hands and leaned on it. "F-f-folks . . ."

He swallowed, and then his voice came out loud and strong. "Folks, Mrs. Rodgers is going to stand for constable of Canelo!"

There was dead silence. Yoss's jaw dropped and his mouth hung wide open. He sort of brushed in the air with his hands. Then he said in a squeaky sort of voice, "She can't do that. Fiddling around playing deputy's one thing . . ."

Pat said, "It was you who was talking about this forward-looking state which gave women the vote. But it ain't been forward-looking enough to elect a woman to public office yet, so me and Mrs. Rodgers, we aim to remedy that."

Yoss had had time for it to sink in good and deep. "She can't do it!" he yelled. "By God, Pat Malloy, this is another of your damned tricks! Well, I'll get you for this one, see if I don't! Rodgers, you stand up and tell them it's a joke and a mighty poor one, or by God, I'll . . ."

Sheriff Paterson's voice stopped him. "You'll what?" the Sheriff asked coldly.

"Yes," said Pat. "What will you do?"

The Sheriff waved at him to keep still. "I'll handle this. As a peace officer, I don't like to hear threats; as a man, I get mad when a woman's threatened. What was it you'll do, Yoss?"

Yoss's face had turned a sort of sick white with rage. But he couldn't stand up to the Sheriff. He didn't say anything; he just turned his back and stomped off. He got on his horse and took off toward Fort Huachuca. I guessed that rotten temper of his ought to cost him some votes.

When people quieted down some, Pat went on. "As I was saying, we aim to remedy that. We think folks'll be proud to vote for a female, proud to prove that they think women are in every way as good as men."

Aggie caught my eye, stood up quick, then sat down. I looked away because it wouldn't be smart to break out laughing while Pat was announcing my political intentions.

"Yes, sir," he said earnestly, "and I'll bet Sheriff Patterson'll agree with me when I say some day not too long from now a woman will sit in the governor's chair in Phoenix and it'll be us who put her there!" He was warming up nicely to the subject. "And I can see a time to come when Arizona will be the first state to nominate a woman for President of these here United States! Yes, by God, and get her elected if we have to go back east and teach those big-moneyed, namby-pamby Easterners what's good for them!"

"Hurray!" yelled Bill Yoel.

"You tell them, Pat!"

"Well, don't you fellers throw off on us when it comes time, is all," said Pat. He sat down.

Sheriff Patterson stood up and smiled at everybody and talked nice and easy. "It's quite a piece from now to election and there's plenty of time for everybody to make up their minds. We came on this picnic to have fun, and it's about time, I guess, we started on the ice cream, if the ladies will let me suggest it. But first there's just one thing I want to say. I didn't appoint Mrs. Rodgers my deputy just for the fun of appointing her. Not just to make her feel she's welcome to ride along with us Westerners, though of course she's done that and done it well. No, it was more than that and something you folks want to keep in mind, too. My feeling is that Mrs. Rodgers' kind don't run in bunches. So we better grab her when we get a chance. We need people like her working for us. Now, who gets the first piece of cake and plate of ice cream?"

"You do, Sheriff!" said Clara, and with that she planked down the biggest slab of cake you ever saw and a whole wash basin full of ice cream in front of him.

So now that everyone knew I was running for constable, I practiced my shooting out in the open. I really worked at it. I had a feeling that some day it might be absolutely necessary for me to be able to hit what I aimed at. I remembered John Yoss's mad face—more than just angry, partly crazy and all evil. There could be a time when I'd have to handle someone like that and maybe the only thing that could deal with it would be a gun. So I learned to stand firm with a steady hand and wrist and bring my sight plumb on the center.

But this wasn't enough for Pat. Oh, no, he had to have frills! He had me riding up and down the road in front of Aggie's cornfield with tomato cans stuck up on the posts, me riding Cowboy full tilt and trying to knock them off with my gun. I could do no such thing; it was just foolish and a waste of time. But it was fun.

Old Satan would sit out on the porch when I did this and seem to take an interest in it. The dogs always vanished at the first shot; they were gun shy. The little black kitten Uncle Tom had brought for a joke at Christmas had shot up rangy and tall and strong as a quirt thong with the good food and milk he got. We called him Limb because he followed Satan everywhere.

"A regular limb of Satan," Aggie had said one time.

Along in the middle of August, I got a message from Sheriff Patterson saying he thought it was time his new deputy came in and reported and that he'd o.k. traveling expenses. I found out later that Artur had put him up to it because he hadn't gotten out to the country since the Fourth. Business affairs had kept him too busy.

So I packed a couple of dresses and put on my very best clothes. B.J. drove me over to Elgin on his regular trip, and off I went. I stayed with the Dunphys, and was there a couple of days. Sheriff Patterson and I talked over the political situation. I liked going to his office in the courthouse. It smelled sour and stale as all courthouse places always seem to, and the desk was all chewed up and scarred where sheriffs before Patterson had sat with their spurs hooked in so their feet wouldn't slide off. There was a cuspidor that no one ever seemed to empty, a busted clothes horse in one corner, a map of the county, some battered golden-oak chairs. It was a room in which lots had happened and I liked sitting there talking man talk and imagining with one part of my mind what had gone on in this room. Murder, sorrow, happiness for a lost one found, all kinds of things had passed through here and left sort of ghosts. But Patterson filled it with his personality, too. He was burly, a chunky, barrel-chested man, a slow talker, kind of slab-faced with small bright eyes and a mouth that turned down at the corners and looked as if he was about to cry. A quiet man, but sure brave—like that time I'd first seen him take the guns from those half-drunk cowboys. I heard he had rounded up a gang of six bandits single-handed. They said he cut his eye-teeth in the Wyatt Earp days at Tombstone when that was the toughest town in the whole world.

He was kind to me, kind and thoughtful and considerate. "Don't think, Mrs. Rodgers," he said, "that I appointed you just for my own sake, though I do want to win this next election and will do anything I can. Not for Pat's sake, either, though he can sure help me a lot, and I like old Pat. He helped me round up a pair of drunk Apaches once. No, I liked your looks first time I saw you, and I've got a feeling this is a mighty good thing for you. Also, I think you'll be a credit to us."

That was about what he had said on the Fourth, and I didn't quite understand it.

"I thank you, Sheriff," I said. "But I'm not such-a-much and I truly don't know why you should bother with me."

He gave me his tight-lipped smile. "Just that I kind of feel proud about this state. So when I can help grab off a good citizen for it, I aim to do so. You do intend to stay with us, don't you?"

"I doubt that even you could run me out, Sheriff," I said, and we both laughed.

"Now, I'm giving you an official order. I want you to come out to my house for dinner tonight. My wife wants to meet you. Said she'd be proud to. And I asked Artur Resswell to come, too, so we could have a fourth for euchre, of course. He wasn't sure he could make it, so I hereby empower you with the force of the sheriff's office to bring, drag, or otherwise see to it that Mr. Resswell arrives in time for dinner."

Naturally, I didn't have to drag Artur.

We had a very nice evening. Mrs. Patterson was a small, slightly faded blonde with a worried look, a laugh like a chime of little silver bells tinkling, and so hard in love with the Sheriff that you might think her a honeymooner. They had two grown, hulking boys, either one of whom could have picked up their mother with two fingers. There wasn't a doubt in the world that the boys and their father would gladly let Mrs. Patterson walk on them.

There was a dance at the Hotel Montezuma the next night and Artur took me and the Dunphys and the Joneses. We had a very gay time. The next evening, Artur persuaded me to go over to Mexico with him. They had an open-air market around behind the calabozo, and part of it was tables with a woman cooking. Artur had brought forks and knives for us; he said he wouldn't use theirs, but of course we used their plates and ate their food. It was good, too. The table we went to had a fat woman running it. Her cookstove was made out of a couple of five-gallon kerosene tins. Cross the top was a piece of sheet iron. She cooked everything on that. We had enchiladas and gorditos, which are crisp and filled with frijoles. They always give you *café con leche,* and before she poured the hot milk into the cup along with the bitter, black coffee that can hold a spoon straight up, she blew back the skin on the top of the milk. Just held the pan up to her lips and blew.

I said, "Gosh!"

"Oh," said Artur, "you can't consider yourself a Nogalesian till you see that happen before you drink it."

He made it seem almost all right.

I went back to Canelo the next day—Elgin on the mail train and a ride across with B.J. and his burro team. Somehow it seemed as if I'd been a long time away. "What's been happening, B.J.?"

"You've only been gone a couple or three days. What do

you think would happen in Canelo in that time, Mrs. Rodgers?"

"Well, I don't know. Lots could."

"In a year," said B.J., "something happens. It's like a glacier moving. You know, those ice rivers. Some of them only move a foot a year, I've read. Can't see much change in three days."

"Yes, you could. Here, I mean. Something quick could happen."

B.J. just shook his head. "Nothing but John Yoss yawping around how he's going to beat you all hollow this election. You and that Pat Malloy, he always says. And you've heard every word of that a dozen times."

"I sure have," I said.

It felt sort of good to see Aggie again. I really had the funniest feeling about that trip, gone a long time, glad to get back, almost sure something had happened.

"What happened, Aggie?" I asked.

She considered a minute. "Well, nothing much. That no-account Limb of yours has been acting up—'cause you weren't here, I 'spose. He jumped up on the kitchen table and stole a chunk of jerky the other evening. I'd have beat the pants off him if I could have caught him!"

But she wasn't really mad, you could see that. She had made a dried apple pie, and the MacBains had butchered, so we had fresh beef cooked Aggie's special way, in a red-hot skillet on salt, the meat sliced very thin. Afterward, we sat around talking—about my trip, the Sheriff, a little about Artur, things like that.

We were sitting in the living room and Aggie thought of something she wanted to get out of the storeroom. She came back, and we sat on either side of the big table in the center of the room. Aggie was darning stockings and I was writing a letter to the children. I'd stop and we'd say a word or two, finish that and go back to sitting quiet and comfortable with our hands and minds occupied. I began to hear a very strange noise after a while.

"Woo-wo-o-o," it went. A sort of moaning sound like a queer, high wind, the queerest wind I'd ever heard. It made my scalp tighten, sent goose-pimples down my back. I looked at Aggie.

She had heard it, too, and she'd just stopped looking at me when I looked at her so I wouldn't see the worry and fright on her face. Neither one of us wanted to speak to the other about it.

But it didn't stop. "Woo woo," it went, and sounded like it was coming from the direction of Aggie's bedroom.

I couldn't help being scared, real scared. I thought of strange sorts of animals that might come down out of the tangled center of the Huachucas; I thought of Apaches—Geronimo, only he'd be a ghost. Well, ghosts, then, except I don't believe there are any.

I looked up again and caught Aggie's eye this time. "Real high wind," I said, just to say something.

"Mighty high," she said. "Guess I'd better see the window in my room's shut."

She went over and opened the door, and there it was! Right outside the window!

Not an animal, not an Apache, no ghost, no wind.

Worse, and more frightening in its own special way.

Fire!

That old, dry, plank-walled lumber room was a blazing torch right outside Aggie's window, up against the house.

I yelled, "Good Lord!" I dashed outside, to see how bad it was, I guess.

The roof of the porch had caught, and little tongues of flames were licking up the roof of the house. Aggie came out with an armful of clothes and threw them in the road.

"It's all going to go, Rodgers!" she screamed.

I started to run to the well and pull water to throw on it.

Aggie yelled, "No, we can't stop it!"

Of course, I could see that was so as soon as she said it. "What'll we do?"

"Hurry up! Save all we can."

We both rushed in and I grabbed up the nearest thing and hurried out. It was a potted plant that Aggie kept near

163

the door. She was almost as bad. She carried out the old split-seated rocker she liked to use.

"No!" she said. "We've lost our heads. The food from the storeroom. That's most important."

She was right, of course. It was stuff we'd harvested all summer, frijoles, dried pumpkin, hams, lard—things we had to have to live on. We ran through the living room, already hot and smoky, and into the kitchen. The storeroom was at the end nearest the lumber room, but it was rock-walled.

I snatched up a hundred-pound sack of flour and felt my fingernails break as it slipped through my hands. But I got a better grip on it and lugged it out. Aggie was right on my heels. We dumped the stuff out a ways, ran back for more. It was hot in the kitchen, too.

I loaded up with preserves, and ran. Aggie had gotten out ahead of me. There was a smoldering patch on the back of her dress. I beat it out.

" 'Bout one more trip," she gasped.

She was right. The whole roof was ablaze. As we ran back into the kitchen flames licked out on the under side of the ceiling. I grabbed the heaviest and biggest sack I could find—it turned out to be frijoles—and dragged it out. I smelled burned hair and grabbed at mine, but it was my eyebrows, we discovered later.

Aggie said, "We'd better quit."

There was plenty of light to see by, and there was my cot still not blazing but close to the lumber room. I ran and dragged it away with one hand, shielding my face with the other. The tarpaulin was almost ready to burst into flame, but it didn't.

We stood off in the road with our arms around each other and watched the house go. When my trunk burned, the couple of boxes of shells I had in it went off like giant firecrackers. Pat said later that he heard them, and said to his mother, "Rodgers is sure shooting off her gun down there. They must be having a celebration about something. She sure is shooting it off tonight."

But we were down in a hollow and no one could see the blaze, so no one came to help us.

When the roof fell in there was a tremendous burst of flame and sparks. We got worried about the barn, and started drawing water and throwing it on it. But nothing happened to it.

And then the walls crashed in and the fire died down.

Aggie sobbed as if her heart was breaking. "Many's the time I've said I wished it would burn down, but now it has and I feel awful!" she cried.

"Well, it could be worse, I guess."

"And all your stuff, too, Rodge, every smidgin of it! Oh, I could kick myself. I must have done it when I went to the lumber room!"

"Aggie," I said, "don't blame yourself. And stop crying. Did we get burned? No. Did the cats burn, or the dogs? No. I saw them all a minute ago. Well, then, there's nothing to weep over. We've just got to start again, that's all. Start again!"

"Oh, Rodgers!" Aggie said. "You'll do. You'll certain sure do!"

chapter 11

WE CAME back early the next morning. We had finally ridden over to Dan's, told them of the disaster, and slept there. We came back early because there were chores to do and animals to tend, and, most of all, we had to get what we had salvaged under shelter.

Clara loaned me an old woolen divided skirt of hers and a jumper because I had been wearing a good blue dress which I had worn coming from Nogales. Aggie had on a cotton dress she used around the house.

When we came down the road I was almost ready to cry again, and I guess Aggie was, too. Dan and Clara just gasped because it was so different. The little barn was there, and so was the corral and the root cellar in the hillside, and further back, with its sheltering trees, the two-holer. But nothing was left of the house except a corner of the wall by the kitchen and storeroom, and the big old rock chimney. Inside was a mess of twisted iron that had been Aggie's bed. The walls had fallen down. The roof was all gone.

Scattered around the house were the things we'd dragged out. Aggie went and sat in the splint-bottomed rocker. She folded her arms and stared at the mess that had been her house. Oh, I knew she was having such a lost and gone and hopeless feeling!

"That's sure no way to get the cows milked!" I said.

We had two at that time, old range cows with big bags that Aggie had made into sort of half-wild milkers.

Aggie never turned. "What we going to milk them into?"

"Well . . ." I said. "Oh, why, a hat." I was trying to joke.

166

"You got a hat?" asked Aggie.

I hadn't, of course. Artur's big, beautiful Stetson had burned along with all my working clothes and everything else. My deputy's badge hadn't, though. I always wore that somewhere, pinned inside my dress if I was in good clothes.

"Just turn the calves in and let them suck," said Aggie. "They can have it all."

The way you milk a range cow is with the calf sucking on one side and you milking on the other.

Well, I did that, and then came back and helped pick up things. The food we put in the root cellar where skunks or coyotes couldn't get at it. The armful of clothes that Aggie had grabbed up we hung over under the mulberry tree that had some of its branches scorched and blackened. But they'd come back next spring.

Dan said, "Ma, we'll build you a new house. But I don't know when."

Aggie looked at him without speaking for a long time.

Clara and I watched. It was as if this was a deciding point. Aggie took her eyes off Dan, stared at the chimney. She got up out of her chair and walked over to it. She put her hand on it. She pushed, then she put both hands on it and pushed again. Nothing happened.

Aggie turned around and said, "We'll start building in the spring. Hire a couple of Mexicans and put up a 'dobe house. Right around this chimney. Use the bottoms of the old walls for foundations. This is one place I'm not giving up!"

"All right, Ma," said Dan.

Clara chimed in. "Thought you didn't like adobe."

"I don't," said Aggie. "But it's quick and cheap. Beggars can't be choosers."

"We can have just as nice a house with adobe as with stone."

"Sure we can," said Aggie. "Rodge, what was it I went to get out of the lumber room?"

"For heaven's sake, Aggie, I can't tell you!"

And neither of us ever did remember.

Pat came over, and he was horrified. "Heard your shells

going off, Rodge," he said. "Thought you were sure riding at them last night!"

"Why didn't you come find out, you old fool!" asked Aggie. Pat didn't answer; he could see she was just itching to find someone or something to be mad at.

"Well, don't stand there gawking," she said. "Can't you see we need help?"

"Sure," said Pat. "Anything you want."

"Ax is there in the chopping block. Woodpile's still there, isn't it?"

Pat scratched his head and looked thoughtful. "I'd think," he said, "you'd had fire enough round here to last you a while."

"Fire or no fire," said Aggie, "we've got to eat. And to eat, we've got to cook."

"That's right," said Pat. "But what you going to cook on, Aggie?"

"Hm . . ." said Aggie. But it only stopped her a minute. "You see that big pile of rock where the kitchen wall was? Well, right under it is the stove. We'll just dig that out."

We did. Aggie and Pat and I heaved rock until we got the stove free and clear. It had been so warped by the heat that the corners all turned up, just like a Chinese-temple roof. But we lugged it out and set it up on rocks. Pat rode home and came back with a length of stove pipe. He stuck it on. I built a fire, and we made coffee on that salvaged stove for lunch, cooked some ham, too. We ate, squatting around, out of our hands and the frying pan. Pat had brought tin cups for all.

B.J. passed on his way to Elgin. Minnie came over with her two kids, Isobel and Fanny, riding before and behind. She had intended to borrow something, but whatever it was had burned up, too. Aggie put them to work.

Isobel was three years older than Cissie, but Fanny was the same age and her blond hair made me think of my own daughter. I'd bet Cissie would work just as hard as either of them. In fact, I was sure all three kids would have pitched in and done all they could— Tim, too, though he was so young. Things like this could happen out here and they'd have to learn to face them.

Quite a few people passed in the afternoon. By nightfall it was all over the country that Aggie Gates had burned out.

Mrs. Barker sent for us to stay the night with them. Old man Barker made some jokes about "you girls burning your house down," but the old buzzard offered us an unused, galvanized-iron chicken house if we'd lug it off. We looked at it in the morning, and saw it would do to cook and live in. Mrs. Barker gave us each a sunbonnet when we rode away. "You don't want to get all tanned up," she said.

Dan went over and with Pat and young Billy Barker helping got the chicken house apart. It took a couple of days, but four days after the fire we were living in a galvanized-iron chicken house about ten feet square, and cooking our meals on our Chinese stove. People had come from all over helping and giving us things.

Bill Yoel brought the old little tent he had lived in when he first took up his homestead. We set it up, and it made a fine bedroom for Aggie. I slept under the mulberry tree. The Duncan boys took some boxes and made us a real good cupboard. Harry Friar came over from the other side of the Canelo hills with a kitchen table he said his mother could spare. Old man Keaton sent a sack of his fine potatoes. An old lady who lived in Fort Huachuca—Mrs. Canning—whom I'd never even seen, and Aggie knew only to hello at, drove herself over in a surrey with a dozen bone-handled steel knives and forks and some nickel-plated spoons.

Charles Jackson drove up in his buckboard with his spanking team and unloaded a set of kitchenware better than what we'd had before. After he left, Aggie sniffed and said, "Easy to see the way his mind runs!"

"Why, Aggie," I said, "isn't that what men get married for? Good home cooking?"

Aggie said, "Stop trying to fool an old widow woman like me!"

Artur came down from Elgin the day before the chicken coop was up. He and I laughed at my burnt eyebrows. He brought a couple of warm sweaters for Aggie and me, a whole dinner set of blue plates and dishes, and a Bible. He never gave any reason for the Bible and he wasn't specially religious, but I was glad to get it. I would read to Aggie about the afflictions of Job and if she needed cheering up—which she did, she'd been grim and clench-jawed ever since the fire—why, Job did it.

"Where do you 'spose he had those boils, Rodge?" she asked.

"It says all over his body."

"Hm. I had one once. It was terrible. Couldn't ride or sit . . ."

Artur took me aside before he left. "Lu," he said, "this is a delicate subject. But would it be good if I loaned you a little money? There are so many things that you need."

I said, "Artur, thanks. But I've still got some in my bank. It didn't burn, you know."

Artur smiled. "Lucky it didn't. That's my bank, too."

"I'll make out all right. But it's mighty nice of you to suggest it."

He made a gesture with his hands. "But if you won't take it . . . Lu, please ask if you need? Please?"

"Of course, I will, Artur. I wouldn't hesitate a minute."

Aggie was working at the stove. Since she wasn't looking, I reached up and pecked Artur's cheek in a way I hoped was a nice mixture of gratitude, affection and plain friendliness.

It was the wrong thing to do. Watching his face as he stood there, thoughts going through his mind, was like watching a row of dominoes after you push the first one. It hits the next and knocks it down, that the next, and so on. I could just see the first thought, "She kissed me . . ." Then that clicked against the next, "She likes me." That the next, "I like—love her . . ." That the next, "Needs help . . ." And then, of course, on with click after click till he'd reach the final one and blurt out, "Lu, why wouldn't this be a good time for us to get . . ."

I didn't want it. I wasn't ready for that question. Maybe I never would be, and I sure wasn't right now.

Very quickly, I said, "That was for being so kind and nice, Artur." I reached up and pecked him again. "And that's to seal my promise that if Aggie and I need anything, I'll ask you. But we'll make out all right, you see if we don't."

That headed him off. The clicks stopped clicking, the thoughts no longer fell neatly into place. One kiss undid what another had done. He was distracted, and since he was a sensitive man, I guess he felt I didn't want to have him speak just then.

He was very right about that.

That evening, Aggie said, "It's none of my business, if you want to say so, Rodge, but when are you going to tell that man about the children?"

"Oh, I don't know—maybe never."

"He'll make it so you'll have to some day. Better do it on your own timing."

I said, "But I'm a little afraid, Aggie, that he'll think me sort of irresponsible, feather-brained, if I tell him I left three kids in Brooklyn."

"Could be," said Aggie thoughtfully.

"I have been thinking about it. I might as well tell you. I think he's going to propose one of these days."

"Might as well tell me!" Aggie snorted. "Think I can't see it for myself?"

"Well, then, seemed to me the better he knew me, the easier it might be for him to think I am responsible. That'll be one thing about winning the election. Constable of Canelo's a pretty responsible position."

"That don't mean you're responsible," Aggie pointed out. "It's just that the voters think you will be."

"I suppose. But it'll look better, anyhow." I'd gain respect, not only from all the people here in Canelo, but from Artur. That was the important part: to have Artur see that I was responsible, solid, dependable, worthy of his admiration and respect.

"Well," said Aggie with a sigh, "everybody thinks they know best."

That was a true enough word, I thought, but I still knew

better than she did, because I knew more of what everything was all about. It looked like a very knotty problem to me, because I knew by that time that I loved Artur Resswell. So somehow I had to be certain that nothing damaged the love he had for me.

John Yoss had been over the day after the fire, looking at the ruins and trying not to grin enough to crack his face. He didn't stay long, and of course, with Pat and Dan there, not to say Aggie in the vile humor she was in, he didn't say much. Just shook his head a bit and said, "Too bad," not even putting his hand over his mouth so we couldn't see him grin. Oh, he was tickled, all right.

A couple of weeks later, though, it was another story. He and old man Barker rode up one noon when Aggie and I were eating frijoles from our luxurious box chairs off our donated kitchen table, using Artur's blue china, which looked entirely too elegant and out of place. Yoss sat on his horse in the road, but old man Barker got off and stumped up to the door in his old, runover boots. He was wearing his constable's badge, which meant it was official.

"Hate to interrupt you folks," he said.

"Well, don't, then," said Aggie.

He had given us the house we were living in and I didn't think she should be so short with him, so I said, "That's all right, Mr. Barker."

He got called mister so seldom that he swelled up like a turkey cock. "That's right nice of you, Rodgers," he said. "Fact is, I come on business." He polished his badge with the heel of his hand. "Wanted to ask if you'd mind if we poked around in your ruins, there."

"Who's we?" Aggie asked.

Barker didn't want to say it. He cleared his throat and jerked his head, kind of pointing with the back of it at John Yoss, sitting there scowling on his horse in the road.

"Me and him," he said.

"What for?" Aggie's voice was crimpy as the air in winter an hour before sunup. Even Barker felt it.

"Well . . ." he said, scraping his toe around in the dust, "well, some folks is saying that fire was set."

172

"Sure was," said Aggie. "I did it."

Barker shook his head. "Not that way. Meaning was that it was done on purpose."

Aggie's mouth just opened and hung there.

"Most foolish thing I ever heard," I said.

"So Yoss asked me to come over with him and find out," said Barker stubbornly. "Figured we might find the kerosene can or something." He stabbed his hand in the direction of the old house.

"But it's none of your business," I said.

"Now, Rodgers, this here's Aggie's house we're talking about."

"You're damn tooting it's my house!" Aggie yelled. "What are you butting in for? If I want to set fire to my house and pour a whole blazing barrel of kerosene on it, who's to say I can't? What business of yours or that fool Yoss's is it?"

Yoss couldn't keep his mouth shut any more. "That Rodgers woman done it a-purpose!" he shouted. "You done it because you thought you could beat me that way! I'm going to prove it! I'll tell everybody you done it just to beat me in the election!"

His face was flushed dark coppery like his hair, his mouth was ugly as a rattlesnake and he had the look of a mean killer bronco in his eyes, but I couldn't help myself. I busted right out laughing. I laughed so hard I felt crowded sitting inside the chicken house, just looking out, so I got up and went outside and propped myself against the wall, and laughed and laughed.

Yoss's face got darker. He came out of his saddle like he had a calf on the end of his rope and was aiming to throw and hogtie it. "God damn you!" he yelled. You never would have thought this man had proposed to me, once.

Old man Barker was a fool to have come with him, but he knew what was right, and he didn't scare easy. He stepped in front of Yoss. "Now, John . . ." he said.

Aggie came out of the chicken house, a kettle in her hand. You could see the steam coming off it. "Get back, Yoss!" she said.

Maybe Barker couldn't have stopped him, but Aggie did.

173

I don't know what he intended to do—slap me, I suppose. I don't know what I'd have done if he had, but I think I'd have kicked him in the shins and scratched his face. I wasn't strong enough to trade punches with him.

"Get up on your horses, the both of you," said Aggie. "Get off of my place. Stay off. Next time you come here, Yoss, I'll have the shotgun in my hands when I say 'hello' and it'll be loaded—not with rock salt, neither!"

"Now, let's all cool off some," said Barker. "I ain't sure but what I've got a right to come on to your property any time in discharge of my duties as Constable of Canelo, Aggie Gates."

Aggie looked him up and down. "I've known you a long time, George Barker," she said. "It ain't your duty as constable to help John Yoss make a fool of himself, though it's your right if you want to. But it ain't your right as man nor constable to come onto my place and pry and poke around to help make a fool out of Yoss. He's a big enough one as it is. What charge could you make to justify poking around in my stuff?"

Barker looked a little stumped. "I guess they call it ar— ar . . ."

"Arson," I said. "But it was Aggie's house, and it didn't endanger any least bit of anyone else's property. She's not asking for insurance, because she hasn't got it, so it's not cheating anyone. I can't see how you could begin to believe you had the slightest right to even cast your eye over those ruins from the road."

"Well, maybe," said Barker. He didn't want to be convinced, but neither did he think he could do a thing, and of course he couldn't.

"And if John Yoss doesn't stop disturbing the peace right now," I said, "or you don't make him stop, as Constable of this township, I, as Deputy Sheriff of Santa Cruz County, will arrest the pair of you, him for disturbing the peace and you for malfeasance in office! Put that in your pipe and smoke it!"

That Yoss was a hard, tough, bad man, all right.

"Rodgers," he said, and his voice was just choked with

174

rage, "I don't give a damn for your fancy badge! I don't care if you are a woman! You lay a hand on me and I'll kill you! So help me God, I'll kill you!"

He meant every word of it, though once he'd almost said he loved me. In spite of him, I wasn't scared, though Aggie said afterward that I should have been. I just stood there, looking at his face, and thinking to myself, "So that's the way death looks."

I don't know how long we stood with our eyes locked. After a while, Yoss kicked his horse, jerked its head around, and walked it down the road.

Old man Barker was flabbergasted. He stood there with his mouth open. When he shut it, all he could think of to say, was "Told him it was plumb foolish . . ."

"So are you!" said Aggie. "What sort of a trick is this?"

Barker gave a little, tight-lipped grin. "Well," he said, "I'm a good Democrat, and Yoss is running on that ticket. I'd like to see a Democrat take my place. Only Rodgers, here, is sure spunky."

"Oh, go home and let us finish our lunch!" said Aggie with a little smile, the first she'd given since Barker got off his horse.

"Might as well," he said. He got on and rode away.

Aggie turned to me. "Rodgers," she said sternly, "you mighty nigh got some real trouble that time. You ought to know better than to bust out laughing at a man like Yoss and then threaten him when he's that mad. Maybe you could make some men feel foolish, but not his kind."

"You're right. But I couldn't help it. Don't you remember the grin on his face the first time he saw how burned out we were, and how pleased he was? And now he's madder than a mean bull with his tail tied in a knot!"

"He sure is!" said Aggie. She gave a short laugh. "He sure is. But he was mad when he got here. I wonder why?"

"Something neither of us thought of. Look how many people have visited since the fire. Why I'll bet everyone in the township . . ."

"Every last one!" cried Aggie, her eyes shining. "They all feel sorry for you, and they all like and admire you, because

175

you're not crying and whining! I'll bet three-quarters of them vote for you!"

"That's what's got Yoss scared," I said.

I hadn't thought of it before that way, but that was the truth of it. People who give things to people in trouble are apt to want to do more, particularly when it's an easy thing like marking a cross opposite their name. It was going to be pretty hard for John Yoss from now on. It had taken him a while to see it, but now what could he do about it?

All he did, of course, was go around saying we had the fire on purpose to attract attention and get votes. It was such a silly thing to say people only had two courses open. One was to believe him, which a few rabid Democrats would, and the other, which would appeal to most, I thought, and so did Pat and Aggie, was to consider this one more proof that John Yoss was a damn fool, a big mouth, and a windbag. In about six weeks we'd know.

But Pat thought that wasn't all. "He's bad, Rodge," he said. "He's a real mean man, and I don't like you taking chances with him."

He made me wear one of his guns. It was a big old .45 and really too heavy for me, but all the work I'd put in with the .38 had strengthened my wrist enough so I could anyway get it level, though I couldn't hold it there too long. It made a lot more noise than the .38, too.

Pat and I did a lot of riding. We went around as if we were looking for lost stock, but we would drop in at places, and sit and talk. It was a sort of hidden way of campaigning, and Pat was certain it would have a good effect. Artur did something that helped a lot, then, too.

B.J. came by one morning with a great big parcel and when I opened it, it was a hat and a pair of fine boots. The hat was like the army campaign hat, only with a broader brim, and I wore it in a peak. The boots fitted fine. Next time Artur came out I had trouble thanking him.

"Lu," he said, "I want you to win this election. I want it because I know you want it and it will be good for you. People are impressed by clothes, so—hat and boots!" He smiled that kind, loving smile of his that made me want to hug him.

I wondered how Artur would be for the kids. I asked myself, "How would they like a stepfather?" Then I thought that Tim wouldn't be apt to have any memory of Greg at all, and I turned away from Artur, because I didn't seem to have too much memory right then, either.

"What is it, Lu?" he asked in his gentlest voice.

We were standing down at the corral where he was unhitching his horse from the buggy. I just shook my head. I was afraid that I was going to cry. It wasn't that I felt disloyal to Greg—I was sure he would have told me to go on living fully every way I could—but that I'd forgotten him. It was all right for Tim; he was a child. But I couldn't really have described what Greg looked like if someone had asked me. And I'd let the feel of him get dim. Maybe because it had been so long, so long . . .

I had to get my mind off it, so I told Artur about John Yoss, though I never did tell him Yoss proposed to me.

"Perhaps someone should speak very hard to Yoss," he said when I finished.

"Aggie and I did. That's enough. Don't you go mixing in it. I just wanted you to know. And I wanted to be the one to tell you because I knew you'd feel that way."

"Did you, Lu?" he asked softly.

I nodded my head.

"You know a good deal about me, don't you? That is, my ways of thought. Do you, then, not know what I most feel and think?"

"Artur," I said, "I'm going to win that election before I stir a hand at another thing except regular chores and such-like."

"And then?"

"Let's see how things are then."

I felt my spine go a little shivery at that because it was the most, the nearest, I had come to discussing us with him.

It was along in September now, and mornings were chilly. I wanted a corduroy riding skirt, wanted it bad. Needed it right away, too. That was one of the reasons that started me riding in to Nogales, forty miles away.

Another part was John Yoss. When he saw how silly he looked with his charge that Aggie and I burned her house down just for attention, he began to talk about how women were all very well in their place, but their place wasn't as a peace officer, no matter what Tom Patterson thought with his female deputies. After a while, Pat began to get worried, because, strangely enough, this argument was taking effect with the women. Maybe they believed it, maybe it made them think that constable wasn't woman's work, but whatever it was, they were starting to talk to their men. This was what worried Pat.

"It ain't the women," he said. "They'll talk and fume around, and when election day comes they'll cast their votes for you because they like you, and because they believe they're just as good as a man any day. But if they get the men to thinking there are things they can do that a woman can't . . ."

"You know what Aggie says," I reminded him.

He unfurrowed his forehead, and his china-blue eyes twinkled, and his face began to get red. He was game, though, this time, or else anxious to knock me down a peg. He took a deep breath. "No, what?" he asked.

"I won't tell; I won't tell. But you can guess . . . Go ahead, guess. I'll bet you know anyhow, Pat."

He lost his nerve then and started to stammer. "I-I-I—"

"All right. You were saying if the men get to thinking?"

"Oh, that." He looked relieved. "Why you know men can be pretty pig-headed. You got to do something to prove you can do things as good as a man. One fine thing would be ride down to Nogales and see Patterson, and let yourself be seen there on old Cowboy. Plenty of people from Canelo go back and forth to Nogales on business of one kind or another. Just let them know you rode in by yourself. I'll bet there's not a woman in the county has ever rid that far alone."

"I'll bet there isn't, either."

"But you could do it! Now, here's the way you'd go . . ."

He hunkered down on his heels and began to draw a map in the dust. I got down and watched him.

"Here," he'd say. "Here you take this fork. Now here you go west around this mountain with red outcrop on top. You'll strike the old river road and you can't, by God, get lost then. Just keep right on and you'll come into the Patagonia road, turn south—that's left—and you've six, seven miles to Nogales. Nothing to it."

"Nothing to it, I'll bet. Well, my sense of direction has improved some, I guess; couldn't have stayed as bad as it was—that's not possible. All right, Pat, I'll take a whack at it!"

His old red face reddened up some more. "Sure glad to hear you say that, Rodgers. If I'd been lucky enough to have a sister I couldn't ask for a . . ." He broke down and began to stutter with embarrassment, so I walloped him on the back.

"Don't try to soft-soap me, you old devil!" I said. "Now, let's go over that map again."

Pat pushed his hat back and scratched at his forehead. "You know, Rodge, maybe that ain't such a good idea after all. There's some renegade Mexes around, I've heard. In fact, you can't tell what you might run into, from bandits to having your horse fall on you—though old Cowboy always was sure-footed. Nope, I guess we better not."

He wiped his hand over his map, making it just plain sand again.

But I wasn't content with that. I talked it over with Aggie, and when she was dubious, I tried to get Dan and Clara on my side. But Dan was dead against it. "Too dangerous," he said. "Too much risk. Pat was a fool to think of it, but not enough of a fool to want to go on with it."

Clara chimed in with, "Rodgers could look at any old Mex with the face she's got on now, and he'd light out for other parts fast!"

"All very well to joke," said Aggie. "You'd not do it."

"You can bet your bottom dollar I wouldn't," said Clara. "Not because I'm scared, but because all that country's pretty rough and hard riding."

"You'd not do it," said Dan, "because I wouldn't let you."

His mouth firmed up just like his mother's; he looked so like Aggie in one of her sour spells that I had to laugh.

"You mightn't let Clara do it, Dan," I said, "but she's married to you and that's her burden. I'm not."

"And that's yours," said Clara, brash as ever.

"I'd train him different, if he was mine, Clara," I told her. "He'd ask me a thing or two before he up and spoke his opinion."

We joked sort of roughly at times, but we all liked one another too well to have any hard feelings.

But I wouldn't let it rest. It was a thing I wanted to do just as bad as anything I'd ever done. I'd never made a real long ride alone, and even if none of the women had ever done it, I was going to. I said so to Pat. I said, "You just better believe, Pat Malloy, that I'm going to ride to Nogales! You might as well make up your mind to help me, or I'll turn up missing one night and you'll just know I've up and done it!"

I pestered him so, he finally gave in. He drew another map and went over it a couple of times. He told me what to do if anyone tried to stop me.

"Man steps out of the brush and grabs for your bridle," he said, "you just pull your gun and bring it down hard on his wrist. The barrel, of course. Then you kick old Cowboy hard as you can, and shoot into the ground, just like you was a good marksman. Ain't a man in Mexico or anywhere else'll take out after you after that. If you come down hard enough on his wrist, anyhow, you're like to break it with that heavy old .45 of mine."

Pat took me part way the first time. He went through the San Rafael with me to show me the trail that led around the mountains and down to the old river road. "You can't miss it so don't get boogery. Stay on the trail, is all."

"You're the boogery one, Pat. I'll make it all right. So long."

"So long," he said, his old, red face puckered up with worry. "Uh, Rodge, you sure you want to do it?"

"Certain sure!" I said. I pushed old Cowboy over the first steep part of the trail. By this time half a day alone in new country wasn't a prospect which would bother me.

It was a good feeling. It wasn't the first time nor the last that I had it—mostly new views would give it to me—but every time it happened it was good. There's just you and your horse—oh, maybe a stray steer or little jag of cows way off on another mountain and them high-tailing for deep brush when they spot you. There's you and your horse and the everlasting hills, the sky, space. Even down in a canyon you can look up and see the sky, limitless, blue, forever.

One place, the trail turned the shoulder of a mountain, the one with the red-rock cap, and here it ran just under the cap which shot up sheer. The trail turned the shoulder and then started slaunchwise down, down, down. I pulled up Cowboy and looked.

Down there, almost half a mile I judged, was a good-sized creek running shallow over red sand, the water flashing in the sun. Off level with my eye, across the creek, was a yellow mountain that came up in a perfect cone out of a hole in the ground. I mean it was ringed with other mountains, so that it looked as if some gigantic hand had scooped out a hole in the earth, then decided to playfully drop a cone of yellow ashes in it, point up.

I could feel my heart swell and get light like a balloon. This was the sort of thing I wanted Jerry to see; I wanted him and Cissie riding on their own horses crowding up behind me, and maybe saying, "Gosh, ma! Oh, gosh!"

If I won that election, maybe I could. There was a salary for being constable, not much, but a steady income for a year or two would sure help.

I had to hurry and work hard, so I pushed Cowboy right along down that narrow, shaly trail, more suited to a deer than a horse.

We were both pretty give out when we reached Nogales a little after sundown. But I was proud of myself; Judge Dunphy, too, said he'd never heard of even an old country woman who had made that ride.

I must have seen a dozen or more men from around Canelo in Nogales. There were a couple of prospectors and some cowboys and even a miner or two from Harshaw. Of course, they wouldn't be voting in my district, but they would be talking to people who were. I'd walk along the sidewalk, and these men would be standing outside saloons, or coming out, or going in, and it was "Hello, Rodgers," " 'Lo, Jim—or Bill or Tom" or whatever his name was.

I stayed with the Dunphys, had dinner with Artur, laid over one day to rest Cowboy, and started back. All the way, forty miles by myself, so proud and tickled. So was Pat.

"Rodge," he said, "Will Levinson saw you there and stopped to ask me how come you were down there and I told him you took a notion to ride down for some women-fixings and he thought that was just great. Great! He said any woman would ride that trail alone in times like these with maybe a Mexican behind every piece of brush had all the guts he thought would be needed for constable. There's one sure vote."

When it got to John Yoss's ears, of course he said Pat went with me. So next week I did it again, and that day Pat made a point of visiting at Barker's about mail time so he'd be seen by plenty.

Artur was both pleased and worried. He liked seeing me in Nogales where we could be comfortable in the Border Café, instead of holed up in the galvanized-iron chicken coop with Aggie and maybe Charles Jackson. But he worried about the danger of the trip.

"Pooh!" I said. "No danger. Anybody tangles with me, I lean over and bust his wrist with Pat's .45."

Lean over, indeed! I'd probably have screamed and leaned backward. But I never did find out what I'd do because I never met any bad men any time I rode alone. I might pass cowboys who would yell and stop to jaw a bit, or some old, shuffling, gopher-hole digger with his beard tangled round his knees shoving his burro to some new place where that great big strike was sure to be made this time. But never did a man, white, yellow, red, or black, ever bounce out from behind a bush at me. Only that one whose boot Aggie and I found that day, the one, who in a way, had got me into this contest for constable because the lawlessness of just killing him sickened me. If I ever got John Yoss where I could squeeze him, you could bet I'd try to make him confess that killing!

As it got closer to Election Day, Pat and I got more and more active. So did John Yoss. Sometimes we'd see him riding up when we were leaning over a corral fence talking to a man, other times, he'd be blarneying a woman at her back door when Pat and I arrived. Night before election there was a dance over at Carl Lucas's, which was outside the township, but all the people went to it. They looked for fireworks, but nothing much happened.

Yoss made a speech between two dances. He waited as long as he could for me to do it, then when he knew if he didn't speak up he wouldn't be let to because people would be too interested in just having a good time, he got up on the musicians' platform and turned his jaw loose.

It was the same old story: women were fine people but they couldn't do what men did, and never would be able to. These were bad times, and it would take a man to handle being constable.

Pat made me wait one dance, and then I just said how fine it would be if they showed their faith in their own state constitution which gave suffrage to women by electing one to office. And how the tradition of the West and particularly Arizona was always forward and upward to new things.

People went on dancing after that, and it was like there wasn't any election coming the next day.

I went to the polls in the schoolhouse early with Pat and Aggie, Dan and Clara. I voted for myself, of course; if I was good enough to ask others to vote for me, I was good enough to vote for myself.

Pat stayed at the polls to watch, but he wouldn't let me. He said, "Go on back and do your regular chores. We got all day to wait. Anyhow, I know you're elected."

I didn't feel so sure of that, not now, I didn't. Aggie said, "I think you'll win, Rodgers." And Dan thought so, too. Clara said she was hoping.

Artur came out that afternoon. Charles Jackson was there,

and it sort of started to get like a party in our old galvanized-iron chicken coop. Couldn't crowd more than about five people inside it, but it was a good, clear day with the sun warm, so you could stay outside. Artur and I wandered down to the swimming place and sat there under the cottonwoods, a little cool but not enough to hurt.

"Lu," he said, "what are you going to do now?"

"It's not over yet. I'm not thinking ahead."

"You must be thinking ahead, Lu. This makes you a real, true Westerner. You couldn't become any more Western than this: Constable of a township! Deputy sheriff, too."

"Constable's better," I said. "Shows they want you. But I'm not, yet."

"I will be very proud of you, Lu."

I said, "I'm glad of that."

We sat there silently, and I felt we were very close, the closest we'd ever been. But it wasn't close enough; there was still between us Artur's old hurt. Winning the election couldn't cure that. Maybe nothing could.

But if anything could, having the kids here could. And winning the election was bound to bring them closer.

I had to get them here. Only they could break down the barrier I knew was between us. The barrier that was invisible to Artur, but which existed as surely as if it was stone. More and more, I wanted to break it down, though I was still a little confused. Being married to Greg had been very, very good; Artur might be even better because I was older and I guessed I had more sense. I was sure I knew more about myself. I certainly had more confidence; I wasn't afraid to try things.

Then, too, there was Aggie and the ranch. We were closer than I had thought we could get. The fire did it, I guessed. While we still rubbed on each other's nerves sometimes, we were roughing it so hard we sort of didn't have time to be picky and mean. We were good friends, hard and fast. Aggie really looked on me as a partner, an equal, I was sure. The part I didn't know about was Charles Jackson.

And that had been working on the way I was thinking

about Artur and me. Smell the coffee someone else is drinking, and you think you'd like some too. Aggie was thinking hard about Jackson, though, close as we were, she talked very little about it. I wondered if having a man in the house wasn't almost a habit, and that she couldn't break it if she wanted to. Not that Jackson was unattractive, of course. But he would be mainly a man in the house.

If he came in, I went out. There couldn't be any other way to it. I wouldn't resent it, either, or be mad at Aggie. No more than she would me if I married Artur.

There it was. I'd said it to myself.

When he asked, "What are you thinking, Lu?" I almost told him. But I stopped in time.

"Wondering how the voting's going."

"I am sure you will win. I wonder what it will do to you, Lu?"

"I'll be just the same," I said. "What could it do?"

Artur spread his hands in a way he had, and smiled. "Perhaps make you wish to go further," he said.

"I just don't know. Oh, Artur, do you think I'll win?"

I did win.

They had the votes counted by nine o'clock and Pat came tearing over to the chicken coop. We could hear him coming from the other side of Barker's; I guess we heard him as he busted out of the schoolhouse and jumped on his horse.

His gun was going off and he was screeching like an Apache when he pulled up in front of us, standing out on the road.

"Hundred and three to twenty-six!" he yelled. "Rodgers for constable! Yeow! Yippee!" He jammed fresh shells in his gun and shot them off.

Jackson and Artur both had brought bottles, so of course we had drinks. Aggie figured the chicken coop wasn't really a house, so we could have them inside. And I hadn't been able to eat much dinner, so Clara and I got out some food. Pat was hungry, too. We made coffee and sat around talking and laughing. The sides of that chicken coop were just bulging.

I don't know how much later it was when there came a yell from outside. "Rodgers, hey, Rodgers."

It sounded mean and like a dirty word or curse the way it was yelled. It was John Yoss, of course.

He didn't wait for someone to open the door. He jerked it open himself and stood there with the light catching glints in his copper-bronze hair. I could see the faces of the Duncan boys behind him, sort of floating in the dark over his shoulder. He was pretty drunk.

"Well, you won," he said.

"She sure did," said Aggie. "If we wasn't so crowded here I'd ask you to come in and have some coffee." Aggie was really feeling happy and good to say that to John Yoss, whom she'd taken to detesting.

"Don't want your coffee," he said. "Just came to congratulate late opponent." He swayed a little and clutched at the door with his left hand.

"Thanks, John," I said.

His eyes focused on me. "Thanks for nothing! Don't never thank me for nothing! Yoss beaten by a woman! God damn you!"

Artur was at the end of the table nearest the door. Clara was next him, with Dan the other side of her. Artur said, "Here, here . . ." gently. He stood up.

"Just stand one side, you," said Yoss. "I want to see that son-of-a-bitch Pat Malloy. She wouldn't have won wasn't for him!"

Artur said easily, "You're drunk, Mr. Yoss. You'd better go home."

Yoss pushed him, tried to shove him aside. Artur stood solid as a big tree. "Now . . ." he said.

"God damn you!" said Yoss. He jerked his gun out of the holster.

There wasn't time to scream. There wasn't time to do a thing. We all sat frozen.

Except Artur. He moved so fast you could hardly see him. He reached out and chopped down with his hand.

Yoss's gun went off, but the bullet ploughed into the dirt floor.

Then Artur's big fist connected with Yoss's chin, and Yoss seemed to lift up and sail away into the darkness.

Pat was struggling with Aggie and Jackson. "Let me go!" he yelled. "It was me he come for! Let me get at him!"

They wouldn't; they had better sense.

Dan went out and broke Yoss's gun open and took the cartridges out. The Duncan boys didn't say much; they weren't so drunk, and they were sort of frightened. Yoss might have shot Pat or Dan and got away with it, but he had nearly shot Artur, who was pretty important in the country. Moreover, Artur was known not to carry a gun, so there could be no plea of self-defense.

"Take him home, now," said Dan. "Sober him up. Tell him what he most done in the morning. Guess it'll take him down some."

They loaded him on his horse like a sack of meal and rode off with him.

"Well," said Aggie, "real warm here for a minute, wasn't it?"

Then I came to. No one was hurt, but I was mad. I started for the door.

"Where are you going, Lu?" asked Artur, not moving out of my way.

"I'm going to arrest him, darn it! I'm constable, now."

Dan's dark, Indian sort of face cracked in a grin. "You better just let him be," he said. "Just let him be, Rodge. He was a little drunk tonight."

But it was more than that. John Yoss had taken a hate on at Pat that he would never get over.

chapter 12

As THE WEATHER got colder, the chicken coop became less and less comfortable. We'd keep the fire going in the stove long after we finished cooking, but it was still chilly and drafty. The floor was just dirt, of course, and when it rained —and we had to have a wet winter, that year—water was likely to run in at one side, meander across the floor, and run out the other side.

Charles Jackson was after Aggie to go into a proposition with him over near Wilcox. It was a combination dairy ranch-milk supply which he thought he and Aggie could buy reasonable enough to make a go of it.

When Aggie first told me about this proposition of Jackson's, I felt pretty bad. There went all my ideas of becoming her partner, and what made it worse was that I really was pretty far along that way, being a person of importance in my own right as constable and deputy sheriff.

We sat there and were silent for a while. I was looking at Aggie, her strong, handsome but worn face. I thought that here was my very best friend, maybe the best I'd ever have in my whole life, and what was going to happen to her? Never mind my little wishes—they could be worked out somehow, concerning only food and shelter as they did. But what about Aggie—would this be right for her; would Jackson make her happy, and treat her right? I wanted this one to be good for her, but how could I ask her questions like that?

So I just said foolishly, "Well, goodness, Aggie, that means you'll move over there to Wilcox."

"Couldn't very well run it from here," said Aggie, kind of snappy because she knew what I was thinking. Maybe she even remembered what she'd said that night the house burned down. Maybe she felt a little guilty.

Well, it didn't matter, I thought, because it was certain that she was going to marry Jackson. Whether she lived here in Canelo and he moved in, or she sold out and moved to Wilcox couldn't make much difference as far as I was concerned. I was out either way. It wouldn't be possible to go on living on a place where Aggie was married to a man. Anybody could understand that, because she and the man would be in a continual state of struggle to see who'd have the upper hand, who'd be boss. And only a deaf mute who was blind, as well, and had no sense of touch could stand being an onlooker at that. Besides, while Aggie might welcome an audience, not many men would, particularly Jackson, who was pretty proud of himself.

"You really are going to marry Jackson?" I said unnecessarily.

Aggie was a little sheepish. "Well, you know, he's been pestering me considerably. Trouble is, Rodge, you get so used to having one of the blame things around the house. Some might say they'd think a woman would be satisfied having tried it three times and never turned out good. Well, the first time I was just like one of these little heifers, walking around switching my tail, wanting something mighty bad, not sure of what it was, but pretty sure the men had it. And Langwood was a handsome creature if ever there was one. Dan takes after him, some. The other two . . ." She gave a long sigh.

I had to say, "Aggie, you don't have to justify it to me."

She gave me a look out of her black eyes. We were hugging the stove; there was frost in the air. "Maybe I'm justifying it to myself," she said. She sat moodily for a time while I brushed out my hair. It was my best feature, I thought. I had a feeling Artur liked it.

"Maybe this one won't be right, either," she said. "Course, the last two died on me—damn them."

"Aggie!" I said. "Oh, Aggie, stop beating yourself! They weren't your fault—or if it's about Jackson, go on, take him if you want to. Nobody's going to say a word."

"Be some snickering, though," Aggie said bitterly. "'Old fool,' they'll say, 'always got to have a man around the house.'"

"The ones that'll say that are the ones who've got men around the house. And often enough you and I've said, 'We don't need a man. Needn't no man come passing by; we get on fine without them.'"

"I've got a notion about you and Resswell, though," she said.

"Well . . ."

"Well, what?" asked Aggie.

"Oh, it's hard to know what to do," I said.

And it was. I didn't know what to do. I pulled on my boots and wrapped my old army overcoat tight around my flannel pajamas and said "Good night."

Limb was waiting for me in the cot under the mulberry tree. He had warmed up the sheets for me; when I got in he purred. Another fellow came lightly up on the edge of the cot, pushed past my face, and slid on down to my feet— Satan. He turned around twice, and lay down, purring, too. They were a good pair of friends to me, though they did take up a fair amount of room. Limb was a long, rangy yearling now, not the little, spiky-tailed poor kitten he'd been when Uncle Tom brought him for a joke.

"My," I thought, "pretty near Christmas again." Trouble was, this one would be different, I was pretty sure. Not gay and fun like last time, but sort of gloomy and with a strain between Aggie and me.

If I only knew what to do about that, at least had someone to talk to.

I did have Someone. I'd been forgetting. "Oh, Lord," I said, "I have forgotten to trust You. I've forgotten my prayers for too long."

I said them then. I said the Lord's Prayer, and I asked Him to bless my children and Aggie and Artur and everybody. And then I said "Now I Lay Me," and I went off to sleep like a baby, and woke up in the morning knowing exactly what to do about Aggie and myself.

I didn't try it on her at breakfast, though. I could see it

was one of her bad days. In fact, for a couple of days, I didn't mention our conversation about the Wilcox place and Jackson, just kept to work and general subjects, till one evening when I thought the time was right. The wind was howling outside, and rain would slat against the galvanized-iron roof and make you glad you weren't out in it. We'd had a good supper and we sat there drinking tea and stoking the stove. After a while, I started.

"Aggie," I said, "are you putting in all the money on Jackson's Wilcox proposition?"

She bridled up at that. "Of course not!" she snapped. "We're going partners, if I decide to do it."

"Sounds like a good proposition, all right."

"What do you know about it?"

"What you've told me," I said. "That's all, but if you're satisfied, I know you're too smart a woman to get into a bad deal in that line, anyhow."

"Well, I guess I do know what I'm doing."

More flies are caught with honey than with vinegar, but Aggie needed a mixture. Just all soft soap wouldn't do; you had to put a little grit in it, too.

"Then you're going to sell this place, aren't you?"

She wouldn't meet my eye. "Well, Rodgers, I hate to do it. I've got a notion you were counting on staying here awhile. And I guess I do get along with you best of any person I ever knew—including the men, too. But, look at it; I can't run this place from Wilcox any more than I could Wilcox from here."

"No," I said, "you can't."

"Rodgers," Aggie said, "Jackson thinks he's got his heart set on Wilcox, but I could make him think different in about five minutes if I put my mind to it. Would you feel happier if I just married him and built that adobe Dan and you was talking about, and just lived right here? You could stay with us. We could use you."

I shook my head. "I don't believe, Aggie Gates, that one of the Lord's bright angels could live in the same house with you and a man. Nor one of his meekest, patientest saints, either. No, I wouldn't stay."

"What would you do?"

"Oh, I wouldn't be surprised if I could make a career in politics."

Aggie snorted. "It was Pat and the novelty that got you elected," she said. "Not to mention the Sheriff. I know what you'll do. You'll just put your strings on Artur Resswell and be all fixed pretty."

"If I could marry Artur some day," I said, "it wouldn't be for that reason. Not just to have a place to stay, to live, my children provided for. My goodness, Aggie, that's almost the same as working in a house. Marry them, and you've got to cook and clean, too."

Aggie burst out laughing at that, and I joined in. "Rodgers," she said, "I do believe you truly think you don't need a man. But there comes a time when a woman does, when she wants someone to love and cherish her, wrap her all up in thick, cotton-wool affection, act for five minutes, anyhow, like she's the most important thing on earth."

"Well, about this place," I said. "Have you asked Dan if he wants it?"

Aggie gave me a look. "You ought to know. Not exactly, because it's a kind of touchy subject. Dan don't exactly see eye to eye with me about Jackson, but he does say that I'm over twenty-one and entitled to make my own mistakes. So we haven't ever talked right out about it, but I know Dan feels it'd be more than he could rightly handle, this place and his own."

"But he's been doing a lot of work on it."

"Not the same as doing all the work on it," Aggie pointed out, just as I'd thought she would.

"That's right. But if you were staying here he'd still help, wouldn't he? You'd still run your stock together; you'd partner on turkey-killing and hog-butchering and all the things just like you did always, wouldn't you?"

"Why, of course," said Aggie, watching me with narrowed eyes.

I couldn't help smiling at her. "Then it's no one's real advantage to sell it, and might be profitable to keep it. Specially with fences going up the way they are, and the talk about Government forest-reserve and grazing permits and all that."

"That's right," said Aggie. "Come on, Rodge, I call. Show your hand."

"Royal flush," I said.

"That beats. Read them for me."

"Easy. Just you go on and marry your Jackson and move over to Wilcox. Take a mortgage on this place—it's safe, so you can surely get one—enough to raise the cash you need for your deal. I'll stay here and Dan can help just like before."

Aggie said, "I just guessed you had it all figured out that way. Rodgers, I hate to say it, but you just couldn't do it. You don't know enough."

"I don't know what you know," I said, "but with Dan around and Pat to holler for, I reckon I could make out."

"Hm . . ." said Aggie.

"My idea would be for me to work on stuff a little easier than cattle. I don't mean cut them out, not that. Dan could handle more and of course I'd help. But I bet I could raise a good flock of turkeys and you know there's money in them. Chickens, too."

"You might have trouble with coyotes."

"Not with a couple of good dogs around the place."

"I suppose you'll send for those children of yours. You'll have to tell Resswell, then."

"If he sees three healthy kids living with me and calling me Mom," I said, "he'll have sense enough to know they're mine."

"I guess he will," said Aggie. "Look, Rodgers, it's a thing I want to think about. It's not as loony as it sounds, but it's loony enough so it needs some sleeping on. And I'd have to talk to Dan."

I said a very thankful prayer that night.

Turned out that Dan was all for it. He hadn't wanted Aggie to sell the old place, but he hadn't been able to think up any good argument to stop her. "Forgetting me sure wasn't very flattering," I told Dan.

"Rodge," he said, "it did cross my mind once, but I

dropped it right away. I was afraid it would turn out like you riding to Nogales— I mean whether you wanted to do it or not, you'd take it as a dare."

"I sure did want to ride to Nogales!" I said. "And I'm going again before Christmas."

"Well, I'm mighty glad it's come out this way. I suppose you'd have moved on somewhere, but Clara and me would sure have missed you."

We made an agreement. I was to work it on shares with Dan, each of us getting one third, the remaining third going to Aggie. So there I was with a place for the children, a ranch of my own—well, near enough so it looked like it, anyhow, though I never would be the owner, though still more than a hired hand.

Aggie was getting ready to go over to Wilcox again one day in December, when I asked her if she and Jackson had set a date yet. I wanted to know, because that would be when I'd take over the place—not that that made any real difference, as I thought then.

"Why, Rodgers, no," said Aggie.

"Oh. I just got the idea the way you were acting that it was going to be pretty soon."

"Well, no, I wouldn't say that . . ."

Aggie was seldom so vague. "Haven't changed your mind, have you?" I asked, as much in favor of her marrying Jackson, now, as I had been against it, before.

She just shook her head.

"Well, then, why don't you get at it? My goodness, anybody'd think you were a little, young girl who didn't know her own mind!"

Aggie smiled at me. It was her whole face, her snapping black eyes, too, as well as her mouth. Aggie could look mighty kind and beautiful when she smiled that way; you were so used to a stern sort of look on her face that this was like having a horse that you knew was all bowed up just amble off at a humble walk instead of pitching.

"You getting impatient?" she asked. "You want me gone?"

"Oh, Aggie, you know I don't!" And that was true, I

didn't, in spite of what it would mean to me to run the place alone.

"Well, then . . ." she said. "Sure, I know you don't, neither, Rodge." She took a deep breath. "Might as well tell you. Remember when I was telling you about Doc Gates and how I came to marry him? I told you then he died in a runaway in a buckboard. Well, Rodge, he didn't. He died purely from liquor. Nothing but whisky. He drank himself to death."

"Oh, Aggie!" That was all I could say.

"Yes," she said, "it was only a couple of years after we married and bought this place. I wondered once in a while —along until you came, Rodgers—what it was I'd failed him in that he should be that way. I could never figure it out."

Her voice was different than I'd ever heard it. It wasn't bitter, as it so often was. She was sitting there with her elbow on her knee, and her chin in her hand, and her eyes staring off into space. The tone of her voice was musing—just musing like someone trying to work out the solution to a difficult problem.

"He was that way before you married," I said.

"Yes. I guess I knew that. But I paid it no heed; I wanted to get married and Doc Gates looked good to me. I was lonesome, Rodge. Dan had gotten married, you know, and I guess any woman feels extra lonesome when her only child, her only son, up and marries. But I guess I made a misjudgment in Doc."

"That why you're delaying on Jackson?"

She shook her head. "I never told you, but Doc died owing a lot of money. I've been paying it off. I can't marry Jackson as long as I still owe some of Doc's debts. There's still one, about a hundred and fifty or so . . ."

"Stock and stuff?"

"No." She wouldn't look at me. "Liquor. Saloons. He died owing every saloon in a day's ride, and that's a lot more than you'd think, if you've got a fast horse."

"But Aggie! Liquor!"

She did look at me then, and her eyes were wide and honest. "Sure, Rodge, liquor. But they trusted him, didn't

195

they? Doesn't matter what he bought, it was a business deal, and someone's got to pay for it."

There wasn't any argument left after that. Nothing I could say. But I could think. There was Aggie, who hated liquor worse than sin and wouldn't allow it in her house, and she was paying for stuff a drunk had killed himself with, to people who shouldn't have sold it to him. It didn't make sense to me.

She saw me thinking. "I know, Rodge, you think I'm a fool. I just couldn't ride around the country knowing that someone who had been near and dear to me was lying in his grave with unpaid debts, no matter for what. Maybe I am a fool, but I've got to feel right with myself."

So we left it at that, and no more was said about it. Aggie went off to Wilcox. "Be home in time for the dance, if you can," I told her as she left. It was the big one before Christmas and Artur was coming. The whole countryside would be there. I hoped Aggie would go, whether Jackson came over or not, because I was pretty proud of myself— Constable of Canelo, Deputy Sheriff of Santa Cruz County!

I had taken a lot of hoorawing about it already. There'd almost always be someone at Barker's when I'd ride over for the mail—even if it was only old man Barker—who'd say, "What are you going to do with your prisoners, Rodgers?"

I had several answers for that. I'd say, "Oh, I never take prisoners."

That would always make them laugh, because, of course, it meant I'd shoot any lawbreaker I caught, which meant I was real bloodthirsty, which I wasn't, as they knew.

Or I'd say, "Hogtie them and leave them out to weather till I get around to lugging them down to Nogales."

Or I'd say, "Rope them round the neck and drag them home!"

Or maybe I'd say, "You know I'm a fraud. I couldn't catch a horned toad!"

They'd laugh. Oh, sure, they'd laugh, but they were proud of me, too. I'd brought quite a lot of notoriety to Canelo and the county. The Tucson paper ran a story about my election under the headline, "Crime Diminishes in Santa Cruz County." The Bisbee paper copied the Nogales idea, which was, "First Female Peace Officer in U.S." Even as far away as Phoenix they talked about it: "Township Elects Woman as Constable."

Aggie came back from Wilcox the day before the dance, and things had gone well for her. She was smiling and happy. She said, "Rodgers, I've got something that's so good for us! You just wait till we get ready for bed!"

The rain was coming down outside, and Limb and Satan were perched on boxes inside the chicken house, their hair all fluffed out by the damp. Arizona sure didn't live up to its name for dryness that winter. The rain was coming down steady, and under the uphill wall of the chicken house, I could see the water getting ready to start running in and across and out the other side.

It was cold, too. I had the stove chunked up and burning hard. We ate our dinner, and the rain came down harder, and there we sat on boxes with our feet up on other boxes. The water had come in now, and was running half an inch deep across our earth floor. When we changed into our night things we had to stand up on boxes.

"Never mind, Rodge," said Aggie. "You just sit there. This thing that I got is going to surprise you, and it's going to do us so much good! Wish I'd thought of it before now. We'd be the beauties at the ball!"

And then she got out a jar of cold cream!

"We're getting to be a pair of leather-faced, old country women!" she said. "We've got to take care of our complexions!"

So we sat on boxes with our feet on other boxes and the water running underneath us in a steady stream while we took care of our faces. No fooling, either. Aggie smeared on the cream very gravely, and so did I, and we sat there working it in.

The rain came down and the water ran. It was wretched and miserable, and still we tried to give ourselves peach-bloom complexions. I began to laugh all of a sudden.

"My Lord, Aggie, look at us! Just look at us!"

Aggie started to laugh, then, too. Taking care of our complexions in a galvanized-iron chicken house in the middle of a wet Arizona winter, one a constable and the other a rancher!

"It's the woman in us, Rodgers," said Aggie.

"The eternal feminine!" I yelled, choking with laughter. "We'll sure conquer them at the dance! We'll sure be the belles of the ball!"

"The men'll flock around!"

"They sure will!" hollered Aggie. "Damn the men to hell! What do we want with them?"

"We don't need a man!" I shouted.

"We sure don't! Don't we look like a pair of fools, rubbing this stuff into our faces, half-drowned out!" With that, Aggie sloshed through the water, opened the door, and hurled that jar of cold cream as far as she could out into the black night and the rain.

"What do we want with a man!" we yelled together.

It was a good joke.

But next night, the joke was on us. You can't have a very good time at a dance without a man. So we forgot our little motto, or at any rate, kept quiet about it. I, for one, was very glad to have Artur there, and Aggie didn't look unhappy with Jackson.

It wasn't raining and it wasn't too cold. Going home, Artur let his horse walk. There was a big, full moon, floating very high up, almost silver, it was so white. It looked quiet and distant. It threw very black shadows in the Huachucas to our left, and shone so brightly on the flat country off to the other side of the road that patches of sand or grass looked like expanses of water. It was kind of lonesome and melancholy, which just made it awful good to sit close to Artur, feeling the warmth of his big, solid shoulder against my cheek.

I told him about my agreement with Aggie. He sighed and said, "I am glad for you, Lu, because it is what you want, but I am sorry for myself. It surely binds you closer to this place."

I guess I was mean to tease him, but I couldn't help saying, "Don't you want me to stay in this part of the country, Artur?"

That gave me my comeuppance right away. He turned to me, his face all clear in the moonlight, a little, earnest frown on his forehead. "Lu, I am always trying to tell you that I want you to stay here forever. Because this is where I want to stay. I belong here, and I know you do, too."

There I was, caught again, and by my own slick tongue this time. The only reason Artur hadn't asked me to marry him yet, was because I'd managed to head it off each time he was getting ready to. Now I'd have to do it again.

"Sure," I said. "Sure, I belong here. Constable, aren't I, and deputy sheriff? This is my place, too. And working out this proposition with Aggie will make it more mine. Only trouble is I don't know when it's going to start. She's got to set the day and she can't seem to make up her mind."

When he started to speak, I said, "You know, Artur, she's one of the strangest women . . ." I rattled along like that for a mile or more, keeping him from saying anything. But I felt so good and close to him, so tender and loving, that I couldn't help snuggling up against him as if I was cold. I tucked one hand in under his that were holding the reins, and looked up at him, driving along, the moon bright on his face, showing his kind eyes, his expression of interest—whether or not he was interested in what I was saying, I knew he was interested in me. I knew I could talk about the most trivial matters forever and any time and he would enjoy listening just because it was me. I think most people know when someone is in love with them, and more important, when someone loves them. Artur was both in love with me and loved me, and I knew it. I had kept him from saying so, though, and I couldn't see anything to do but keep on keeping him from saying the words that were right on the tip of his tongue.

I sure couldn't afford to let him know I loved him, either. I did, I knew.

It wasn't the way I had loved Greg, as well as I could remember that. This wasn't as wild, but it was just as exciting. I was happy to have discovered that I could love a man again, love him all through, and up, and down, and crosswise. But I was very unhappy that I didn't dare tell him.

Feeling sad because I didn't know what to do, I put my head on his shoulder, and closed my eyes.

I had almost fallen asleep, when Artur began to hum and then sing. I couldn't understand the words—German, I guess—but there was no mistaking the tune. It was a lullaby. I almost sat up straight and told him about my children.

Then I realized the song was meant for me; he was feeling protective and loving about me.

I reached up and kissed his ear.

chapter 13

For Christmas that year, Artur gave me a beautiful double-action .38. It was a Colt, of course. It was silver-plated with a pearl handle. On the backstrap was engraved, "Lucretia Rodgers, Constable of Canelo."

I was very proud of it. Pat had advised Artur on it. Pat gave me a black-leather holster and belt, tooled with steer- and horseheads. It made a mighty good-looking outfit. I guess I swaggered around in it some, though nobody seemed to mind, not even Aggie.

She was still putting off deciding about both Jackson and the Wilcox proposition when spring came. There'd been so much rain through the winter that it didn't matter that the spring rains were scanty. One night when we went to bed, the hills were still tawny with what was left of the old grass, the scrub oak were dark, worn-down green, the Huachucas were nearly black. Somehow next morning it had happened. By noon the sun was shining down on hills that had a fuzz of bright, shouting green; the oaks had lost their sleepy look and put out new little leaves overnight; the Huachucas were two tones lighter, specially along the top where the pines were growing long, yellowish-green tips on their branches. It was spring, all right: the pair of blue herons that lived down near the swimming hole came winging in from their winter quarters in Mexico.

The calf crop began to appear. We were busy all day, riding, looking for poor cows that were having trouble, though there were few of these, due to the plenteous feed this year on the range. Dan and Clara had brought over a tent and set it up next to Aggie's so they could stay and work with us. It was a lot like the first summer, riding day after day, full of no thoughts but the cattle. Aggie had softened some, too; she'd mellowed.

I don't mean she was exactly gay and radiating sunshine, but she wasn't so snappy, so hard-headed. It was as if she was putting out a few little new leaves too; the spring had gotten to her also. It was Jackson, of course. Not that he was such a wonderful shower of life-giving rain—just that it was doing Aggie good to know someone loved her enough to want to be with her.

Once in a while, it made me feel a little sorry for myself. But not often. I kept thinking about Artur and what to do about him, but that wasn't always in the front of my mind. I'd say to myself, "Well, just take it in your stride. Handle it as it comes. The more time you have, the more you put off a decision, the easier it'll be." Whether that was true or not, I didn't stop to consider. The prospect of taking over the ranch made everything so much simpler. Probably in a year or so I could get Jerry, Cissie, and Tim out here. Although that seemed like a whole lot longer than I could wait.

Time, I thought, was on my side.

The big outfit that ran to the north, the Rail-X, decided to include the Huachucas in their spring roundup that year. They figured, I suppose, that since they hadn't worked south that far in a couple of seasons, there would be a lot of their stuff running loose in the mountains. Dan and Pat figured that if the Rail-X got in there alone, there was a reasonable possibility of them making mistakes and taking out a lot of yearling stock that maybe hadn't been branded, but was running with their mammies who might wear Canelo brands. Old man Barker felt the same, and so did the Duncans and Bill Yoel and Pete Stolley. So they all banded together and threw in with the Rail-X men, and went into the Huachucas. John Yoss went along, too. Soon as he had heard about it he began to talk big about how much of his stuff had drifted in there and he was going along to protect his interests.

MacBain, Minnie's husband, left his carpentering in Bisbee for a week and went, figuring there'd be enough of his own stock to make it worth while. Phil Sowers took his eldest son, Fred, along. He was a nice, quiet boy and I wished Jerry would develop, at his age, a lot of his qualities. Harry Friar figured he could find a stray or two, so he showed up. A couple of others went, too. It got to be a real big roundup for that part of the country.

As they were going to start about ten or fifteen miles south and drive right up through the mountains, Pat fixed the wagon he and I had used on our prospecting trip for a grub wagon. He agreed to cook and feed the other Canelo men in return for them rounding up his stock for him.

"But you won't be doing any riding, Pat," I said when he told me, grinning all over as if he'd made a fine deal.

"Rodgers, the greenhorn will come out every so often! What for do I want to wear out my pants polishing a saddle, when I can get the rest of them to do it for frijoles and biscuits?"

"That all you going to feed them?"

"Oh, a little jag of something else now and then," said Pat, who was proud of his camp cooking.

"But look at all the fun you'll miss," I said.

Pat just gave me a disgusted look and Aggie laughed. "Pat Malloy was born tired, Rodge," she said. "The less he can do the better he likes it."

"After all the cords of wood I've chopped for you," Pat said reproachfully.

"The food we fed you for it!" said Aggie and I together.

Next morning, he came past with his wagon, leading a saddle horse behind it. He stopped. "You ought to come down in a day or two, Rodge," he yelled. "Something to see."

"You bet I will!" Nothing could have stopped me. It was the first real big roundup since I'd arrived in Canelo and I sure wasn't going to miss it.

"Two days from now we ought to have worked up to that old corral a couple of miles south of Uncle Tom's. That'd be a good place to come to; they're likely to start cutting there."

"I'll be there!" I hollered. "I'll be there."

When the day came, I pinned on my badge and buckled

on my gun and stuffed some jerky in my pocket just in case I got hungry. At the last minute, Aggie decided to come too.

"Could be there might never be another of these, ever," she said. "The way people are building fences and all this forest-reserve stuff, stock won't be ranging so far afield. Couple of years more, and they'll have automobiles in place of horses, and it'll be all done. Man like Pat'll ride around on springs and cushions, and never fork a saddle or set foot to the ground."

"Oh, it'll be a long time yet," I said.

"You'll see," said Aggie. She felt a little gloomy that morning.

But there was nothing gloomy about me. I was anxious to get there and see a big bunch of cattle and men and horses working. The sun was warm on my face, and old Cowboy was feeling fresh enough to jig his feet and snort and roll his eyes at a jack rabbit that jumped up under his nose. I was the constable of Canelo and a real Westerner, somebody who counted in the community, somebody who would count more and more pretty soon when I started raising turkeys on Aggie's place.

"Aggie," I asked, "when you going to make up your mind?"

"Stop pestering me, Rodge! I'm not ready yet, but I might be soon if Dan turns me up enough salable stock this time."

That made me feel even better. I thought of meeting the kids at the train in Tucson. Jerry would be very serious, because, of course, he'd have been the one responsible for getting there. He'd have charge of Cissie and Tim; he'd be the one to talk to the conductor, to pay for meals in the diner.

"Aggie," I said, "Aren't kids wonderful things!"

"I've always been mighty proud of Dan, Rodge. He's turned out to be a fine man."

"He sure has. Oh, Aggie, I do want you to see my kids!"

"Three is a lucky number. I think you are a lucky woman, Rodgers. Only I think you ought to give Resswell a little more consideration. He'd make you a fine husband."

"I'm scared to tell him about them, Aggie."

"I can't see why. Not with the way he looks at you. You know, Rodgers, you don't look like the old-maidish woman who came here. You're pretty near pretty now. When you get excited about something you are pretty, I guess. I'd bet you're really in love with Resswell. Why don't you marry him? He would if you'd lead him on a little."

I shied away at that. "Oh, stop picking on me about him!"

"Well," said Aggie, "I guess you think you know what you are doing. You sure are an independent cuss, Rodgers!"

The trail went right past Uncle Tom's, so we stopped to say hello. He told us the men had made their headquarters at the old corral and were working out from it. "They're really combing the hills this time!" he said. "Most likely I'll have to eat venison from now on, and I don't like it in hot weather."

"Why, Uncle Tom," I said, "you don't kill other people's beef!"

"I sure can't kill my own!" he said. " 'Cause I ain't got none! Why, I just make a natural mistake now and then. When I take that old Winchester of mine and go out stalking a deer, I'm mighty apt to let fly at anything that moves. Eyes are getting dim, and a lot of these cattle is dun-colored anyhow, just like a deer. So if there's a yearling killed by mistake, I might as well take a quarter as leave it for the coyotes and buzzards."

"Just don't make a mistake where I can see it," I told him. "Remember, I'm constable. I'd have to do my duty."

"Wish you'd follow down that blamed woman that trimmed my beard all slaunchwise a year or so back, then. Took it a long time to grow straight."

"If I ever find her, Uncle Tom," I promised, "I'll let you know."

"Don't go looking in any mirrors, then," he yelled, laughing, as we rode off.

There was a lot of commotion at the old corral. It was full of spring calves, put in it as the easiest way to make their mammies stay around. In a canyon to the right of the trail was a herd of mixed stuff, cows and steers with a couple of bulls. There must have been a hundred or more. A couple of strange cowboys were holding them, and Aggie said they were Rail-X hands.

Off in a little glade with short grass and a spring, nice high-branched oaks round it, Pat had set up his wagon. The men's bedrolls showed they camped there. Pat was working away at preparations for dinner. He grinned all over his homely face when we rode up. "Light and give your saddles a rest!" he hollered. "Men'll be in for dinner 'bout an hour from now."

"What you got to eat?" Aggie asked.

"Roundup food, of course!" Pat said. "Fried beef and frijoles, biscuits and coffee. What more's a man want?"

"Woman either," said Aggie. "I'm a little empty right now."

"Beans is ready," said Pat.

"Nope, we'll wait, won't we, Rodge?"

"Oh, sure. How's it going, Pat?"

"Pretty good. You must have seen the stuff we've already found. 'Nother couple of days and we'll move them all up and out of the mountains. This here's a real good roundup."

"Getting along with the Rail-Xers all right?"

"They ain't a bad lot," said Pat. "Not for hired hands, they ain't."

Aggie snorted. "What's wrong with hiring out?"

"Not a thing for most," said Pat. "Me, I like being independent, running my own stuff. I may not be better than anybody else, but nobody's better than me."

"That's a cattleman for you," said Aggie. "Big or little, that's the way they feel."

"They eat with us?" I asked.

Pat shook his head. "They got their own setup. It's down that little canyon a ways."

"Get indigestion from your cooking, anyhow," said Aggie. "Any of our boys down sick yet?"

Pat laughed. "I put out the best grub in Southern Arizona," he said. "Maybe the whole of it. Of course, somebody's always got to complain, but it don't mean nothing."

"Who's kicking?" Aggie asked.

Pat said, "Oh, well, one of the Duncans didn't seem to like the coffee. And somebody else was complaining that the flapjacks was heavy. Nothing important. Men have got to bellyache about something, and it's generally the food. I never yet had to part someone's hair with a skillet, though, so I guess what I give them's as good as I ever did."

I had a sort of feeling that it wasn't quite as friendly as Pat made out. There was something in the way he didn't look up when he told us that, but just kept stirring his beans. Pat had a way of looking at you when he told you something that made you feel wrong when he didn't. But I guessed, as he said, that it wasn't much wrong.

Aggie must have felt something too, though, because she asked, "How's John Yoss acting?"

"Well," said Pat, "Yoss is big-mouthed, we all know that. I doubt that he means much . . ."

"What's he said?" I asked.

"Nothing particular. I don't notice him much."

"Pat Malloy, don't be so minchy-mouthed!" said Aggie, but Pat just shut his mouth and his old face got red.

"Whyn't you go look for Dan?" he asked. "I got to get my dinner ready. I ain't got time to flapjaw with a couple of ignorant women! Dan'll be coming that way. . . ." He waved at the shoulder of the hill over the corral.

"Come on," said Aggie. "Come on, Rodge, we'll leave this old sullen turkey gobbler and find Dan."

We hadn't gone a mile when we heard noises in the brush. We pulled up and sat quiet so as not to turn whatever was coming. Pretty soon a couple of wild-eyed steers came out of the brush, snorted, tried to reverse themselves, but Pete Stolley was right on them and hazed them past. Then came five cows, wild-eyed, too, with their calves bawling behind them. Dan was driving them.

"Hello," he said after they got by and we had ridden up beside him. "Kind of thought you'd be along, Rodge. Didn't exactly expect you, Ma. How's Clara?"

"All right," said Aggie. "You're picking up a lot of stuff."

Dan nodded. "We're really combing the hills. See those steers? Rail-X four-year-olds."

"Yes," said Aggie. "Dan, how's it going?"

"Work's all right. Rail-X is keeping honest—maybe they are, anyhow. And all our bunch is working fine."

"Together?"

"Well, no. Tell the truth, Yoss and the Duncans kind of make a team, and that's all right. Nobody wants to work with Yoss if they don't have to."

"Look here, Dan," I asked impatiently, "how are he and Pat getting along?"

"Pat's handling himself real well. I told the Duncans that Yoss was trying to make trouble and they'd better hold him down. He sure is trying, because even they agreed with me. But Pat just acts like he can't hear."

"Pat doesn't want trouble?"

"He doesn't." Dan gave me a long look. "Rodge," he said, "just you be careful how you behave at dinner, that's all. You'll be gone before supper."

"I'm not going to do anything," I said.

"I know you're not," said Dan. "Maybe it would be better if you took off that badge. No use rubbing Yoss's face in it."

I didn't like that. But I said, "You really think I ought to?"

Dan nodded. "It won't make Yoss forget, but it won't seem like you're trying to rub it in."

So I unpinned my badge from my shirt and pinned it inside my jumper where it wouldn't show.

We helped Dan and Pete run the calves into the corral and the steers down to the Rail-Xers who were holding the main bunch. "Mighty kind of you," they said.

"Guess your boys might pick up some more of ours," said Pete, and the Rail-Xers guessed they might.

Before we got back to camp, we heard Pat beating on a skillet with a spoon and yelling, "Come and get it! Come and get it 'fore I throw it out and spit in the skillet!"

Old man Barker and Bill Yoel rode in from the other side with Sowers' son. Four men were already squatting in the shade of the oaks eating. One was MacBain and the others were the Duncan boys and John Yoss. Yoss looked up and saw me and gave me a black, black look. It made me sort of nervous, almost made me wish I hadn't come, not because I was frightened, but because he muttered something to one of the Duncans that seemed like a curse. When he looked back at me, his face had a bad, mean expression that reminded me of the night of the election when he pulled his gun.

MacBain didn't intend to make trouble, I know, but he sure didn't help any by singing out, "Hello, Constable!"

Yoss's green eyes filled up with all the old rages and resentments.

While we were getting our plates of beans and beef, our biscuits and mugs of coffee, MacBain left Yoss, who said something sneering as he did, and came over and spread his bedroll. "Come sit on this," he told us.

We were sitting there eating peacefully and catching up with each other. Pat was dishing up for Barker and a couple of others who came in. All of a sudden Yoss let out a howl that was pure anger.

We looked that way.

John Yoss stood up and flung his plate on the ground. He spat out a mouthful of food. "Stone in the beans!" he yelled. "I busted a tooth! God damn that damn fool cook!"

Pat never even quivered, just went on dishing beans, but his face turned bright red.

Yoss shouted, "I'll learn you, Pat Malloy. God damn you! I'll learn you!"

One of the Duncans must have said something to him, because he bellowed, "Tend your own business!" He picked a rock the size of his fist off the ground and walked quickly toward Pat. "Turn round and see what you done to me!" he shouted.

Pat put down his spoon and wiped his hands on his floursack apron and turned around, all deliberately. He had his back to us. John Yoss yelled, " 'Nother one of your damn tricks! But the joke's going to be on you, this time!"

He raised the rock and brought it down hard as he could on top of Pat's head. It knocked Pat's hat off. Pat staggered, and sank slowly in a crouch, partly stunned, his left hand reaching the ground and bracing him.

Without thinking, I had put my plate down. I jumped up and ran toward them, trying to get my gun out of its holster as I ran.

"Stop that, Yoss!" I shouted.

He looked up at me. I knew he hated me. Every line of his face meant murder. His hand started down for his gun.

"You're asking for it, too, Rodgers!"

I couldn't get my gun out, and I kept wondering desperately why someone didn't do something.

Yoss's eyes were hard on me and his gun was out of the holster.

A gun went off, but it wasn't his.

He dropped his. His hands went to his belly, clutching it. He crumpled in the middle and fell down in a heap.

Pat was sitting there on the ground, his gun in his hand, and it was still smoking. Of them all, it was Pat who had done something. He had saved my life.

Everything was so silent you could hear Yoss's breath go out in a long sigh. Then he drew it in again; you could hear him draw it with a great rasp. It went out; he moaned; his hands fell away from himself.

A .45 bullet at six feet tears quite a hole in a man. John Yoss was awful dead.

Pat got to his feet and put his gun back in his holster. "Well," he said, "maybe that'll learn him." He put his hand to the top of his head. "Going to be a right good knot he gave me."

Old man Barker stepped over to Yoss. "Sure is dead," he said. "Deader'n buzzard bait."

"He brought it on himself," said Aggie. "Here, Pat, let me see your head."

"Rodge," asked Pat, "you all right?"

"Yes," I said. I wasn't. I wasn't hurt, but I knew there was something I had to do. It was a thing I wanted to do least in all my life, I guess but I had to.

"Pat Malloy," I said, "I arrest you for killing John Yoss." I put my hand on his shoulder the way I thought you were supposed to.

Aggie had wrung out a rag in cold water. "Here, Pat," she

said, "put that on your head." She pushed my hand off Pat's shoulder. "Stop fussing, Rodgers! It's the clearest case of self-defense I ever saw."

"Sure," said Bill Yoel, "and he saved your life, too."

"I know he did," I said. "But there's laws in this state. You can't just shoot a man and walk away. Pat's got to stand trial."

"That's just going to cost the county money it could spend better on lots of more important things," said MacBain.

"It sure is a no-account idea," said old man Barker. "You're taking yourself too seriously, Rodgers."

Harry Friar said, "I don't see no reason . . ."

Any other time, I guess I'd have gotten mad at them, but all that violence, Yoss still lying there, sickened me. I said, "But can't you see he's got to stand trial? You just can't do this sort of thing." My voice was pretty shaky, even I could tell that, myself.

Phil Sowers said, "Look here, Mrs. Rodgers, right's right."

Pat interrupted him. "Rodgers is right!" he said. "By God, Rodgers, you're right! That's what we got laws for. I aim to stand trial, and no one's going to stop me! I'm your prisoner, Constable. You tell me what to do."

"You're carrying it too far, Pat, you crazy old poke," said Bill Yoel.

"No he's not!" said Aggie. "Rodgers and him are right, and I'm with them. It's self-defense and defense of a duly elected officer of the law—that's Rodgers—and still he's got to stand trial. People might start calling Pat a killer if it wasn't legal."

"They sure might," said Pat, of a sudden all indignant and hurt. "They sure might, and I know none of my friends and well-wishers would want that!"

"By God," said old man Barker, "there's sense in that, too!"

So they finally agreed that the law had to take its course. But I'd certainly not been popular for a few minutes, there! Pat had the last word. "I'm not a bit sorry I done it," he said stoutly. "He brung it on himself! Like I told you, John

Yoss thought he was big enough to hunt bears with a switch."

We made Pat comfortable with the wet rag on his head and a cup of his own strong coffee. I intended to take him down with Aggie and me. I'd take him to Nogales in the morning. It bothered me a little about where I ought to put him during the night, but I figured I'd think of something.

"Now what are we going to do with Yoss?" I asked Aggie and Dan.

"I never heard he had any relatives," said Dan.

"No, you're wrong, Dan. I think I heard he had a brother up around Salt Lake City."

"Right smart ways," said Barker. "Ain't much sense lugging him around. He'd hardly keep till we turned up the brother—if there is one."

"Let's dig a hole and stash him away up here," said Bill Yoel. "That way if anybody wants to claim him, they'll know right where he is and can come and get him. Besides, it ain't dignified to go dragging a corpse around the country."

They decided on that, and the Duncan boys went to work over on the other side of the clearing digging a grave. The men decided to move camp, anyhow, though. "One more night and we'll be through," said Dan.

"What you want to take Pat down tonight for, Rodgers?" Barker asked. "It ain't like he was going to run away."

"He's under arrest for shooting a man," I said, "and it's my duty to put him into the county jail as soon as possible. Mur- . . . " I didn't want to say it; it felt too queer to say in connection with Pat, who wouldn't hold a corset over a fire. Anyhow, it wasn't technically murder. "Killing's a serious offense," I said instead. "I'm taking him tonight."

"Oh, all right," said Barker. "We'll go visit Uncle Tom for supper. He's probably lonesome, anyhow—or he better be!"

The Rail-X foreman and one of his hands had come up to find out about the shot they'd heard. They were being told the story with all the details, and the hand stood there shaking his head when they finished. "I've wanted to shoot many a cook," he said, "but this is the first time I heard of a cook shooting a boarder!"

Pat began to stir around and gather up his stuff. It was decided that Bill Yoel would drive the wagon and team down to Uncle Tom's, and then on down to Pat's in a day or two. Pat would ride down with Aggie and me.

"Though I don't see what you're in such a hurry about," he said, shaking his head. "Ain't as if you could change it any."

"I ought to deliver you to the Sheriff as soon as possible, Pat." I wanted to add that I certainly didn't want to, but that might take too much explaining after the fuss I'd made. Besides, the explanation would only embarrass Pat.

He sort of knew what I was thinking and tried to make a joke of it. "Oh, all right, all right, I sure ain't going to make trouble for my own constable," he said, "the one I campaigned for and got elected."

I knew he wasn't trying to hurt me, but he did. I was upset some, anyhow. For the first time in more than a year, I found myself crying. Not hard, thank the Lord, just wet in the eyes and so choked up I couldn't speak. No one except Aggie noticed it. She gave me a cup of coffee, dug around in Pat's private box while he was talking with Dan, and found a bottle of whisky. She put some of it in my coffee, and poured herself a little.

"Shakes you to see a man shot," she said.

It had surely shaken me, and I thought that with her memories she ought to be all broken up. But Aggie was stern stuff.

We didn't talk much as we rode down the trail. It wasn't like the ride up in the morning. Uncle Tom came out and hollered at us, but we jogged on past with just a wave, leaving him mad, no doubt. He'd feel better when the rest came down.

We were going across the canyon, past Barker's, and in sight of our galvanized chicken coop when I said, "I don't know where I'll put you tonight, Pat."

"Put me?"

"Yes, you're my prisoner."

213

"Why, don't be crazy, Rodgers. I'll go home, of course, and you can pick me up in the afternoon. We'll ride over to Elgin and get the train."

"That's a whole day...."

"Sure, I told you you were in too much of a hurry. Hell, Rodgers, you ain't thinking I'd ride to Nogales, are you?"

"Well," I said.

Aggie gave a short chuckle and Pat laughed out loud. "Why, now, Rodge, if I was taking a desperate prisoner like me to justice, and I was you, I sure wouldn't go riding no rough mountain trails with him where he could make a break for freedom. Train's a lot safer and lots easier for me."

"Oh, go chase yourself, Pat," I said.

I didn't sleep well that night. I kept seeing the surprised expression of John Yoss's face just before he fell down. He had never thought that anyone would do anything to him; he was a fool who, because he was young and strong, thought he could bully anyone. I wasn't sorry for him; just disturbed because I had seen a life wiped out so quickly. It was so final, a thing that could never be undone. And then I began to worry about Pat. Would they want to condemn him for murder?

I asked Aggie about that first thing. "Goodness, Rodgers," she said, "you think of the silliest things! Didn't you see Yoss slam him on the head with a rock? Hasn't he threatened Pat time and again? Didn't a bunch of us see him try to shoot Pat on election night, and would have if Artur hadn't moved fast? Wasn't he about to shoot you when Pat shot him? Not a jury in the county would call that murder. Wait and see, they'll not do a thing to him."

Going down on the train that afternoon, Pat said, "Rodgers, I was rawhiding you a little about being in a hurry, but you did just right. It was right to arrest me right away, and take me down as soon as I could ride. It'll teach some of them wild young boys like the Duncans a respect for the law."

He sat there so serene, chewing on his tobacco and once in a while spitting out of the window. The cinders blew in on us, and the little old car swayed and rocked along the tracks. It didn't seem possible that this man—this gentle and considerate Pat, this man who was shy in his kindness, who stammered to women and could be wound round your finger, who made me feel at times that he needed my care just like Jerry did—it didn't seem possible that he had killed a man about twenty-four hours ago.

"Pat," I asked, "don't you feel queer?"

"Oh, my head don't hurt at all today."

"No. I mean about—about the shooting."

"Shooting Yoss? Why, no, not hardly."

"But, Pat, you killed him!"

"That's what I meant to do!"

I shook my head. "I could understand Yoss acting this way. Look at that Mexican he killed."

"What Mexican?" Pat asked.

"The one Aggie and I saw the shoe of sticking up where Yoss hadn't buried him deep enough."

"Oh, that one," said Pat. "Why, Yoss never did that. I done it myself."

"You did?" I gasped.

"Sure. He bothered you, didn't he? He was dangerous. You can't have men like that running around loose."

I quit, then. I guessed I hadn't understood Pat very well. I wondered if I was as wrong about other people, Aggie, say, or Artur? Maybe they were just as wrong about me, maybe they had totally false ideas about what I was like. Only mine hadn't been totally false about Pat; I just hadn't wanted to believe he could kill a human being—even one he might despise—the way he would a chicken or a steer, and not be the least bit disturbed by it. I remembered now seeing him ride past that morning when Aggie and I were going over to Keaton's for feed. I remembered the shovel on his saddle. He'd gone looking for the Mexican just like he'd go out to kill a mad coyote or hydrophobic skunk.

But he'd done it to protect me—me and Aggie and Minnie and his own mother and maybe some men, too.

That meant I had a responsibility. My actions had to make it worth-while that a human life had been taken—however unnecessarily—in my name. Yoss's, too. Pat had killed him to save me.

Pat and I walked into Sheriff Patterson's office just as he was getting ready to go home. "Here's a prisoner for you, Sheriff," I said.

He thought we were joking. "Well," he said, "you been horse-stealing again, Pat?"

"No," I said, "I guess you'd call it manslaughter. He shot and killed John Yoss yesterday when Yoss was about to shoot me."

Patterson said, "Sounds like a warm time." Then he sat down and wrote him up, called the jailer, and had him locked in a cell. "Hate to do this to you, Pat," he said, "but it's the law. Rodgers and I'll go right up to Judge Dunphy and see about bail."

The Judge wasn't disturbed much. "Too bad it had to be Pat for your first prisoner," he said. "I'll fix bail at five thousand dollars, Sheriff. Rodgers, why don't you go down to Resswell's place and see if he wouldn't like to go bail for an old friend? That'd give Pat a chance to have some fun this evening."

It was really moving too fast for me. But I went and sent one of the men who was lounging outside the saloon doors in for Artur. He came right out, and we walked up the street toward the courthouse. Artur said, "Is it trouble for you, Lu?"

"No," I said, "it's Pat. He shot and killed John Yoss yesterday; I arrested him, and Judge Dunphy fixed bail at five thousand and said you might like to stand it. The Sheriff went back to the office in case you did. Yoss was going to shoot me."

Artur never said, "I told you so," or, "Now, you see," or anything like that. Instead he gave me a long, loving look. Then he said, with his whole soul in his voice, "Thank God for Pat!"

On our way to the Sheriff's, I told him just what had happened. It relieved my mind to do it, too.

When I finished, Artur said with complete understanding, "It must have hurt, Lu, to have to arrest Pat. It was a very responsible thing for you to do. You see, I was right when I first knew you."

I was so happy and glad that he felt that way about me that I couldn't speak for a while. I just held on to his arm and walked along.

Artur said, jokingly, "Well, this evening we must mark your first arrest by a real big dinner. The Border Café's very best."

I shook my head. "No, we'll celebrate bailing Pat out. Not me!"

"You will celebrate that, then," said Artur with a smile, "and I will just celebrate being with a very nice lady, the lady I like best."

"Your favorite peace officer?" I asked.

"My most favorite," Artur agreed.

Artur put up Pat's bail, and he went back to Canelo on the morning train. I stayed at the Judge's forty-eight hours. I felt a little tired, as if I'd ridden for days on end or done a lot of work. Artur seemed to sense it, because he talked quietly of nothing in particular, just made me feel good by acting careful and kind.

The Nogales paper wrote a story on the first page about "Prominent Canelo Citizen Charged with Shooting. First Arrest by Constable L. Rodgers." It was picked up by the Tucson paper and I didn't know for a while what happened to it after that.

Pat's trial was set for three weeks later, on the first of May. Everyone who had been present went to Nogales and testified that Pat had killed Yoss in my defense and in self-defense, and after many threats from Yoss. The jury was out just ten minutes, and came in with a verdict of "Not Guilty." Judge Dunphy, who presided, thanked them and told them they had acted as reasonable and sensible citizens. We all went back to Canelo.

Three days later I had a letter from New York, on the stationery of the National American Woman Suffrage Association. It said, "Dear Mrs. Rodgers: In the name of all women we salute your courage in taking into custody a desperado immediately after he had performed a killing.

We applaud your industry and ambition in attaining your elective office. We want you to tell your story to all so that our campaign for votes for women may be furthered. Therefore, we offer you travel expenses and a fee of fifty dollars per lecture for a series of six lectures here in New York. Please reply at your earliest convenience."

It was signed by the secretary.

Well, here it was! My chance to go back and get my kids. My chance to kiss them and hug them and just love them till we all laughed and danced and shouted.

My chance to bring them out here!

My chance to break down that barrier between Artur and me!

You can bet I answered that letter right away.

chapter 14

I WAS IN New York for three months, July and August—which were hot, muggy and uncomfortable—and September—a lot better. It was a good trip, a fine experience which all pulled together and made sense, but I was sure glad to be back in Arizona.

I wasn't quite home. I was on the train going down from Tucson to Nogales. Over to the right was the high peak of Old Baldy, the mountain that's always in sight from one end of the seventy-mile trip to the other. Sticking their heads out of the windows in an effort to be the first to see Nogales were Jerry and Cissie. Tim was drowsing on the seat beside me, tired at the fag-end of a long, long trip across lands that he hardly knew existed. But he had come through without a whimper, and the other two had been good as gold. Mostly, that was. They did make trouble once in a while, of course.

"Jerry! Cissie!" I said. "Come back in here! It'll be an hour before we get anywhere near Nogales."

"That certain sure, Ma?" Jerry asked. I wondered again, as I had several times, where he had picked up these bits of Western slang.

"Oh, very well, Mater," said Cissie. She'd gotten that fancy name from some English girls in the school old Mrs. Rodgers sent her to I guessed. It didn't matter; the country kids would soon knock that sort of nonsense out of her.

Tim moved around and mumbled sleepily. He was such a sweet youngster, with his yellow curls and his pretty face, pretty as a new colt. It was just wonderful to have them all with me, to realize that in little more than two years I'd fixed things so my children were coming out to the place I wanted to be our home always. They helped me to forget, a good deal of the time, that now it wasn't very likely that their presence would accomplish the one other thing I'd counted on. I had thought, "Just let him see me with Jerry, Cissie and Tim, and he'd see a mother who wanted her children with her all the time, who slanted all her actions and thoughts toward their good." Now, I wasn't sure that would make any difference.

It was the second Saturday before I left for New York that I told Aggie I was going to bring my kids back with me. I'd been thinking of Artur and myself because he was coming out to see me that day. We were going to one of the regular Saturday dances. Also, I had planned to tell him that I was going back to New York—just for a trip, of course. I hadn't told him before because I was afraid that when I did he'd say the words I had to have an answer for. But as Aggie pointed out, I'd have to face it sometime. I couldn't put it off forever.

So I was very proud and pleased with my simple, sure idea. It solved everything, I thought.

I was bubbling about it at breakfast. I started telling Aggie before she'd even finished her mush. She just went on pushing it in her mouth. When she put her spoon down at last, she gave me a long, hard look from those black eyes of hers. Usually, that made me uneasy, meant she was going to tell me what a fool I was. This time I felt so good, I paid no attention. Pride surely does goeth before a fall.

"Rodge, you ought to tell the man first, not shock him."

I waved my hand at her. "Oh, you don't understand." I reminded her of Artur's ideas of women and how they stemmed from the bad acts of his mother and sister.

Aggie looked thoughtful. Finally, she nodded her head. "Yes, I can see how it would be hard to tell him about you doing the same thing."

"Not the same!" I said.

"Looks the same," said Aggie, plainly trying to keep her patience. "So just coming back with your kids makes sense that way. But you've forgotten something else."

"What?"

"The reason you're going to give for going."

"Easy!" I said. "Just what the letter said. To speak at suffragette meetings."

Aggie let her face get long. "Hm. Well, all right. But if I was you, I'd start with that, and start as soon as he gets here. You being kind of famous and all is going to make him touchy—worried—even a little uncertain about himself."

"Shoot!" I said. "I'll handle it all right."

I was so pleased to see Artur's good face arrive at sundown that I said to myself, "Lu, before a dance is no time to talk seriously."

And the dance was extra good. People were pleased with me; I'd made Canelo famous, for a while, at least. Stories about me in the New York papers! Even a very snobbish West Point officer from the Fort asked me for a dance.

Driving home with the horse just trotting and the moon high up over the Huachucas was almost too good to interrupt with serious talk. Every five minutes, I'd say to myself, "Well, tell him now you're going back for a little while, that you won't be away long." Then I'd be too lazy and content to take my head off his shoulder, to stop talking about how the moonlight on the new grass that was still green made it look like quiet water, a lake or pond.

It was a nice, cool night, not too cool, but when we'd cross the mouth of a wash coming down from the hills, there'd be a river of cold air pouring out on the road toward the flats on the other side. So naturally Artur put his arm around me at one of these.

Then before I knew it, he kissed me.

That was all right. He'd done it before, though never as hard as this time.

The trouble was, I kissed him back. I don't know how long.

Then he pulled back and said, "Lu, Lu, I want to marry you! Please! I love you!" His voice had a tremor in it.

I reached up to him. If I could kiss him again I could stop him, I thought. But he was so far away, so tall! Before I could reach him, he said again, "I want to marry you! Will you, Lu?"

There it was and I wasn't ready for it.

"Am I too sudden, Lu?" he was asking gently. "But I am sure you know how I feel about you. Won't you tell me, Lu, please?"

It was terrible. I had nothing except the weak, mean words. "I can't. Not now."

"You want time? I was too abrupt. I should learn."

"No, Artur," I said, "don't blame yourself." I put my hand on his mouth to stop him and he kissed my fingers. "Look."

I knew what I had to say and I knew it was all wrong for him. Oh, God, Aggie was right! But I said it, and it was like cutting myself.

"I'm going back to New York two weeks from today. I'll be back."

Artur laughed, "Oh, a fine honeymoon, Lu! We must be married right away!"

"No, no!"

"But yes, lovely, foolish Lu! So we can go together."

The trouble was, we couldn't. The kids had to come here with me. They had to come here so Artur would know I hadn't abandoned them. Besides, I couldn't marry him and not tell him about them first. And I couldn't tell him now.

"No," I said, "I can't." I thought wretchedly that maybe this was the time to be brave—that the right word now might save everything. I was foolish, no doubt, but I was so afraid of losing Artur.

How can it be a burning, fiery pain when someone takes his arm from around you? I don't know, but it was. Everything was pain; even the moonlight hurt my eyes.

We jogged on for a long time in wretched silence. We crossed the ridge, and on the other side, over there against the side of the hollow, the chicken coop gleamed like silver in the moonlight. There was a light shining through the door so I knew Aggie was waiting for me.

Artur said stiffly, "Is there someone there you do not tell me of, Lu?"

"No," I said miserably. Looking back, worrying it over later, I knew I had been silly. But just then it seemed right.

"I wonder . . . " said Artur. "All my life I am afraid that women are not trustworthy. Then I meet you. . . ."

It hurt unbearably. I said, "Don't, Artur. Don't say anything more. You don't understand."

"You don't try to help me understand."

"Maybe I can't."

"Maybe you should try, though."

Because I had no answer, again, I kept still. We turned down the road, we stopped in front of the house. "Come in and have a cup of coffee, Artur," I said. I sounded dull and bewildered to myself.

"Then you will tell me?"

"There's nothing to tell." It was so hopeless, now. "Just that I'm going to make some money talking at suffragette meetings."

"That," said Artur carefully, "is more important to you than what I have asked?"

I shook my head.

"Well, then?"

I couldn't say anything.

"Perhaps I was too sudden," said Artur. "Perhaps you need more time to think. Very well, then, you will tell me whether you go to New York or talk to me. Good night, Lu."

He drove away without looking back, though I stood there in the road as long as I could hear the sounds of his rig, as long as I could see it on the moonlit road.

Aggie looked at my face. "You been making a fool of yourself, Rodgers?"

"Maybe," I said. "I just don't know."

But somehow when I found Limb all warm and furry on my bed under the mulberry tree, I picked him up and hugged him and was able to cry bitterly.

When things get bad, they're apt to get worse. I wrote Artur a note and said again I was sorry but I must go back for the suffragette speeches. I packed. Aggie and I went down to Nogales. I would get the train to Tucson there, and at Tucson the train for New York.

We stayed overnight at Dunphy's and though I'd told Artur I'd be there, I heard nothing from him. I knew I'd hurt him badly. I felt so horrible and sad and bewildered that Aggie didn't have the heart to tell me how wrong I'd been. And she, too, could see how I couldn't do anything else now. Just keep my mouth shut and go to New York, come back with the kids, hoping I hadn't wounded Artur so much that he wouldn't be reasonable and at least talk to me.

"Only one thing, Rodge," Aggie said. "You've got to remember some men don't exactly take to being father to another man's kids."

"That's one I sure don't have to worry about right now," I said. "Besides, I guess I can go farther and fare as well alone, if I have to."

"If you have to," said Aggie. "But remember this: You can go as far with a man as without him—maybe further— and he'll be there to catch you if you fall."

I tried to joke. "We don't need a man, Aggie, you know we don't."

That was what I was telling myself right now, here on the train on the last lap of a long journey, my kids swarming all around me, Nogales, Canelo, home, ahead. I was telling it to myself pretty strongly because the thing that happened that day two months ago when I left Nogales made things seem even blacker.

The Judge and Mrs. Dunphy and Aggie and I had all gone down to the train. It left at noon, and we were there about fifteen minutes early. There had been no sign of Artur, so I was surprised and pleased, when just five minutes before train time, here he came, striding down the gravel platform.

He lifted his hat and greeted everyone. I said, "Oh, Artur, I'm so glad you've come!"

He didn't smile. He said, "If we may be excused, I would like a word with Mrs. Rodgers in private."

"Of course!" I said, sure he was going to let bygones be bygones. We moved up the platform a little.

He stood very stiff. "Lu," he said, "will you not reconsider, even now, at the last moment? Will you not marry me, now, quickly, so I can go with you?"

If I'd been foolish before, I had to go on being foolish. I said, "Artur, you've got to believe me. I simply can't."

224

Those blue eyes of his hardened like ice. "I think you have good reasons!" he said.

"Artur . . ."

"Perhaps you lie. Perhaps you did leave a husband behind you."

I lost my temper. I said, "I hate you, Artur Resswell!" I stamped my foot. "You God damned fool!" I shouted.

The conductor yelled, "All aboard!"

The engine bell began to clang. Aggie hollered, "Rodgers!" I ran for the train.

Artur kept pace with me. I jumped up on the steps of the car and turned. "I am sure you have left someone there!" he said.

Aggie heard him. "You're a fool, Resswell!" she said.

"You keep still, Aggie!" I called. "Yes, I did leave someone, Artur! I left two men, not one! Two sons and a daughter! My children!"

Artur's mouth dropped open. He stepped backward. The engine whistled; the train jerked and jangled and picked up speed. I hung off the steps and looked back. Aggie was talking to Artur, but he didn't seem to be listening. He was staring after the train.

So I was afraid that I'd done everything wrong. My temper had gotten the better of me at just the very worst time. Artur was undoubtedly convinced that women were worthless. If he hadn't been, why hadn't he written me while I was in New York? Aggie had my address.

To make me feel even worse, New York had settled a lot of things for me. One of them was my feeling for Artur. I knew beyond the slightest doubt that I loved him, that he was the finest man I could ever meet. I'd met some others in New York, and they were so far behind in comparison to Artur that there really wasn't any similarity. Not that they hadn't been fun, but alongside Artur they were a weak, guttering candle beside the noonday sun. What little light they gave was swallowed up in his cheerful glare.

Aside from feeling low about Artur, my stay in the city had been a very good time for me. But the nearer we got to Nogales, the gladder I was to be getting back to my own stamping ground.

There might have been a minute or so when New York seemed pretty appealing, a big, wonderful place and me with its tail in my hand and a twist in the tail. But those were only short moments; I couldn't even identify one. Oh, maybe when I finished my first speech and the hall full of people stamped and clapped, and some yelled, "Bravo!" Maybe that first time that Mr. Simms, very handsome in his dark way, took me to dinner at the Waldorf, where the head waiter bowed and scraped, and people stared, because Mr. Simms was a well-known man about town, and my face was familiar since my picture had been in the papers.

But, however flattering those things had been, I always remembered as soon as they were over that it wasn't me and New York that made them happen, it was me and Canelo and Nogales, Arizona. So if, even for an instant, I was crazy enough to wonder, to think about staying in New York and gobbling down some plums and peaches, I was sensible enough to remember that the fruit would turn sour and spoil pretty quick without my Arizona sunshine.

No, I never really wanted to do anything but collect the kids and come loping back to Arizona, to the place that made me what I was and that I was helping make what it would be. Helping hard, now, bringing in three future good citizens. It made me glad I was a peace officer; here were three more arguments to back up my argument that lawlessness must go.

Real lawlessness, I mean. I remembered sitting on Judge Dunphy's porch after Pat's trial and telling him how puzzled I was. I'd been terribly mixed up. I knew Pat shot Yoss to save me, and most likely himself, but there was always the chance that Yoss could have been stopped some other way. Like the time Dan stopped him.

I said that to the Judge.

"It was a pretty close thing, wasn't it?" he asked.

I nodded. "But it did work, Judge. And it isn't just that, it's a man being killed."

"You wouldn't have wanted Pat convicted of murder, would you? Or even manslaughter?"

"Oh, no."

"Good," said the Judge. "Laws and courts aren't necessarily served best by convictions, you know. In fact, our law is supposed to consider a man innocent until he's proved guilty, though more and more I notice to my sorrow that politically minded prosecutors—and sometimes judges, which shames me—with their eyes on politics rather than justice present their cases with the air that the man is guilty because he's charged with breaking some statute. You heard me say that to the jury. No, Rodgers, the ends of justice would have been shamefully misused were Pat to suffer the slightest penalty for this."

"That's right, Judge, but doesn't it mean there's something wrong with all of us, that things like that can happen? I mean, aren't you and me responsible for Yoss and Pat?"

The Judge smiled. "I like the way you think, Rodge. We're still in the midst of change here, Rodge. There aren't enough people like you, yet, to raise the moral pressure to a point where men won't think and act like Yoss. But there are enough Pats, who are in a stage of transition from the old, rough frontier to the new civilization, who resent Yosses and kill them off. It's rough, and I suppose indefensible on high moral grounds, but it works. Yoss had no respect for anyone, male or female. Pat has the typical idolatry for the good woman you find all through the West. As time goes on there'll be fewer and fewer Yosses. Meantime, you can help by just doing what you're doing: letting people see that a woman can be a woman and still think of things further away from her than the kitchen, a husband, children."

"But those are important."

"Oh, sure. Got to have them. Don't neglect them, either. But don't confine yourself to just them. I don't mean you —you don't—but women in general."

That had been a good talk, and I hadn't forgotten it. In fact, I'd used some of what the Judge said in my speeches and gotten plenty of applause for it. Those New York women—and men, too—had clapped real hard when I said, "Take your eyes off the kitchen table and look out the kitchen window at that horizon off there. It's got hills and mountains on it, and you ought to find out what they're like, because your menfolks know and it's your business to know about what your menfolks do and think. Get into politics! Take your broom and mop out of the cupboard, lug them outside your homes into city and state and national affairs! Let's show them it's a woman's touch that'll clean up all these dirty politics they seem to think they can't do anything about!"

Sometimes they cheered.

It had been real good, but it was better with the hills slowly wheeling past outside the car window, knowing that soon I'd be home. I looked at Tim, at the back of his head, I mean, because he had his face in my lap and was sleeping hard. I looked at Cissie and Jerry, still busy staring out the window. Here they were. I'd done what I set out to do, little more than two years ago. I remembered how scared and weepy I'd been, a mousy little city woman. Now I was a Westerner and a peace officer.

"We really going to live in a tent, Ma?" Jerry asked for the thousandth time.

"That's what I figure," I told him.

We'd have to because the new house hadn't gotten built yet. Aggie was still hanging fire on the Wilcox deal, but she had set a date to marry Jackson in November. I wasn't really too worried about where to live because having my children with me meant I'd just have to get workable ideas, or the good Lord would have to put them into my mind. "He sees the fall of a sparrow." He'd surely see my kids.

The way it looked to me I couldn't lose. If Aggie decided against Wilcox and kept the place, I would homestead a place of my own. There was a nice quarter-section up beyond Sowers' on the way to Uncle Tom's. I'd stand for road supervisor next election. There were dozens of things I could do. But there was only one thing I really wanted to do. Somehow, I must make Artur see I'd been right to go without him. Somehow, I'd have to bring us together again.

Maybe the kids still would do it. I could only hope. Anyhow, I had them at last.

The first thing I'd done when I reached New York, was to call on Greg's old lawyer friend, Will Saunders. It had been good to see Will, and not too painful. Greg was so far away and long ago, now; he'd always be with me as a loved and cherished ghost, but I could only regret he was gone, not spend my days in endless weeping.

Will advised me to go see old Mrs. Rodgers, and tell her I was going to take my children back to my home with me when I left at the end of September. "She can't stop you," he said. "Aside from being their mother, the fact that you're an elected public servant proves you're perfectly capable of taking care of them. That was the only point she could have stopped you with when you left. Your lack of competence. It doesn't exist, now,"

"I guess she'll be pretty mean about it, though," I said.

Will looked at me. "I guess any woman who can capture a bloodthirsty killer can handle Mrs. Rodgers."

"Pat Malloy's about as bloodthirsty as a cow," I said, somehow remembering the look of terror on his face the time I waved my wet corset at him.

I found out later that about this; Will was like everybody I was going to meet. They wanted to believe that I'd arrested a desperado armed to the teeth.

"You're just modest, Lucretia," he said.

I was wrong about old Mrs. Rodgers. I don't think she was exactly glad to see me, but she was reasonable. She said, "I've been reading about you in the papers. I never thought you had it in you, Lu, but you did. Real backbone and courage. I congratulate you."

I did something I'd never been able to do. I put my arm around her stiff old shoulders. I said, "Grandmother, thanks for all you've done for my children. I want to see them now."

"Are you going to take them away with you?"

I nodded. "You know they've got to be with me. That's what I went out there for."

"It's only right, of course." Then her stern old face crinkled up a little. "But I'll miss them terribly."

"I know. I did."

"I mustn't be selfish, though. It's right, Lu, they should be with you. I hope you feel I've cared for them properly."

"Oh, Grandmother," I said, "I know you have!" Then I bent down and kissed her wrinkled old cheek. "Please," I said. "I've waited so long."

"Of course, Lu. Right upstairs. They're all together in the nursery."

Golly, it was good to see them! When I opened the door, they just stared till Cissie yelled, "Mother!" Then all three came at me in a high lope.

They stayed at Mrs. Rodgers' of course, till I finished the lectures. And when it came time to leave, catch the train for Nogales, there was weeping and wailing and "Why doesn't Gram come too?" So much of it that Mrs. Rodgers cried over them and I cried too and she came to the station with us and stood there waving till the train pulled out. Promised Cissie she'd come visit soon. She had to or Cissie wouldn't have let go of her.

She was a good woman and kind to my children. Some of the sweetness Greg had was in her, but buried deep under her sternness and stiffness.

Of course, next morning when they woke, with the excitement of traveling and the new place they were going to, the kids had gotten over missing her. They were sure wild about the idea of living in Canelo on a ranch, and if I wanted to stay in Nogales, I was going to have a hard time changing their minds. But I guessed I could do it if I tried. To a Brooklyn kid Nogales would be plenty wild and Western.

But they were looking forward to Canelo. Jerry asked, "Ma, are we going right out to Canelo on the next train?"

"Yes," said Cissie. "We are. Mater has promised it."

"No, I never," I said. "I sort of thought we might stay around Nogales a day or two. Judge Dunphy said he sure wanted to see you kids, and he can't get out to Canelo often."

"I want to see Pat," Jerry said.

"Well, you're going to. You're going to see lots of people and learn to ride a horse and . . ."

"Where are we going to school?"

"There's a right good school close by. You'll like it."

"What are the other children like, Mater?"

"Oh, you'll like them," I said vaguely.

"Do they come to school on horses?" Jerry wanted to know.

"They sure do." I wished they'd shut up and stop pestering me because we were getting closer and closer to Nogales, and I was feeling worse and worse. I wanted Artur back. I wanted him because I loved him and wanted him in my life and my children's lives forever and ever.

There wasn't a thing I could do except hope, and my hope was pretty faint. Suddenly I felt as desperate as I did when I was tugging at my gun with John Yoss about to shoot me. Pat Malloy saved me that time. There was nobody to save me now, though.

Yes, there was. The best and most helpful of all. I closed my eyes.

"Mater's tired," said Cissie.

I wasn't tired. I was praying.

I wanted to run Aggie's place and I wanted to be independent—some. I might even try to go on in politics after I got settled down and the kids got used to the new country. But what I wanted more than anything was just Artur.

I knew I could do everything I had ever planned to do and still do it better with Artur than without him.

I loved him. I'd make him understand. I wouldn't let pride hinder me. I'd go right down to his saloon and if I had to I'd go inside and find him!

"We're here!" Jerry yelled.

I opened my eyes. We were pulling into town. There was the courthouse, high on its hill; there was the string of little adobe stores; there was Artur's saloon.

Jerry was counting the baggage checks for the tenth time. Tim was sitting up, staring around, hanging on to my arm. Cissie was straightening her dress.

The train slowed, stopped.

"Nogales!" yelled the brakeman. "All out!"

I hoped Aggie would be able to meet us, though I doubted it. More than likely, she couldn't get away from the place. If the Judge was free, I guessed he would. I had written and asked Mrs. Dunphy if she could put us up for a day or so.

We were the last ones out of the car because we had a couple of pieces of hand luggage and I had to carry Tim. The odd dozen people who had got off ahead had scattered so the platform was pretty empty. There wasn't a soul I knew on it.

We stood there in a little group. I said to Jerry, "Just let's wait a minute and we'll get a Mexican boy to carry our stuff."

"I can do it, Ma," he said. "I'm plenty strong."

"Too much for one boy," I said, smiling at him. I looked for one of the kids who always hung around the station.

There, coming around the last car of the train, was Artur. He came striding toward us, and I couldn't figure out if he recognized me or not. There wasn't a bit of expression on his face.

He stopped two paces from us. His eyes met mine, then they traveled over Jerry, jumped to Cissie, moved to Tim.

The kids stared back at him.

Finally, Cissie asked, "Who are you?"

He spoke then. "I am Artur Resswell. Are you Mrs. Rodgers' children?"

Jerry said, "Of course."

"Anyone can see that!" said Cissie, a little pertly.

Tim just turned and hid his face in my skirt.

"Yes, I can see that," said Artur. He took his hat off. "I have come to beg your mother's pardon," he said slowly.

"Oh, you don't have to, Artur!" I said. "You don't have to say that!"

"I was very wrong," he said, "and you were very right. You are responsible, and I always knew it. I think I can even understand why you would not tell me why you were going back to New York."

He was so solemn that I wanted to shake him, to do something to make him smile.

"Wouldn't you, for these?" I asked. "Pretty good-looking family, isn't it?"

Artur began to smile, just a little, just enough to curl the corners of his mouth up and make him handsomer than ever. He shook his head. "No, Lu," he said. "There is something missing."

"What?"

"A father! I would like to be the father! Lu, please, will you . . ."

I didn't let him finish.

"Artur," I said, "I'd never let you get away!" I flung my arms around his neck and kissed him. I thought the kids might as well get used to me doing it; they'd see it happen pretty often.

Feeling him close to me that way was the best thing I could possibly imagine. I had sure come out on top of the heap.

PEARL S. BUCK

Author of THE GOOD EARTH, etc.

PORTRAIT OF A MARRIAGE

A novel to touch everyone's heart. Probing, deeply sensitive, it tells of two passionate people caught by love and stirred by its meaning.

C-419 • 35¢

OTHER NOVELS BY PEARL S. BUCK:

- C410 — Command the Morning, 35¢
- C111 — The Good Earth, 35¢
- C387 — The Hidden Flower, 35¢
- GC41 — Imperial Woman, 50¢
- C308 — Letter From Peking, 35¢
- C372 — The Long Love, 35¢
- GC35 — My Several Worlds, 50¢
- C105 — Pavilion of Women, 35¢
- C388 — Peony, 35¢
- GC46 — The Townsman, 50¢

If your bookseller does not have these titles, you may order them by sending retail price, plus 5¢ for postage and handling to: MAIL SERVICE DEPT., Pocket Books, Inc., 1 West 39th St., N. Y. 18. Enclose check or money order — do not send cash.

PUBLISHED BY **POCKET BOOKS, INC.**